WRIGHT MORRIS

THE
DEEP
SLEEP

UNIVERSITY OF NEBRASKA PRESS · LINCOLN

Library of Congress Cataloging in Publication Data

Morris, Wright, 1910–
  The deep sleep.

  "Bison book."
  Reprint of the ed. published by Scribner, New
York.
    I. Title.
PZ3.M8346De4   [PS3525.07475]   813'.5'2   75-5746
ISBN 0–8032–5823–2

First Bison Book printing: 1975

Most recent printing shown by the first digit below:
1   2   3   4   5   6   7   8   9   10

Bison Book edition published by arrangement with the author.

THE DEEP SLEEP

NOVELS BY WRIGHT MORRIS IN BISON BOOK EDITIONS

Date of first publication appears at the left

1948 *The Home Place* (BB 386)
1949 *The World in the Attic* (BB 528)
1951 *Man and Boy* (BB 575)
1952 *The Works of Love* (BB 558)
1953 *The Deep Sleep* (BB 586)
1954 *The Huge Season* (BB 590)
1956 *The Field of Vision* (BB 577)
1960 *Ceremony in Lone Tree* (BB 560)

In Preparation

1942 *My Uncle Dudley* (BB 589)
1945 *The Man Who Was There* (BB 598)

For
HARRY FORD

THE DEEP SLEEP

And the Lord God caused a deep sleep to fall upon Adam, and he slept; and he took one of his ribs, and closed up the flesh instead thereof: and the rib, which the Lord God had taken from man, made he a woman, and brought her unto the man.

And Adam said, This is now bone of my bones, and flesh of my flesh: she shall be called Woman, because she was taken out of man. Therefore shall a man leave his father and his mother, and shall cleave unto his wife: and they shall be one flesh. And they were both naked, the man and his wife, and were not ashamed.

THE LIQUID NOTE of the thrush entered the house through the flowering privet, through the clumps of rhododendron, from where he whistled in the bed of pachysandra, but the Grandmother, eavesdropping on the stairs, wished he would shut up. When he whistled again, sweet and cool, she unhooked her cane from her arm and shook it at him. She had heard the paper boy, and she was waiting for the paper to fall on the porch. From the landing on the stairs, her listening post, she heard it swish through the privet, and through the cataract blur she saw the branches part, close again. Years ago, when she had eyes, the Grandmother had seen a scared bat do as much. She had shooed him through the kitchen, through the parlor, and then through the window where the lilac bush, as if it saw him coming, just opened wide and swallowed him up. Now the Grandmother was blind as a bat herself, and she couldn't seem to hear some people when they shouted, but it might surprise you what she heard if you let it drop. In her ninety-ninth year, the Grandmother sometimes surprised herself.

The Deep Sleep

The arrival of the paper, like the rising of the sun, was one of the things that she observed, but she was under oath not to step out on the porch and reach for it. At that time in the morning it was known that she looked a sight. The heels and straps were worn off her shoes, and her apron, the loose strings dangling, hung like a curtain from her gobbler's neck. But there was no law to prevent her from fishing for the paper with her cane.

If it fell within reach, *that* was what you heard next. If it fell out of reach, what you heard was considerably worse. In the dining room, seated in her rocker at the sunny bird box window, the Grandmother would slip her cane between the slats of the bird box, then give it a wag. That was all, she would do no more than give it a wag. It was hard to believe that such an old lady could make so much noise. But there was nothing whatsoever to be done about it as she had been *asked* to do it, and if she didn't do it the only birds in the bird box were pigeons—and squirrels. The awful racket indicated that they, like the Grandmother, were now up. Judge Porter, the Grandmother's only boy, would get up out of bed and squeeze the morning orange juice, and Mrs. Porter, who had set the alarm, would shut it off. There had been no need to wind that alarm for fifteen years. Not since the summer that the Grandmother had come to make her home in the house, and the daughter had left it to marry an artist, a painter named Webb. The Grandmother's racket, winter and summer, indicated that a new day had begun, as well as the fact that the morning paper was out of her reach.

This morning it lay, as the Grandmother could tell you, on the rim of the porch. A photograph of Howard Porter, widely known as the Judge, stood at the head of an article running two columns, and he seemed to gaze from the rim of the porch into his own house. Over this picture the caption read, CITY MOURNS HIS PASSING, and beneath it the weatherman predicted another summer day of humidity and heat.

WEBB

The clatter in the bird box came through the window that still vibrated as if the house shook, and Webb could hear, as if trapped in his pillow, the tremor in the springs. The racket made him wince, but it also made him feel at home. After fifteen years he had a certain feeling for the ghosts in the house.

Webb had never spent a night in the bed when he hadn't been awakened by the unearthly racket, and once awake he had never been able to get back to sleep. He would lie there and listen. He would go over, once more, the same old ground. He would begin with that summer fifteen years ago, when he had come home after a year in France to marry the girl, to paint, and to live on a mountain—in that order. The mountain had got away, but the girl had driven down to the boat and picked him up. She had met him in the roadster which belonged to her brother, the windshield covered with Ivy League stickers, and in the cool of the morning they had driven through the country—the historic, haunted, big-name country— to the modest, as her mother described it, Porter house. Actually it was, but it looked big and comfortable on the wide green lawn. Dark clumps of rhododendron, heavy with flowers, shaded the porch. All the windows were open, and as they came up the drive Webb could see the music lying open on the piano, a framed picture of the Judge, and a bowl of pansies that had just been cut. The front door stood open, but the girl led him around the house to where her father, with his bird binoculars, sat on the steps of the back porch. From there into the kitchen, where the coffee was perking, then into the dining room where the Grandmother, her lethal cane in her lap, sat quietly at the bird box window. She had one eye on the birds, and the other (as Webb was to discover later) on the bowl of dinner mints on the sideboard. From there up the stairs to where Mrs. Porter, speaking to him with her head in the closet, gave him a towel, a washcloth, and a bar of soap without once glancing at his face. Then into the guest room—which was the girl's room if she happened to be home for the summer— with the short high bed that looked like a buggy without the fringed top.

There Webb had stopped, as the year in France had made him wary of beds, but before he could speak the girl began to giggle and left the room. He had been left there with the monogrammed guest towel and the bar of soap in his hand, gazing at the bed that looked, for *him*, about a foot too short.

The Deep Sleep

Upright, in his fashion, Webb was just six feet, with the stoop at the top that he had never corrected, but stretched out in bed he ran three to four inches longer than that. In France he had never solved this problem, and he had even written the girl to say what a fine thing it would be when he could sleep in a bed stretched out. So he had looked at the bed, then he had turned and faced the mirror on the dresser, where everything in the room seemed to be gathered, as if seen through a lens. There he saw himself, more stooped than ever, thin to the point of being skinny, but a man now in the suit he had put on as an over-grown boy. Gathered around him, as in a composition, were the photographs on the walls of the room, show-ing the daughter of the house at various stages of her life. As Pan, in some school play, as a Sea Scout in her crisp nautical costume, and as the owner of "The Best Home Library" for girls under twelve. As a co-ed, almost a woman, waving from the boat taking her to England, and as the sober student, Baedeker in hand, on the steps of Chartres, and on the beach at Mont St. Michel.

It was all there in the mirror, but Webb could not describe the impression it had made on him. He had been led through the house, room by room, so that this room had come as a symbolic climax, as if the house had gathered itself together in the lens of the mirror. Beginning at the back, beginning with the kitchen, each room seemed to open on a wider vista, a deeper, more ambitious prospect of American life. A sense of summer leisure, of sweetness and bounty, of innocence and promise without melancholy, seemed to pass through the house, blow in and out of the windows, as if he stood within a grove that Inness might have painted, and gazed out at life.

It had seemed to Webb, right at that moment, that he had gone abroad not to find himself, or other such prattle, but in order to return to this room and rediscover America. To find in this house the spaciousness of American life. There in the mirror, as neatly ordered as a painting, were the sentiments that painting had failed to grasp, and it seemed to Webb that the heart of this secret was the house. It was the house, the house itself, set in its miniature surburban forest, that brought the conflicting forces together and gave them shape. It added up to more than the sum of the separate lives. It had struck Webb as a sort of revelation, the challenge he had awaited as a man and an artist, and at that very moment the ear-splitting racket rang through the house. And for the length of that moment, like reflections on water, the images in the mirror all ran together, the pattern was shattered, and the house itself seemed about to fall. But as suddenly as it had occurred, the tremor passed. The mirror stopped vibrating, the house was serene, and in the summer quiet Webb heard a voice say—

"I sometimes wonder if your Grandmother has *any* feathered friends."

To whom was it speaking? In Webb's opinion it spoke to the house. The daughter, Katherine, was out in the yard, the son, Roger, was not at home, and the Judge himself, with the hired man Parsons, was backing down the drive in his car. Webb saw them wave as they drove off down the street.

The voice belonged to Mrs. Porter, and there were times when she spoke to herself. If anybody was listening he was free to answer or to let it pass. Webb had let it pass that morning, but he had thought of it again, nearly fifteen years later, when he had climbed out of bed to answer the phone. They were out on the Cape, in a place called Wellfleet, and the operator said, "This is Bryn Mawr calling," and then he had heard Mrs. Porter's sober voice.

"Your father-in-law, Paul," she had said, "is a very sick man."

They had known that, known it for two years, but the thing that struck Webb was the way she had put it; it had made him think of the first morning he had spent in the house. The terrible racket, followed by the peace, then the calm voice of Mrs. Porter saying—

The Deep Sleep

"I sometimes wonder if *your* Grandmother has *any* feathered friends."

Webb had felt it had given him the key to something, one he had looked for many years, but the morning she had called, he had had nothing to unlock with it.

"Here's Katherine, Mother," he had said, "here's Katherine, Mother—" and that had been that.

The call had come on a Sunday, in March or February, and five or six hours later they were in Boston, where they made reservations on the night train. In the late afternoon it began to storm, the south-bound train was an hour or two late, and Webb had passed the time listening to a pair of old hack drivers. They had come in out of the storm to warm up a bit. The blizzard got them to talking about old times, and Webb took it for granted that they were reminiscing, like any pair of old cronies, about the good old days. But they were not. He found it hard to credit what he heard. The old men before him both held the opinion that old times were lousy, old weather was worse, and a horse-drawn hack was enough to leave them speechless, wagging their heads. They were in sober agreement that they lived in a truly marvellous age. That to have died when they were young would have been a fearful calamity. The very world that frightened Webb out of his wits, the gadgets, the machines, and the cybernetic wonders, brought an awesome religious note into the old men's speech. They looked forward, through bleary eyes, to the new age. They thanked the Lord for quick cab heaters, for engines that would start, for roads that were paved, for garages that were heated, and for the hot cup of coffee they could get at any hour of the night. In considerable detail they reviewed all they had to be thankful for. It took time. It added up to quite a bit. If men were still losing their sons in wars, where else in the world, and at what other time, could they fly a boy home from Korea to die in his mother's arms? No, it was a great world, and they were glad to be alive in it. The old man who seemed to love it the most wiped a hole in the window so he could gaze upon it, and through this hole Webb could see flares burning along the tracks. He could see shadowy men, with burlap wrapped around their feet, holding long oil cans with spurting flames at their tips, as they fought to keep the switches open, and the trains on time. Such an unreal scene, by Webb's standards, that it reminded him of Bosch and Breughel, or any nightmare world rather than the actual scene itself. And so it crossed Webb's mind, while that view was before him, and while they both stood there gazing at it, that this deluded old man had a better grasp of real life than he had himself. He saw only what was there. He therefore preferred it to anything else.

The real flares hissed, the real wind howled, and the snow blew from the scene into both of their faces, but Webb had the feeling that the old man had the best of it. That he felt it, that he lived it, with more authority. The painter Webb, the hack driver Steve, gazed through the same hole at the same world, but it was clear that they did not see the same things. Webb had put his hand on the old man's shoulder—around his shoulder, as his wife said later—as he had felt their strange predicament as fellow mortals, each with two eyes in his head, each staring, but neither seeing the same thing.

"Think that's her comin' now," the old man had said, and walked from beneath the arm not quite on his shoulders, into the wind that puffed out the pockets of his coat.

That might have been that, but when they boarded the train something had gone wrong with their reservations, so that Katherine had a berth, but he had to settle for a seat in the coach. He had thrown his bag up on the rack, then walked through the train, which proved to be a long one, as if through compartments of summer and winter, of real life and chambered withdrawals, to the lounge car, where he should have ordered a drink. The drink would have relaxed him, made him sleepy, but he had got a little cold sitting around the station, so he had ordered coffee instead. A pot of coffee, as it turned out, since that was how they happened to serve it, and he had sat there all night puzzling over the pattern of the Judge's life.

The Judge had lived for sixty-nine years, not a long life by the Porter standards, but a good long life in terms of experience and accomplishment. The blow, the big blow, had been the loss of his son. When the boy was killed, the second year of the war, the Judge began to write Webb the long monthly letter he had once, more or less fruitlessly, mailed off to his son. It had been up to Webb, in one way or another, to take the boy's place. The triumph of his life, if he could be said to have had a triumph, was to appear successful enough to have justified the Judge's love and confidence. To have given the Judge a glow of pleasure when he spoke of his son-in-law, the artist, and took him to the better clubs of the city and showed him off. It had been *their* triumph, they shared it together, as there had been plenty of people to scoff when Webb had been on the WPA and the dole. They had got by, they had just got by, because the Judge had found a way to keep them from starving when they had had nothing in the cupboard but their goddam pride. It had been the Judge, the Judge himself, who had come to New York with some Philadelphia bigwigs and bought the first five paintings out of his first big one-man show. The Judge had mulled around, he had made quite a fuss, and he had managed to create the impression that this fellow Webb was not just a man to watch, but the man to buy while his prices were low. That seemed to have done it, as eighteen paintings were sold, eighteen out of twenty-one, and they were over what the Judge liked to refer to as the *hump*. But the high point of that hump was right in the house. Mrs. Porter had been harder to sell than anybody else. In the opinion of the Judge, Webb had made it thanks to an issue of the *New York Times* where his name appeared in a column-long list of promising young men. On finding him there Mrs. Porter had admitted, once in public and several times in private, that her son-in-law, Webb, *ought to be encouraged*, her highest form of praise. If that was true, Webb had been obliged to take it on faith. He had never felt encouraged in the Porter house. He usually felt, if the truth were known, like the battered grackles on the roof of the bird box, living in the shadow of some unseen power and the swish of the Grandmother's lethal cane.

The Grandmother, a living Rock of Ages, was a symbol of the strength of the Porter line, but also a daily reminder that the Judge was failing fast. And

[13]

then the war, coming when it did, had finished him off. Right when he should have retired, he had taken on the work of three or four men. That was what Webb kept telling himself and his wife, but they both knew that the Judge would not have retired, war or no war, but would have gone on doing something. *That* was the pattern, as a matter of fact, as the Judge needed something to draw him out, to keep him going, and the war had given it a nice patriotic twist. He got to be something of a national figure, heading first this committee, then that one, and forever being called in to settle some crisis, and to arbitrate. Which he did. He could settle every problem but his own. It was *that* little problem that troubled Webb, but he felt that the Judge had overcome it in his mastery of every life except his own. If he had been broken, it had been on the wheel of his choice. His present illness, locking him in the house that he had spent his life escaping, had been worse, Webb felt sure, than death itself. There had been nothing left for him but to die.

So the news that he was dying—might be dead when they arrived—was the kind of sorry news that made sense. That was the picture as Webb saw it, and as his wife Katherine would tell you, he had to make a *picture* out of everything. That was what twenty years of painting had done to him. Katherine pointed this out in such a manner that it was clear, in her opinion, this was the type of fiction a woman knew better than to take seriously. The fictions that women took seriously always struck Webb as evidence that the suffragette movement would never benefit the human race. On receiving the news of her father's condition, Katherine had put the telephone down and said, "Well, I'm sure it's all for the best."

That kind of thing nearly drove Webb out of his mind. He had had to leave the room to keep from shouting, "And just how the hell do you know?" although he knew that it might be perfectly true. There was no shred of evidence to the contrary, not one bit. But the way a woman would settle, when the time came, for the worst of all possible worlds, made him feel a real despair at the core of human life. "Let's get on with it," they were saying, "to hell with it and get on with it!" which was very likely a fairly sound biological point of view. Have another child, another man, another lover, and get on with it. Well, Webb insisted on mulling it over, which was *his* biological business, and he would not consign a man to his grave until he was dead. Particularly, let it be said, in the case of the Judge. Whenever that case seemed to be closed, he reopened it. He had been given the facts, such as they were, right at the start. Years ago the Judge had bought one of Webb's best paintings—had bought it from a show and paid cash for it—but it did not go home to hang in Mrs. Porter's house. The Judge had had to find a place for it in the drafty annex at the law school.

"It's her home, son," the Judge had said, when he had felt obliged to say something about it, "it's her place. I let her run it on her own principles."

Mrs. Porter's principles, in Webb's opinion, were just so many shadows in a hall of mirrors, but they were part of the picture the Judge had in mind. Webb had thought about this picture so much there were times he thought he might even paint it—a sort of Grant Wood-Norman Rockwell version of the All-American home. The sober protestant colors, the air of summer leisure, the *Saturday Evening Post* look of innocence and promise, with all the lines, in an orderly perspective, converging on the house set in the background, the morning paper on the steps, and the luminous wicker furniture on the porch. Out in back would be the Judge, an inconspicuous figure, leaning on the hoe in his own Victory Garden, surrounded by a cloud of birds that were pointing up the moral and feeding from his hand. It was quite a picture. Webb had almost reached the point of admiring it.

In the club car, kept awake by the coffee, he had had all night to brood over the moral, and for something done with mirrors, it looked pretty good. Then, a little after daylight, they arrived in Philadelphia where Dr. Barr, the family's spiritual adviser, had come to tell them that the Judge was still alive. Webb had heard the news with mixed feelings, as it meant that he had to reopen, for a time anyhow, a case that he considered closed. Nobody seemed to know, Dr. Barr said, where the Judge had found the strength, but he more or less implied that it had not been from the Lord. The Judge had been a man who stood alone, and he meant to fall that way. Webb liked Barr, that is to say he liked that kind of honesty, but he was always ill at ease with a well-educated religious man. The Judge had once hinted, in a roundabout way, that Dr. Barr had once been a great one with the ladies, and that among the ladies Katherine Porter Webb had played her part. But there were always such hints, it seemed to Webb, about the girl who played the piano or the organ.

Dr. Barr had got up at dawn to meet them, had a hot cup of coffee with them in the station, then drove them through the gray winter morning to the Porter house. They had been obliged to leave the car in the road and wade through the snow that had drifted in the driveway and had even made it hard to find the steps to the front porch. Then they stood there five or ten minutes, ringing the bell. They knocked, Webb pounded on the door till the windows shook. When that got them no answer, he went around back and tried the kitchen windows, but everything had been locked up tight. Mrs. Porter was sleeping the sleep of the dead, or was dead herself. Then Katherine thought of the bird box window, and Webb waded around to the side of the house, under the tree where the wrong birds hovered, from where he could dimly see, through the frosted window, the Grandmother at her watch. So he had called to her, which gave her quite a start, but in due time, which seemed forever, they could hear her fumbling with the door key. That took more time, but she finally managed to get it unlocked. Then Webb had rushed for the stairs, with Dr. Barr behind him, as he expected to find the Judge dead and Mrs. Porter in a crumpled heap in one of the rooms. He had gone on ahead, made the turn on the stairs, and had looked up to see the hall nightlight burning, just as Mrs. Porter appeared on the landing, then disappeared. She walked from the sick room into the hall, and in spite of the racket they had been making she passed them by without a word, without a glance. A moment later, like a phantom on the landing, she was back with a bottle of Air-Wick, walking in the remote dreamlike trance of Lady Macbeth. Shock—Webb had thought—a case of shock, and he had exchanged glances with Dr. Barr, then he had said—

"Oh, Mother—oh, Mother, here we are."

She did not reply. In the quiet they could hear her hands tuck something in, smooth something down, and the cat-like padding of her bare feet. So he called again, "Oh, Mother—"

"Would you mind—" Mrs. Porter replied, in her customarily sober voice, "would you mind waiting until he is presentable?"

Webb could think of nothing. He could think of nothing at all to say.

"I didn't know it was customary," she went on, "to make calls on the sick so early in the morning. I suppose we're just old-fashioned in this house."

Webb did not speak, so Dr. Barr said, "I'm afraid you're right about the time, Mrs. Porter. We are very early. It's not yet seven o'clock."

"He's asleep right now," she said, "I suppose he should sleep."

"By all means," said Dr. Barr, and then they had turned and gone down the stairs, but on the landing she spoke to them again.

"I hope you've had your breakfast," she said, "I simply haven't had the time for shopping. Your father-in-law always did the shopping, and he's been sick."

"No, we've all had our breakfast, Mother," he had said. "We had it on the train."

"We've had to let things slide a little," she had said, and they had stood there in the cloak room, the three of them together, neither speaking nor raising their eyes from the tile floor. Dr. Barr had put a hand on Webb's shoulder, squeezed it, and then had gone. Webb could hear the iron ring of his feet on the porch. Then he had raised his eyes to the room, gray with the light of the winter morning, and saw that the Grandmother stood there looking at them. Nothing showed on her withered face, nor seemed to look through the flecked lenses of her glasses, but Webb knew that a judgment, an everlasting judgment, had been passed on them all. On Dr. Barr, on his Lord, on the grandson-in-law and on the granddaughter, and on the woman upstairs who had spoken, and the man, her husband, who lay in the bed. A judgment that included not merely the inhabitants, but the house. What this judgment was Webb had no idea, beyond the fact that it sent them all to hell, to an everlasting fire; but that was not the worst of it. The hell of it was that Webb agreed with it. The verdict was right. He could feel in his bones the truth of it. He didn't like the Grandmother—she kept him off as she kept the squirrels out of the bird box—and her simple-minded world no longer held any charms for him. But this judgment, whatever it was, came from that point anchored in time where the Grandmother weighed the world and found it wanting, and so did Webb.

But the Judge did not die, he slept through the morning, he joked and laughed in the afternoon, but early in the evening, out of nowhere, he shouted WEBB! It had been a command and a cry of woe at the same time. By the time Webb got to the room the Judge's front had collapsed, his guard was down, and he looked like a figure seated at the very bottom of hell. On his enormous head the hair was tousled, giving him a wild, nearly rakish air, but the haggard, ashen face beneath it was not his own. Nothing that belonged to the Judge peered out of it. Nothing but fear, fear on such a plane that Webb had just stood there, staring and speechless, as if he had just witnessed some terrible crime. Then it passed—no it did not pass, but was merely replaced, superseded, by an even greater fear—the fear of showing how he really felt. To spare him that, to spare them both *that*, Webb turned and left.

It came as no surprise to Webb, three months later, when he heard that the Judge, although a dying man, had seized the smooth round knobs on the bed posts, one in each hand, and snapped them off with his bare hands. Hearing the crack of the wood, Mrs. Porter had gone in and found him dead.

The Deep Sleep

*　*　*

"You children asleep or awake?" Mrs. Porter said. It gave Webb quite a start, as he had not heard her come up the stairs. He opened one eye, and saw that she was wearing her pre-war bathrobe with the faded dragons, and carrying the clothes she would put on following her bath.

"I'm awake, Mother," Katherine replied.

"We're going to have to be on our good behavior," Mrs. Porter said.

Katherine did not reply.

"Katherine—"

"Yes, Mother—"

"Would one of your father's shirts fit him?"

"We've gone into that, Mother. You know his arms are about a foot longer."

Mrs. Porter picked lint from the sleeve of the blue frock she held.

"I know what artists are wearing," she said, "but I do not know what they're wearing at funerals."

She waited to hear if her daughter did, but Katherine did not. Turning from the door, Mrs. Porter stopped to jot down something on the phone pad in the hallway, then she crossed the hall and entered the bathroom, closed the door.

KATHERINE

There had been a time when Katherine Porter Webb thought of only one thing when she entered a bathroom, nearly any bathroom with a window on the yard at the back of the house. The Porter room was square, with an oversize tub, and not much like a bathroom in some respects as there were also a chair, a chest of drawers, and throw rugs on the floor. In the morning it was sunny, in the winter it was warm, and she had come to the bathroom whenever she cried as it was the only room in the house that she could lock. Her own room had a lock, but there was no key, and if her mother found the door closed she always opened it to help circulate the air. No one had the right, her mother said, to keep the air in a room to herself.

Katherine thought of the bathroom as her room, and she had gone there the morning she had decided, as the note to her father declared, to take what she referred to as her own life. She had taken all the bottles with skulls on the labels, climbed into the tub to keep from being messy, and then started with the one that recommended no antidote. *That* one, she was sure, would really kill her, but all it did was burn her throat badly

[23]

and then she had fainted climbing out of the tub. Her father found her lying on the floor as though she was taking a nap. Her mother had not been at home at the time, so her father first rushed her to a doctor, then they went to hear Myra Hess and Stokowski play César Franck's *Symphonic Variations*, which her mother had said was just an extravagance. Which was why she had made up her mind to take her own life. There were other reasons, but that had been, as she said in her note, the last straw, and there was no point in living if she had to do it without Myra Hess. Dame Myra was English, so she knew that in England there were human beings, and lives worth living, and when the time came her father sent her to England to school. That was not easy, but it was her father who had found her on the floor of the bathroom, and he didn't want to find her there again. More than that, he didn't want her mother to find her there. So she had gone to England, she had gone to camp, she had gone to college in California, but her brother Roger had not gone anywhere. Until the army took him, he had lived right there in the house.

Her brother, Roger, had been the kind of boy who would stick hot match heads under his nails just to see how long *she* could stand something like that. It had never been long. She was not what he called his type. And when he had learned that she had taken poison, he had not been impressed. She had gone, he even hinted, over to the enemy. She didn't know where she had gone, or where she was going, and the truth was that she didn't much care, that last summer, so long as it took her out of the house.

But she had been worried, at the time, about going to school in England, since her brother always wanted whatever it was she had. She knew that her father could not afford it for both of them. But the only things he wanted were the things she had in the house, such as her books with her name plate at the front of them. He would steam her plate off and put in his own. Her album of stamps, her collection of shells, her wooden cases of bugs, moths, and butterflies; no matter what it was he took it for his own. He was her brother. He was also very brilliant and they had to humor him. Even with him life had not been worth living until she found out how quickly he tired, how quickly he lost interest, the moment everything he wanted was his. He would let her borrow them back, as *his* things, and play with them. Why she loved him like a brother nobody knew, she hadn't the slightest idea herself, until she found him hiding in the piano box behind the garage. He didn't look like her brother. He looked like a little monster, as he was wearing a World War helmet, and he had a bayonet, with a World War rucksack on his back.

In it he said he had everything that belonged to him. Naturally, she thought he meant her stamps and her shells, and when he saw that she might put up a fight about it—at that time she had been an inch taller— he opened the rucksack and showed her everything. Not a thing of her own. Everything he had belonged to her father: his pen and pencil set from the top of his desk, his bird binoculars, the knife he used to trim his nails, and at the bottom of the rucksack, in the leather case, his fine Swiss watch. They both knew that the watch was a sacred thing, though they had no idea why, but when she saw that he had it she just gasped, sucking in her breath. It had been the only thing she ever did that had made an impression on him. He was such a clever boy that he was never impressed by what she said, or what she thought, but he watched her very closely, and he was sometimes troubled by what she did. The gasp did it. He had been so impressed that he hadn't run away. She had been able to persuade him to put it off till another time.

She disliked him so much in general it had never crossed her mind that she might love him, or that it was possible to love anybody she hated so much. But when she found him behind the garage, she could see very clearly that he needed something, and it must be love. She was old enough to know that putting on a war helmet and stealing a watch wouldn't really help matters, but it had made her wonder why he took just the things that he did. He stole only from their father. He hadn't touched a single one of her mother's things. Their mother had a gold watch, with a snap-lid face, that Katherine liked better than the Swiss one of her father's, and there were five one-dollar bills at the bottom of the box that held her loose hair. He knew that, but he never touched any of it. It was not that he liked her, because he didn't. When Katherine needed help she turned to her father, but her brother Roger never turned to anyone. She had a father, but he didn't seem to have anything. That was why she found him in the World War helmet, prepared to go to France and join the Foreign Legion, which was something he had dreamed up after reading one of her books. It had been over his head, and he had the whole story a little mixed up.

Her brother had been just eleven that summer, and in the fall she had gone to school in England, from where she wrote him letters she knew her mother would open and read. But she was very clever, she never said a thing except what a terrible time she was having, and how lucky he was not to have to take the cold morning baths that she did. But when she came home, two years later, he was already such a grown-up person that she had been ashamed of the silly letters she had sent. He was almost a man in some respects, with a croak in his voice that did something for him, and she could see that their father was very proud of him. But there was no way of telling whether her mother thought well of him or not.

"Pride goeth before the fall," she had said, when she saw the picture of him as an athlete and honor student in the paper. It made her brother laugh, but there was something about it that Katherine didn't like. Nor did she like the way he spent all his free time around the house. He didn't seem to have friends, or to care much for girls, and when he went into his room in the evening to study, he hung a sign on his door which said—

GENIUS BURNING
QUIET
Please

Then she had gone off to college—off as far as she could get—and a week or so later, at the first college dance, she had seen a tall boy so badly stooped she thought he must have curvature of the spine. But most of it was due to the little, dumpy girl he was dancing with. The girl was very gay, but ordinary, and Katherine had made a mental note of the fact that the tall, lean-looking boy simply had no taste. She had made other notes during that evening, one to the effect that he seemed to stoop as much as he did in order to keep in touch with the world. There was that about him—he *looked* above it—it seemed to cost him an effort to come down to it, and she was thankful she knew better than to fall for an unpleasant type like that. She hadn't been dancing herself, that evening, as she had cracked her knee open in a hockey match, and was sitting on a table with her bandaged leg stuck out in front of her. It gave her a good chance to look over the boys—they were certainly not men according to her standards, nor the standards of any girl who had been educated in England and on the Continent. She *had* noticed the tall one, as he *did* stick out, but he was just a big boy, with fairly nice teeth, but from the side he had this posed, observant air. *Au dessus de la mêlée*—as she told him later on. That was why she happened to be looking at him when he suddenly turned, for no reason on earth, and gave her a great big knowing smile. That took her so much by surprise that she had probably flushed, as he said later, and then he had crossed the room to the table and sat down on it.

"Name's Webb—" he had said, nothing else, and when she tried to find that name in the phone book, when she sat up half the night looking for it, there was no Webb, and she thought it must be his first name. So she went through more than eleven hundred names looking for it. It was not there, and the only dark days, the only really dark night in the whole business, was the one she spent thinking he must be a teacher and married to someone. England had put her out of touch. Young American men could be very strange.

Even the year abroad was not so long as the two or three days before he called her, and she heard his voice, heard him say "This Webb," as if introducing someone who stood beside him, and she had come to see the terrible truth in it. His name was Paul, a good name for him, but he always referred to himself as Webb, as that was the half of the man that interested him. Webb the painter, Webb the thinker, Webb the persevering, dedicated artist, Webb the great and holy pain in the arse, as he described himself. In the corner of each painting, like the print of a paw, he put the name Webb. That was the man he fancied he was —and perhaps he was. It was not her business, since the man she had married was known as Paul.

"Webb—" he would say to himself, loud enough for her to catch it, "just what the hell you up to now?" and she would have to put her own work down and come to his room and look. She seldom knew. His painting had got very advanced. She was apt to like what he described as his weaker things. So she had just half a man, in some respects, the Paul half of the painter Webb, but the better half in so far as she was able to judge. Not that he was not a fine painter; it was

known, now, that he was, but Paul, rather than painting, interested her. It often crossed her mind that she
had given a whole life, or almost a whole one, for his
half, but that seemed to be a woman's lot. One of
the first things he had said to her, when they were
married, was that a *just* marriage was impossible, since
one of the partners always gave, and the other one
took. He was not cruel about it, but he was awfully
detached, and she had once thought it was more than
she could bear, but that always turned out to be an
overestimation on her part. She could bear him, rather
than not have him at all. There had been other men;
there had been Dr. Barr, there had been the conti-
nental who wrote her French love letters, but they
were only good letters while there was some chance
of Paul reading them. They were only good men if he
was there in the room competing with them. But when
he turned and left the room—as he usually did—all
the interest she felt went right along with him, and
she would either look for him, or ask somebody to
please take her home.

But there had been one summer when she came
to the conclusion that for the good of them both,
for his work especially, they had better go their separate ways. Which meant that *she* had gone (when
they had talked it over she had the absolute conviction
that he wasn't even listening). She had got as far as

Philadelphia, when the idea of leaving him to all those women, the bohemians and the harpies who just *loved* his painting (he was such a ninny when it came to women) made her leave the train and take the next one back to New York. She didn't give a hoot, she realized at the time, whether she was good or bad for his painting, whether she had just half of him or a quarter, or whether he was not, as her friends pointed out, doing much for her. But when she got back it was clear that he hadn't even been outside the apartment, and he seemed to have forgotten that she might have been leaving him for good. If he was painting he never showed the slightest awareness of her own state of mind.

But the worst trial (hearing the screen door close she drew the blind and stepped back from the window) the worst trial was when they had to spend a week or two in this house. She had worked this out very carefully, she knew exactly why he was utterly hopeless, and if she knew anything, she knew that he would never change. Nevertheless, it was always worse than she had been led to expect. He was often shrewd, he could even be kind, but he had a mania to figure things out, and there were some things that he would never understand. A family, nearly any family, was one of them. He had never had a family himself, he had almost been an orphan, he had made his own way and it had certainly made him a better painter, but it left him nearly blind to the family side of life. The Paul side, *her* side, he was inclined to treat as a good humored joke, with the kind of infantile frankness of which he was so proud. After ten years of marriage, and right here in this house, some busybody had asked him if he had any children, and the room had gone quiet to hear what he had to say.

"Kids?" he had said, in his booming voice, "I'm afraid it's been up to me to have them, my wife's more than had her hands full taking care of me!"

God knows that was what everybody knew, absolutely everybody, but just for that reason he didn't have to shout it, but he would always blurt it out if it struck him as the *truth*. This mania for the truth, which she had once admired, which she had thought was such an index to his character, now led her to feel that *the truth* was just about the biggest lie of them all. It was just a fancy way of covering up the facts. She had made the mistake, when they were just married, of telling him the long story of her life, all about her family, and how she had even tried to take her own life. She had never told a living soul these things, and it had been a great relief to her to tell it, but of all the people in the world to tell, she should have never told *him*. She had given him what he called *the picture*, and by that he meant he thought he had the facts, he thought he could see just how it worked. But she had told him before she knew that, before she realized that he thought a family, or anything else that had to do with people, was supposed to add up and make what he called "sense." Supposed to fit into the picture like the various colors were said to fit into his paintings, so that if one went wrong, all the other colors would have to be changed. If she had known *that* she would have told him that she was a motherless orphan herself, had no family at all, and simply written all of them off. She would never have permitted him to set a foot inside of the house. As it was he had the *real picture* of her father, two or three theories concerning her mother, and very likely an expanding set of sketches and plans in regard to herself.

It was perfectly true that her mother was strange in a way that had warped the life of the family, and that a force of some kind, as if the place were haunted, seemed to drive people from her house. Neither Katherine nor her father had been able to live in it. They had worked out a way of doing their living somewhere else. That was perfectly true, there *was* something in the house, but there was no doubt whatsoever in Paul's mind, as there was in hers, just what this strange power was. It seemed to her that all powers were strange. Why she ever lived with

Webb was one of the strangest powers of all. If she could go on doing something like that, living with half a man on a half time basis, there was nothing very strange about her father's life. He had settled for *something*. Perhaps he alone knew what it was. So had her mother settled for something, and if it seemed a strange thing to other people, if it drove her own children nearly crazy, that was certainly too bad, but there was nothing *really* strange about it. That was merely how it looked to other people, and the whole world was made up of other people who puzzled over their neighbors but never raised an eyebrow about themselves. There was nothing in all the world so strange as the happy marriage of Paul Webb to Katherine Porter, but her husband, in fifteen years, had never given it a thought. All his wonderful powers of analysis he turned somewhere else. He simply *couldn't* understand how Judge Porter had lived with his wife. Well, Katherine couldn't understand it either, all her life she had loved and pitied her father, and only very recently had she given her mother a serious thought. What, for thirty-five years, had her mother's life been like? Nobody seemed to care. It was about her father that they talked. Her mother never talked, never broke down, nor had she ever given any indication as to whether her own life was good or bad. She had never, so far as Katherine knew, ever said a kind word to them as children, or ever shown the need for such a kind word herself. That had not been her mother's role. Whatever this role had been, Katherine had had the feeling, since her father's illness, that a role—a role of some sort—was what her mother played. She played it without a hitch, which was perhaps the trouble, as most people stumbled and fell, but her mother never missed a day, never missed a cue. She was never, as Webb liked to say, out of character. Never, no, not once, and thinking of that she turned back to the window, as she could hear, right there below her, voices in the yard. Drawing a corner of the curtain she could see Mr. Parsons, a Sherwin-Williams painter's hat on his head, standing in the yard where her mother threw the bread and the melon seeds. He stood with his head cocked to one side, facing the back porch. He was listening, she knew, to what her mother had to say to him. Katherine was fond of Parsons, and with her father dead she wondered if another human being, beside herself, knew what Parsons had meant to the family. He looked older and grayer. She could *see* what it had taken out of him. A little deafer, too, as she could tell by the anxious cock of his head. Mr. Parsons—if anyone could be said to be—was a member of the family. For more than twenty years, maybe thirty, he had kept up the yard, opened the clogged drains, repaired

the drive and the leaks in the roof, and found time
to listen to her mother on civic affairs. She was about
to tap on the window—he was fond of her, and called
her *his* Porter—when the clothesline, the double line
that was strung from the post on the porch to the
sycamore tree, began to move as her mother put
something out to dry. The line moved slowly, just a
foot at a time, and she saw that Mr. Parsons, his head
wagging, had his eye on what was coming down the
line. A moment later it appeared, a square sheet of
paper, the center damp and one corner torn, but
otherwise, as her mother would have said, none the
worse for wear. A faint orange-juice smudge showed
on one corner of it. Mr. Parsons watched the towel
come down the line, pass jerkily just to the left of his
head, into the spot of sunlight, without anything
showing on his face but serious concern. The towel
was held to the line by a red plastic pin, of the pincer
type. Parsons showed no surprise that the wife of
Judge Porter, many years after the war and the paper
shortage, still put a single sheet of slightly used towel
paper out to dry. If any man had the picture, the real
picture, of what life was like in the Porter house,
of what the Judge was like, of what his wife was like,
of what living in the house had really been like, it
was this old man who never took the trouble to say
anything.

The Deep Sleep

Katherine turned from the window, and across the hall, through the bedroom door that she had left open, she could see Paul sitting on the bed, scratching his head. A light fall of dandruff had already sprinkled the rug. It happened to be one of the things, of all the aggravating things about him, that led her to feel that one day she might really give him up.

"Paul—" she began, but as she left the bathroom she could hear her mother's voice in the stairwell.

"Katherine," her mother said, "don't you think it's about time he was getting up?"

"He's up," she replied, "he's up now, Mother," and as she stepped into the bedroom she added, "Paul—"

"Yes, Mo-thurrr," he replied, but she said nothing, no, not a word, for no matter what she said to him, in *this* house, it would only make him worse.

PARSONS

Parsons could have told you the day the Judge took a turn for the worse. He never admitted as much to himself, but a day or two later, going into the garage to pick up the grass catcher for the mower, he had slipped the pair of pruning shears into the pocket of his coat. Imported shears, stamped *Made in Germany*. Parsons was a reasonably honest man—that was the opinion he held of himself—so he must have wanted that pair of clippers pretty bad. He had walked into the garage for the battered grass catcher, but his hand went out and picked up the shears as if he had had that steal in mind for many years. Which was true. He had wanted those clippers from the first. The Judge had brought them home from Germany at a time when he did a little clipping himself, but that hadn't lasted long and they just hung there on the hook. When Parsons used them he always took the trouble to wipe the blades when he was through, and leave a thin film of oil on the handle when he hung them up. He was free to use them, but that hadn't been enough. He had wanted that pair of clippers for himself. So his hand went out and took them, but as he came through the door of the garage he realized, all of a sudden, what he had done. He had put a nail in the Judge's coffin.

He had put in a nail, on the average, once a week. After the clippers came the oil can with the fancy trigger action, like a revolver. He didn't have the slightest use for such an oil can, but he liked its looks. After the oil can came the screw driver, with the assorted tools in the cherry-wood handle—all of which he had, but not in a cherry-wood handle. After the screw driver, the brass water-nozzle, after the nozzle the tube of Ant Killer, and then, one book at a time, the five-volume set of *The Rise of the Dutch Republic,* in old calf. Parsons didn't read books, but he had always wanted them around the house. After that he slowed up, and took only things that he could replace. On the empty hook he would hang some old tool of his own. The last thing he took, before the youngsters arrived, was an almost new South Wind car heater, although he had never owned or driven a car himself. He hid all of these things in the dark fruit cellar of his own house.

A reasonably honest man, Parsons didn't find it easy to steal, but he found it easier than letting the place just go to pot. Letting other people steal the things that he really deserved himself. If he didn't, some shyster lawyer, or some bird-club friend of Mrs.

Porter's, would make off with what was really his by rights. Parsons had, as a matter of fact, his principles. He never took a cent of money. He never touched a thing inside the house. But the garage, as the Judge said himself, was his bailiwick. Anything that really belonged in the garage was his by rights.

If he had asked the Judge, the Judge would have said, "Parsons, you help yourself." That's what the Judge would have said, but he was a hard man to ask. It would lead him to think that he should have thought of that himself. The Judge was the kind of man it was easier to steal from, in some respects, than to hurt his feelings by coming right out and asking for something.

In the early thirties, when the Judge got so busy he couldn't spend enough time in the yard, he had asked Parsons if he would like to keep an eye on the place. He offered to pay him what he, Parsons, thought it was worth. Parsons had said about fifteen dollars a month. In the early thirties that was money, the dollar really bought something, and on top of all of that Parsons could do a lot more work. He was just twenty years younger then himself. But in those twenty years Parsons had reached the point where he worked day and night on the Porter place, but all he got, right up to the last, was the fifteen a month. He couldn't bring himself to speak about it to the Judge. It would make the Judge see that he should have thought of that himself.

When the war came along, the second war, that is, and the Judge might be gone for as long as a week, Parsons more or less lived in and out of the Porter house. Nobody knew that, but it was a simple fact. The Judge knew it, of course, but he seemed to think Parsons was one of the family and had forgotten that he was once a hired hand. When the Judge said keep an eye on the place, he never troubled to mention Mrs. Porter, but they both knew that that was what he meant. Not that she couldn't run her own house, but there were things she left to the Judge, and the Judge naturally left these things to him. The Judge did the shopping for instance, he bought the meat, the vegetables, and the Kleenex, and when there was a melon to be picked out, he had to pick it. Over the years Parsons had learned to do these things. He could pick a frying chicken for Mrs. Porter, but when he tried to pick one for himself he didn't seem to have the same sort of confidence. That sounded mighty strange, but he had found it to be a fact. He didn't understand it, but it helped to explain certain things. When Parsons *represented* Mrs. Porter, when he bought her ground beef, or picked her a melon, he had an inkling of things it was none of his business,

really, to know. He had an inkling, that is, as to why
the Judge had married her. He knew what it was to
really be married to a woman like that. There were
people who found that something of a puzzle, but it
had never been a puzzle to Carl Parsons, and when
they questioned him about it there was just one thing
that he troubled to say.

"Mrs. Porter's a remarkable woman," he would say,
and let it go at that. He was seldom contradicted.
People could sense the truth in it. Parsons never said
much, but he had never said more than when he said
that.

Toward the end of the summer they had gone
abroad, Parsons had got a letter from the Judge himself. They were going to be needing, the Judge in-
formed him, a bigger place. He didn't say why, but
here and there in the letter he referred to Mrs. Porter
as Mother, so it wasn't too hard for Parsons to puzzle
it out. The Judge went on to say that he had put
some money on a fine new place, a little further down
the Main Line, and he wanted Parsons to be the man
to look after it. So he was there in the car, a month
or so later, when the Judge drove them over to look
at the place, a big fifteen room Norman type house
with a half acre pond. It was supposed to be a surprise
for Mrs. Porter, but even while they were just idling
up, stopping alongside the big SOLD sign, Par-

sons had the feeling that the shoe was on the other foot.

"Well, how do you like it, Mother?" the Judge had said, then turned on the seat to wink at Parsons. Mrs. Porter looked at it, she looked it all over, the house, the grounds, and the fine big pond, then her eye seemed to fasten on a concrete urn full of a lot of dead ferns.

"Howard—" she said, "don't we *already* have a concrete urn?"

The Judge had turned to Parsons, as if he didn't know.

"Think maybe there is," Parsons had said. "Think maybe there is one around somewhere."

"I remember an urn—" Mrs. Porter had said, and though her eyes were on the new house, Parsons could see that she had already forgotten it. "If we have a perfectly good urn of our own—" she said, and took off one of the gloves she was wearing, and picked the lint off one of the Judge's sleeves.

"If you think you like your own urn better," said the Judge, and since it was perfectly plain that she did, he turned the car around in the road and drove back home.

Not a word was said, all the way back, but when the car turned into the drive the Judge pulled to a stop at the front of the house to let her out. Then

Parsons and the Judge drove around in back. Parsons climbed out of the car to open the garage door, and he was still there, a minute or two later, when the Judge came out of the garage and stood at his side. Looking down the long drive, and the hedge of privet, there was no sign anywhere of Mrs. Porter, but she had left her hat, her gloves and her purse at the edge of the drive. For one terrible moment an awful thought had crossed Parsons' mind. It was like the pile of clothes that suicides leave on the edge of a bridge. Then he saw, they both saw, the fluttery movement through the crisscross slats that went all the way around the bottom of the front porch. It was Mrs. Porter. She was back under the porch waving at them. They both went forward—the Judge actually took a hop or two, as though he might start running— then he slowed down and they went along together down the drive. They stopped where they could see Mrs. Porter's face through the slats. The porch was pretty high, but not so high she didn't have to stoop.

"Howard—" she had said, as she had never got around to calling him *Judge*, like other people, "Howard, if they're really coming back, we'll use our own."

"What's that, Mother?" the Judge had said.

"Urns," she had replied, and they could hear her pat her hand on the concrete bowl stored under the porch. It had come with the land. Nobody had ever laid claim to it. Then she had made her way from under the porch, coming out with her hair full of dust and cobwebs and walked to that spot in the yard where she would like the urn to stand. There were some dandelion greens in the grass—Parsons had let them grow, since he figured they'd be moving—and as they stood there, watching, she stooped over and began to pull them out. The Judge did not speak, but Parsons knew that the scene, for both of them, was a revelation, one of the type that passeth understanding, as the Scripture goes. Nor was there in it anything he could put his finger on. Mrs. Porter was indeed a remarkable woman—he had known that from that point forward—and what they knew was a bond between Parsons and the Judge. Even though what they knew was a hard thing to pin down. In his mind's eye Parsons had two pictures, Mrs. Porter picking lint from the Judge's sleeve, and Mrs. Porter picking dandelion greens in her own yard. They were related in such a way that it truly passed his understanding, but remained, nevertheless, a remarkable thing. There they had stood, with this knowledge between them, until Mrs. Porter, without turning, had said—

"One of you men want to fetch me a paring knife?"

* * *

The Deep Sleep

Parsons seldom entered the garage any more without wondering what he ought to take next, and he seldom left it without taking a look down the drive. Down to that point where Mrs. Porter had left her hat, her purse, and her gloves. This morning, however, the drive was blocked by Webb's car, an old Ford coupe, that had never really looked right in Mrs. Porter's yard. She considered a car as old as that dangerous. But with the Judge gone, the children would now get the family car. The very thought of that made Parsons turn and take another look around, as if he might have missed something, since the idea of Webb getting something for nothing didn't appeal to him. All the times that Webb had been around the place he had never cut the grass, he had never raked a leaf, or so much as swept the snow off the porch. He took it for granted that Parsons was the hired hand. Parsons had never liked Webb much anyhow, and if the honest truth were known he had really hated to see the boy make good. He looked lazy. He didn't seem to know how to work. He would sit on the furniture out in the yard until he'd worn away the grass that Parsons had planted, but it never crossed his lazy, good-for-nothing mind to put it back. He would drive his fool car up on the lawn so the oil and rusty water would drip on it, and just walking down the drive he would break twigs off the pyracantha bush. Parsons couldn't figure out what a girl like Katherine could see in him. The terrible truth of the matter was that he even hoped Katherine herself would show it, and look a little bit frowsy and worn like most married women did. Why she didn't, he couldn't figure out. He would go crazy married to a loafer like that himself. As he stood there in the yard, watching the piece of towel paper come down the line toward him, then pass over his head, he couldn't help thinking what a boy like Webb would make out of that. A kid who never turned to pick up what he had dropped. It was a fine example of Mrs. Porter's patience that she seldom spoke to him about it, and that she did what she could to make him feel at home. Parsons could hear her calling up the stairs, asking if the big loafer was still in bed yet, and then he could hear Katherine answering back that he was getting up. Still a young woman's voice. Nothing old, or cracked, or bitter in it. Nothing like the tobacco croak of the loudmouthed, horsey set. He headed toward the house, he wanted to see her, but his head was down when she suddenly cried—

"Why, Mr. Parsons, you're looking wonderful!"

And there she was, there she was on the porch, looking more like the Judge every living minute, and so far as he could see showing hardly any wear and tear. So he came forward, holding out his kisser, and not until she hugged him did it cross his mind how much he must have slipped since she had seen him last. Never before had she cried out how wonderful he looked.

MRS. PORTER

Not exactly frail, nor the sort of person you would describe as delicate or anemic, right up until her marriage Millicent Ordway had never looked very strong. But she took very quickly, as her father said, to responsibility. The youngest of Sherman Ordway's five daughters, she had been the first to attract much attention, but the last to pledge her troth to any one man. Almost petite, with a waspish waist and her hair piled so high she looked top heavy, Milly Ordway appeared to be both smaller and frailer than she really was. This came from something once described as her bearing, and the habit she had, as the youngest daughter, of gazing on the young men gathered in the hallway from the top of the stairs. She had observed that Howard Porter, as a rule, preferred to look up at her. Just as she looked her best at the top of the stairs, he looked his best somewhere near the bottom, and he had been something of a problem from the moment he stood at her side.

A Finlay boy, he had come to Mercer as a member of the Wesleyan debating team—resolved that the

Cuban Imbroglio had been a mistake. Michael Leahy, her escort, had cried at him—

"Remember the Maine!
The deuce with Spain!"

but Howard Porter, she had remarked, had paid it no heed. He had passed the night in her father's house, and in the morning he had pointed out, in Xenophon's *Anabasis*, the modern usage of the word *presbyteros*. Before Howard Porter there had been Michael Leahy, a Divinity student from Pittsburgh, and after Howard Porter there had been, for longer than she cared to remember, the problem of the bone hairpins found in the rented buggy seat. A joke, as it turned out, put there in jest by Michael Leahy, but taken in earnest by Earl Caddock, who came for the horse. Howard Porter had pressed her for her answer, but for his own satisfaction she had kept him waiting until Michael Leahy cleared the matter up.

"Mornin', Mrs. Porter," she heard Parsons say, and she turned to see what her daughter was wearing, saw what she was wearing, and that it was closed at the front.

"Isn't Mr. Parsons looking wonderful, Mother?" her daughter said.

"I've seen you both looking better," she replied.

"When I saw her on the porch—" Parsons said,

waving the hat that he held toward her daughter, "when I saw her through the winda, why, I thought it was the Missus." He closed his eyes, as if in pain, then opened one and winked.

"Hmmmm—" Mrs. Porter said, and took a dish from the pan, rinsed it, then turned to look at her daughter. She was a well-formed girl but a little heavy for her group and age.

"Now what do you think of *that*, Mother?"

"That's just what I thought, so help me," said Mr. Parsons. "When I saw her through the winda I said to my—"

"Win-*dow*," said Mrs. Porter.

"—when I saw her through the win-dow," Parsons said. He put the hat he was holding on top of the box full of crusts for the birds.

"You've had your energy, Mr. Parsons?" she said, although she could see plainly enough that he hadn't. On the sides of his mouth was the goo from Freihofer's sticky buns. Bulk, sugar, and starch, but no sustaining energy.

"Had a bite when I got up—" Parsons began, then stopped there, took out his watch. "Don't tell me it's a quarter to nine already?" he said.

"If you'd had en-er-gy," Mrs. Porter said, "you wouldn't be looking so hungry already. One breakfast a morning would be enough."

"Mo-*thurr*!" said Katherine.

"Mr. Parsons and I," Mrs. Porter said, "are old enough to speak frankly."

"Thing is," said Mr. Parsons, "I got it bass-ackwards. I got the wrong energy at the wrong time. One breakfast is enough if you happen to get the right one first." He slapped his hand on his leg.

"Katherine," she said, "if you'll lift the basket maybe Mr. Parsons would like to sit down."

"Got it!" he said, "already got it," and held up the basket to show that he had it, then sat down on the stool with the basket in his lap.

"You can't eat holding *that*!" Katherine said, and took the basket from him, looked around the kitchen, then looked through the window at the porch. There was no place, anywhere, to put anything down. Parsons waited till she saw that, then he put out his hand and took the basket from her.

"Oatmeal," said Mrs. Porter, "oatmeal for energy."

"Cup of hot coffee suit me fine," Parsons said.

"Sugar, cream *and* coffee, that is," Mrs. Porter said.

"Guess your mother knows me pretty well by now," Parsons said, and drummed his fingers on the sides of the basket.

"Sugar, cream, coffee and a melon," Mrs. Porter said. She was making out a list.

"You want to get that down, young lady?" said Parsons, and pointed with the basket at the pad on the table. "I get up from this seat, 'fraid somebody else sit down on it."

Opening the bread drawer Katherine said, "We're going to need bread too, Mother."

"Tobacco——" said Mrs. Porter.

"Tobacco?" Katherine said, and turned to look at Parsons.

"He would be alive now," Mrs. Porter said, "he came from a simple, long-lived family."

Parsons stood up, took a match from his pocket and scratched it on his pants leg, then passed it to Mrs. Porter who was waiting for the pilot light to light.

"Next thing I got to look into," Parsons said. "Check pilot light."

"Salt," Mrs. Porter said, dropping a pinch into the oatmeal, "salt will taste good."

"We been doin' without salt," Parsons said, "we been doin' without it since the Judge couldn't eat it. Easier to do without it than try to keep track of where it is."

"Your Grandmother thinks that she needs it," Mrs. Porter said.

"How she seem to be doin'?" Parsons said.

"We need some Carter's Little Liver pills," said Mrs. Porter.

Pushing up from the stool, Parsons made a note of it on the pad.

"Think we can use a can of Drano, too," he said, and wrote it down.

"Is it all right if I boil all of the eggs?" Katherine said.

From the shelf above the stove Mrs. Porter took a plastic leghorn chicken, with a weighted bottom, and a glass tube in a hole in her back. The tube contained fine sand, like a miniature hour glass, and operated on that principle. When it passed from the top to the bottom, a soft-boiled egg was done. Mrs. Porter turned the tube, then said—

"You would think anybody might have thought of it."

"That the coffee I smell boilin'?" Parsons said.

Katherine lowered the flame under the coffee, and dropped the eggs into the boiling water. Then she turned from the stove and looked toward the stairs, where somebody was coming down. At the bottom of the stairs the feet turned to the right, into the living room. They crossed the living room to the screen, where one foot kicked the screen open, and they heard the sigh as he stooped for the paper on the front porch. Then he came back through the house, slapping the paper on the furniture, to where he stopped, suddenly, at the door to the dining room.

"Good morning, Grandmother!" he boomed, loud enough to scare her to death, but the Grandmother gave him no reply. "The cat got your tongue?" he said, as that was the Grandmother's expression. One that she used on him quite a bit of the time. "Well, if the cat's got your tongue—" he went on, and crossed the room to the door of the kitchen, pushed it open, and stood there looking at them. Holding the morning paper up he said, "See they got a picture of him on the front page."

Mrs. Porter, facing the stove, did not turn to look. Katherine, watching the eggs, did not turn to look. Mr. Parsons took out his watch, passed his thumb across the crystal, then said—

"If you want them eggs soft boiled, think the time's about up."

THE GRANDMOTHER

Good morning your night nurse! the Grandmother thought, thrust her battered cane into the bird box, and came within an ace of beaning the lady cardinal, one of the *good* birds. There were good and bad birds, friendly and unfriendly, but through the cloudy cataract blur the Grandmother found it hard to tell them apart. More and more, now, all of the birds looked about the same. Feathered friends as well as feathered enemies. She gave the cane a wag, cuffed it on the window, then sat there, her eyes half closed, listening to the racket that the birds made in the trees. The fuss she made had a soothing effect on the Grandmother's nerves. Good morning your old hat! she now said, which was a milder form of swearing, and indicated that she was not holding a grudge. She placed the scuffed cane in her lap, then took from the pocket of her apron a piece of half-sucked, lint-covered, hard candy. She had started it earlier, but she had had to spit it out. The Grandmother was not supposed to take sweets until after she had had her breakfast, but it was nine o'clock and she had been up since five. Good morning your night nurse! she muttered, loud enough to make her plates clack, then she slipped the piece of hard candy into her mouth. As the raspberry flavor soaked through the lint, she began to rock.

The Grandmother was born in a Conestoga wagon that had red sides and a bright blue bottom, and when she was twelve the *Monitor* fired upon the *Merrimac*. Not a woman to be rushed, she married at thirty a man with Confederate money in his pocket, and two years later her first and only child was born. As a woman who had set eyes upon Abraham Lincoln, Angela Rautzen Porter had her standards, and her son, Howard Porter, had his work cut out for him. The town of Finlay, in western Pennsylvania, had lawns he could mow, papers he could deliver, circus animals that had to be watered, and several trains daily that whistled, but did not stop. They were headed for Pittsburgh, Philadelphia, and New York.

Howard Porter did not split rails, nor grow to be very tall and ugly, but he early showed a knack for settling the problems other people brought up. The Law came fairly easy to a boy who could read a page of Blackstone, and, if the need ever came, find it filed away in his mind. He had that from the Rautzens, who were good at figures and all problems that began, *Now if a farmer had three donkeys—*. From the Porters, a close-mouthed clan, he had the knack of listening. A little shorter than average, a little broader than average, he was a young man who had never really been a small boy. A fellow student had been the first one to refer to him as *The Judge*.

In weekly letters to his mother, Howard Porter never mentioned his rise in the world, or when the world came to him, since he knew that his mother, Angela Rautzen Porter, merely expected it. What she didn't take for granted she could find for herself in the Finlay *Nonpareil*. There were people who wondered what Mrs. Porter's boy would be up to next.

He spent the holidays with her in Finlay, cutting back the vines that were pulling down the porch, or sowing new grass seed where other people's children crossed her lawn. But in her eighty-fourth year a deep fall of snow kept her son from getting home for Christmas, and she might have nearly frozen if the three cats hadn't slept in her lap. In the spring she went to live with him and help keep the squirrels out of the window box. She got up at five, but she couldn't eat until somebody remembered to feed her, since the last time she cooked for herself she had caught on fire. Her apron the first time—then one of her sleeves. After eating she would go into the basement where she would pound with her cane on the plumbing until somebody heated one of her irons and brought it down. Then she would iron—for two or three years it had been the same shirt, and nobody wore it—and when she was through they would dip it in water, muss it up.

Sometimes the Grandmother would pound on the plumbing till she thought the house would fall all around her, and spiders and cobwebs would have to be brushed and combed out of her white hair. But most of the time she just took the shirt and ironed it. She found it wrinkled, and she smoothed the wrinkles out. The iron was never hot enough to burn it, or to scorch it so she could smell it, but if she dropped the iron on the floor it made a big noise. The talking would stop and one of them would come to the top of the stairs.

"Oh, Grandmother?" they would say.

Grandmother your hat! she would think, but she wouldn't answer.

"Ohhhh, Grandmother?" they would say, and come down the stairs to where they could see her. Sometimes she was there, and sometimes she was hiding in the fruit cellar. If she wasn't there they would all come running, turning on the lights so they could see her, and finally they would find her sitting on the tub she once made butter in.

"Grandmother!" they would say. They were all alike. They were young, they grew up, they grew old, without learning anything. Her son was poorly.

The Deep Sleep

Then he had died. Everybody did. Everybody, that is, but the Grandmother.

"Oh, she's the same as usual," Mrs. Porter would say, and though there were no birds at the window, good or bad, friendly or unfriendly, the Grandmother would put her cane into the bird box and give it a wag. There were no birds now, not a one, but that's what she did. There were people who marvelled that such an old lady had so much strength. In the quiet that followed the Grandmother could hear the silence in the kitchen, the coffee perking, and then the tinny noise as they put the dishes on her tray. Then the door opened, and Mrs. Porter said—

"Canned cream, you know, less fat in the coffee—" and then one of them came through the swinging door at her.

"Here you are, Grandmother," said Webb, "here's your one thousand two hundred and eighty-seven calories."

WEBB

Here you are, you old battle-axe, thought Webb, and put the tray of food at her place on the table, then drew out the chair with the padded cushion tied to the seat. The cushion, two inches thick, was not there for the Grandmother's comfort, but to lift her high enough to keep her chin out of her plate.

Webb stood behind her chair, watching her make the movements that were preliminary to rising, the claw-like hands seeing that everything was in its proper place. She would not let them help her. She would *not* be beholden to anyone. Webb admired that streak in her, he admired quite a few of the things about her, but he also had the urge to give the rug a jerk while she was standing on it. She was so damned *intact*. She was like a turtle clamped tight in its shell. From where he stood, towering above her, she looked like one of the snapper variety, all dolled up for the ball in Alice's Wonderland.

"There you are," he said, giving the chair a nudge, and to show just exactly what she thought of that, she put her old hooks on the table, pushed herself away. Her face was so close to the bowl of oatmeal the steam rising from it fogged her glasses, and gave an oily, nearly polished gloss to her leathery skin. One dish at a time, one snoop at a time, she looked over the tray. She waited till Webb moved from behind her, then she placed her hands in her lap, lidded her eyes, and stiffened the tight line of her mouth.

"What's missing, Grandmother?" he said, as he

knew something was. She did not move. She did not answer. Turning to face the kitchen Webb said, "Hot oatmeal—doesn't she eat it?"

"Tell her that it is *not* the three-minute kind," said Mrs. Porter.

Webb had another look at her, then said, "There's oatmeal, prunes, toast, and coffee."

"If you just let it set, she'll eat it," said Mrs. Porter.

Webb doubted it. He looked at the tray again.

"She likes a tablespoon for the oatmeal," said Katherine, "a *big* tablespoon."

"Hold on a minute," Parsons said, and they all held on a minute while he crossed the kitchen, came into the dining room. From the kitchen door he looked at the tray, then he turned and said, "She's got no spreadin's—"

"No what?" said Webb.

"Spreadin's—" said Parsons, "she won't eat without her jam." Mrs. Porter took a jar of applebutter from the cupboard, spooned out a little, and gave it to Parsons. He made a place for it on the Grandmother's tray.

"Like it spread?" he said softly, as if she wasn't deaf.

"No," said the Grandmother, and spread it herself.

"Paul," said Katherine, "you have to stand there and stare at her?"

"I am not standing and staring," he said. He came

back into the kitchen and stared at his egg. It looked cold.

"Nobody likes to eat with someone standing and staring at them," Katherine said.

"You asked me to take in her tray," said Webb. "You like me to walk it in with my eyes closed?"

"I see they gave him front billing," Mrs. Porter said, but when Webb turned to look for her, she was not in the kitchen. She was out on the porch, where the old icebox—now used to store onions, clothespins, and potatoes—served as a lectern for the paper she had spread out on the top.

"Gave who, Mother?"

"Howard Rautzen Porter," she replied, "your father." Then she added, "I see they have *him* born in the wagon. Will they ever get it right?"

Looking at the watch on his wrist, Webb said, "Well, it's nine forty-five, what's next on the docket?"

From the porch, Mrs. Porter said, "He's sounding like his father-in-law already, Katherine."

"As I understand it, we have a lot we've got to do today," said Webb.

"Three columns in the *Inquirer*," Mrs. Porter said, "was it the *Bulletin* or the *Inquirer* that didn't like him?"

"Don't think the *Bulletin* favored his policies," Parsons said.

"If there's nothing on tap right away—" began Webb, but he was cut off there by a racket in the next room. The Grandmother was drumming with her spoon on her coffee cup.

"Guess she's ready for her second cup," said Parsons.

"No sugar at *all*, this time," said Mrs. Porter.

Webb waited for somebody else to do it, then said, "If you don't want me to be staring at her, dear, suppose you serve the coffee?"

Katherine pushed her plate away from her and said, "You've been up just twenty minutes, and already—"

"Born in a covered wagon," Mrs. Porter read, "Judge Porter early showed an aptitude for jurisprudence, in the now celebrated case of *Man* vs. *Dog*. Attacked by a large dog, the defendant protected himself with a pitchfork that he found handy. As this damaged the dog, the owner sued the gentleman for damages. Asked why defendant could not have used other end of the fork, Judge Porter's ruling, now a classic, was that defendant would have used other end of fork, if plaintiff would have used other end of dog."

Webb looked at Katherine, and she said, "Why, Mother, I never once heard it mentioned."

Mrs. Porter turned the page, as if to change the subject, then returned to the kitchen for a swallow of her coffee. Perhaps the steam, rising from the coffee, brought the flush to her face. Her eyes seemed to focus in the middle distance somewhere. Webb took a cigarette from the pack on the table, then stood up as if to look for matches, standing with his back to the table and facing the clock on the stove. He had suddenly remembered that Howard Porter was now dead. That his wife, Mrs. Porter, was now a widow and eligible. It embarrassed him to think that such a thought had crossed his mind, but it had. He found a match, lit the cigarette, then turned to glance at the face of Parsons. He looked old. There were bags and circles under his watery bloodshot eyes. What eyes he had, however, were on the back of Mrs. Porter's neck, still white with the powder she had puffed there after her bath.

"Why didn't Daddy ever mention it?" Katherine said, as her mother seemed to have forgotten the question.

"Your father didn't do it," Mrs. Porter said.

"Then who did?"

"Abraham Lincoln," Mrs. Porter said. "It was Lincoln who did it."

"I don't understand, Mother," Katherine said.

Clearing his throat Parsons said, "It's one of your Grandmother's stories, Kathy. Guess one of the reporters heard her tell it."

Since he was already up, and facing the stove, Webb

picked up the pot of coffee and pushed through the swinging door into the dining room. Until the door swung back, sucking the air and rattling the closed French doors behind her, the Grandmother, seated at the table, had been asleep. She had bent over so low that her forehead rested on the edge of the tray. Webb thought she might be dead—it might happen any time —till he noticed the tremor that came from the beating of her heart. At that moment, precisely, the Grandmother realized that she had been caught. That Webb stood there in the room and was looking at her. So she didn't budge her head an inch, she left it right there, as if she were playing possum, and with the spoon she still held she gave a smart clack on the side of her cup. Webb had never remarked before in the old crone any real resemblance to Judge Porter, but now he seemed to be sitting there himself, aged ninety-nine. He had seen the Judge play the same foxy game when he dozed at cards. Put on a foxy air, cock one eye wide, lid the other one tight as if meditating, then play some card as though he had been planning that move all along. Webb had not moved a step when he heard the chimes at the front door.

"I'm afraid I'm simply not presentable," Mrs. Porter said.

"Oh, honey—" said Katherine, "it's the door, you'll have to answer it."

The Deep Sleep

Webb set the coffeepot on the table, and on his way through the house to the door he saw the car, a black limousine, parked in the drive. Through the glass in the door he could see the chauffeur, in full uniform. The chauffeur held before him a large gleaming package, and Webb was so sure that it would be flowers, flowers in one form or another, that he put out his hands before he saw what the parcel was. The chauffeur held a large, gleaming aluminum roasting pan. Heat, waves of heat, were rising from the lid.

"The Judge Porter residence?" said the chauffeur.

"Why, yes—" Webb replied. "Yes."

"Compliments of Mrs. Crowell," the chauffeur said, and as Webb just stood there, "if I can just put this down, sir—" he said, and Webb opened the door wide and got out of his way. He walked into the house, looked round for a table, and seeing none in the living room, he walked on ahead to where the Grandmother sat with her tray. Webb got there in time to slip a newspaper underneath. "It's warm, but not hot," the chauffeur put in, then took from the crown of the hat he was wearing an unsealed envelope, bent it straight, then placed it in Webb's hands. "Mrs. Crowell—" he paused to say, "will have me call for the roaster when you are through," and with that he headed back for the door, Webb following him.

"Thank you, thank you very much," Webb said,

stood there while the man walked down to the drive, and was still there when the limousine eased into the street. When he turned from the door the women were gathered around the roasting pan. Katherine held the lid in her hand, and they were gazing at an enormous turkey. It had just been roasted, and the savory smell filled the room. Mrs. Porter took the letter Webb was holding, removed the card, and held it off at arm's length. From the chair to the floor seemed to be her ideal focusing length.

"Crowell—" she said, "Mr. and Mrs."

"There's something on the back, Mother—"

Turning the card, Mrs. Porter read, "Deepest sympathy." She stopped there, pursed her lips, then continued—

"Sorrow eats the heart a-way
And anguish sucks the mar-row,
But we must dine tonight, my dear,
If we shall weep tomor-row."

From the sleeve of Katherine's robe, and the arm that held the lid, Mrs. Porter picked something, rolled it between her fingers.

"Who are the Crowells, Mother?" said Katherine.

"Quail people," Mrs. Porter said, promptly.

"That's a mighty big quail," Webb said and laughed, then stopped laughing. The women didn't seem to have heard him. Katherine returned the lid to the roaster.

"It must be what they're doing now," Mrs. Porter said. "The Crowells are modern."

"That a quail in the box?" the Grandmother said.

"No, Grandmother," said Katherine, "it's a turkey."

"It's a *what?*" the Grandmother croaked, but on her face Webb saw the expression she had worn, many years ago, when Mrs. Porter tried to tell her that tuna fish, in the small round cans, was not rattlesnake meat. "Now lookey here—" she said, but they turned from her, they all turned, to hear the phone ring. Mrs. Porter, the Crowell letter in her hand, took a seat facing the telephone table, lifted the receiver, and placed the palm of her hand across the mouthpiece.

"Thank you cards," she said to Katherine, "something very simple," then she took her hand from the phone and said, "Yes, my dear, we have just been discussing it. I was just telling the children what a shame it is that *he* couldn't see it. The *Inquirer* always supported his policies, you know."

The Deep Sleep

KATHERINE

She left her mother on the phone, her Grandmother at the table, and carried the roaster into the kitchen, where she held it while Webb cleared off the dishes, made room for it. She waited for him to say something sarcastic, but he seemed to be preoccupied with what he was doing. Without turning to face her he said, "Will it be all right if *I* have a cup of coffee?"

She didn't give him the satisfaction of an answer.

He put water in the pot, the pot on the fire, then said, "I go in there—" he nodded toward the door, "I go in there with a pot of coffee, with at least two good full cups, then I set it on the table, then I answer the door, then I come back and find no coffee. I find the pot—" he said, making a face, "but the coffee's gone."

"She could *not* have drunk two full cups of coffee," Katherine said.

"Nope—" he said, and before he went on she knew very well she should have kept her mouth shut. She knew exactly what he was going to bring up. "Nope," he repeated, "it's out of the question, it's simply out of the question and ab-so-lute-ly silly to think an old lady could drink a pot of coffee or eat a two-pound box of chocolates at a crack." He smiled. She had been the one who told him about that. It had so

[71]

astonished her at the time that she simply had to tell someone, but it had been a mistake, as usual, to tell him. It had been a terrible and fascinating sight to see the Grandmother, over ninety at the time, eat a whole box of chocolates and then top it off with a full Christmas meal.

"Any old girl," Webb went on, "who can finish off a two-pound of Whitman's—"

"It was a one-pound box," she said.

"Well, that's still pretty good," he said, "if you consider the roast duck and the gravy, the buttered carrots and the creamed peas, the two helpings of cranberries and the hot mince pie—"

"I'm going to ask you—" she said, and it actually made her shudder to think about it. "I'm going to ask you to please stop bringing it up."

Turning up the heat on the fire, he said, "Like a swallow of this before she gets at it?"

"I would not."

"Well—" he said, in that way he had that she had once thought so wonderful, "Well, my dear, we've just *got* to keep up our en-er-gy!" He made a pious face, wet his lips, then began—

> "Sorrr-roooow eats the heart ah-way
> Annggg-wish sugs the marrr-ow—"

"Paul," she said.

"Yes, my dear?"

"Paul, I'm going to leave right now if you—" she stopped there, as she could hear the dull tapping on the kitchen floor. She could both hear it, and feel it through the soles of her shoes. It grew louder, and one of the pipes beneath the sink began to twang, indicating that the knob on the end of the chain pull, in the basement lavatory, was striking on the thin plywood walls and the water pipes. Someone was sitting there in the dark, groping for it.

"I was wandering where the hell he'd gone off to," Webb said.

"Just for this once," she said, "you might be a little more respectful."

"All I said was—" he replied, "I wondered where the hell he was."

"I don't know what Mother would have done without him," she said. She watched him pour some of the coffee into his cup, see that it was weak, and return it to the pot.

"Just so there's no viewing," he said, "if there's a viewing, you can count me out."

"Why do you keep harping on it? There will be no viewing. You heard Mother say she thought viewings were barbarous."

"They taking that line in the *Reader's Digest* now?" he said.

Katherine turned to the sink, turned on the water and let it run cool over her hands, then she turned it off and waited for Parsons to come up the stairs. Near the top, to warn them he was coming, he stomped his feet. In the landing at the top, where the rubbers were stored, he blew his nose. Stepping into the kitchen he started for the door, then he saw the roaster on the table.

"Well—" he said, "what in the world we got here?"

"Mr. and Mrs. Crowell have given us a turkey," Katherine said. She removed the lid from the roaster, showed him the bird.

"That's about a twenty pound bird, anyhow—" Parsons said.

"I don't know when we'll ever eat it," she said.

"They got money all right," Parsons said, "they take a half a year off just to fool around with birds."

"Paul's made some more coffee," she said, "you like a hot cup?"

"Nope, I guess not. If I take it now, have to do without it later." He turned back to the roaster and said, "That's a twenty dollar bill or I'll eat my hat."

Katherine looked at Paul, and saw that he was gazing at the milk bottles in the driveway window. "While Mother's busy," she said, "why don't you two sneak off and get the papers?"

"What papers?" said Paul.

"We've got to have extra papers," she said. "Every one of the relatives will have to have one."

"Think it adds up to about three dozen, don't it?" Parsons said.

"*Three* dozen *what?*" said Paul.

"There's thirty-some people in the family," said Katherine, "and if one of them should get what the other one doesn't—"

"Oh my God!" said Paul.

"Don't think there'll be more than five or six left at the station," Parsons said.

"Then you'll just have to drive into town and get them," she said. "We've got to have them, and there's no use arguing the point."

"Look—" said Paul, but the kitchen door opened— that was all, it merely eased open—and after several moments, backing through, the Grandmother appeared. She made the turn at the sink, then she waited till whoever it was had got out of her way, moved from the corridor between the table and the stove. When Webb had moved, her cane thumping, she proceeded to the basement stairs, where she hung the cane on her left arm, prepared to go down. Slowly, a step at a time, they could hear her heels come down with a click.

"By god, it almost gives you the creeps," said Webb.

"Judge was always worried that she might stumble.

Judge, I used to tell him, a *mole* don't stumble. Took him quite a spell," Parsons said, "to see that I was right."

"What the hell time is it getting to be?" Webb said.

When he couldn't speak without swearing, she knew that she had to do something about him. "Mr. Parsons," she said, "will you show him where the *Inquirer* building is?"

"Look—" began Webb, but Mrs. Porter, with the Grandmother's tray, came in from the dining room.

"She's leaving her prunes," Mrs. Porter said. "That is not good."

"Mother," Katherine said, "Mr. Parsons and Paul are going after the papers. How many papers do you think we're going to need?"

"Mrs. Lockwood was saying how little the picture looked like him," Mrs. Porter said.

"Mother, we've got to know just how many papers."

"You know how the Porters are," her mother replied.

"I'm saying thirty-five," Katherine said. "Is that all right?"

"There's thirty-three in the family," Mrs. Porter said. She put the tray on the table, then said, "No, there's just thirty-two now."

"I think we might just as well get three full dozen," Katherine said.

"If we get 'em today, they're still a nickel," said Parsons. "Wait till tomorrow think they go up to ten cents."

"Mrs. Lockwood also thinks it's barbarous," Mrs. Porter said.

"Think it's barbarous myself," Parsons said, "but he don't look at all like they got him in the paper. Makes you sorta wonder what it was he really looked like."

"If he was alive," said Webb, "I'd walk on my hands and knees all day to see him. But I don't intend to walk anywhere to see him dead."

When he said that, Mrs. Porter slowly turned and looked at him. Katherine had the feeling that it might as well blow up now, and get itself over, than blow up later, out in public, where nothing could be repaired. As her mother gazed at him, she saw him blink, then fall back a step.

"You say he has another shirt along with him?" Mrs. Porter said.

Paul did not speak, he nearly seemed to be pinned right there to the wall by her mother's calm gaze, her eyes fastened where the plaid sports shirt opened on his chest. He seemed unable to move, or to speak, until her mother turned back to the tray she had come in with, and then, with a spoon she took from the drawer, ate the Grandmother's prunes.

"Les's get out of here, Parsons," he said, and then the screen door would have slammed behind him but Parsons was able, by hustling a little, to catch it in time.

"See you people later," Parsons said, and then they were gone.

PARSONS

"Birds can be a dang nuisance," Parsons said, and wagged his head at the bird-spotted hood there before him, sucking the air through his teeth to make clear just what he meant. Webb didn't seem to hear it. He had his head out the window, backing up the car. It gave Parsons a chance to edge off the seat, that part of the seat where a spring protruded, and spread his legs in such a manner that *that* particular problem ceased to trouble him. He didn't like Webb, and he felt a little cornered to be cooped up in the car with him, but it wasn't often, these days, that he got a chance to ride in a car. The Porter car hadn't been out of the garage in more than a year.

Up till that time both Parsons and the Judge, at least

once, and sometimes twice a day, got in the car and went shopping. They certainly went a long way to do it, and there had been a time when he thought the Judge did that to economize. It was one of the words that both he and Mrs. Porter liked to use. Then it just crossed his mind one day—they were sitting in the car at the new shopping center—that the Judge had a way of putting off getting back to the house. He liked to take, on his way home, what he called a little spin.

This usually meant a ride along the Schuylkill, or in the hills around Mannyunk or Conshohocken, and sometimes this so-called little spin was along the Brandywine. The Judge knew that country quite a bit better than Washington did. They might dawdle around on the narrow back roads for a couple of hours or so. The Judge was fond of wildflowers, and flowering trees like dogwood, and in the spring they would wangle a little jaunt, just the two of them, over to see the trees at Valley Forge. The Judge was a well known nature lover, and he could name you any bird or flower you could see, but it had crossed Parsons' mind, that summer, that there was more to it than that. What the Judge seemed to like, and where he really felt at home, was behind the wheel. He was always at his best, it seemed to Parsons, when they were on their way to and from somewhere, and it was usually a letdown when they had to get out of the car. He was like a kid in the way he liked to drive around and put on mileage, and nothing pleased him more than to see another thousand miles turn up. "Well, Parsons," he would say, "let's run up to 30,000 before we get home," and so they would drive around, just any old place, till they had run it up. It was never any money in Parsons' pocket, and it just put off the work he still had to do, but there were famous people who would give their eyeteeth to spend their time like that. Riding around in the country with as big a man as the Judge.

"You'll have to tell me how to get there, Parsons," Webb said, as he swung the car into the road, then he turned and said, "You don't mind my calling you Parsons like that, I hope?"

"Why no," said Parsons, "why no. Judge always called me Parsons."

"I get so dam' sick of this Mr. and Mrs. business," Webb said.

"Make a left right here," said Parsons, taking him east on Old Gulph road, then he said, "You in a hurry to get down and back?"

"Parsons—" said Webb, but he didn't go on. Then he turned and said, "No—why?"

Clearing his throat a little, Parsons said, "Judge sort of liked to go along the river."

"That's longer?" said Webb.

The Deep Sleep

"Little," said Parsons, "but not so much traffic. Seems a little cooler." He felt Webb eying him, so he added, "Judge seemed to like going in the back way."

"I don't know what we need to hurry for," Webb said, and the way he settled back, slumped back in the seat, was so much like the Judge that it startled Parsons a little bit. "You're the boss," he went on, shaking out a cigarette, "you just say when."

"We go along here to City Line," said Parsons, "then we drop down and go along the Schuylkill."

"You smoke?" said Webb.

For a moment, Parsons wasn't sure. He did and he didn't. He had given up smoking to make it easier on the Judge. "Well, I guess I might try one," he said, "guess at my age it won't likely stunt me." He reached for one just as Webb said—

"Have 'em rolled for me personally," and Parsons more or less accepted it for a fact. He just took it for a fact till he saw the word CAMEL printed on the cigarette. Then when he glanced at Webb, he was just sitting there with a deadpan look. That was what he didn't like about the younger people, that kind of thing troubled and upset him, as how was he to know what in the world they really meant?

"Left here?" said Webb.

"Right," said Parsons, then he hurried to add, "I mean *right,* turn left!" and when he heard Webb laughing at that, he grinned himself. When a man was with youngsters he certainly had to be on his toes. He managed to get the cigarette lit without being too awkward about it, and while they were smoking it gave him a chance to look around the car. There seemed to be paint smears on just about every inch of it. He had actually seen Webb take one of his brushes, which had a dab of color on the tip of it, and drag it down the cloth on the inside of the door to wipe it off. There were pieces of what he recognized as charcoal sticks stuck into the ashtray. It looked like a bunch of kids had gone wild in it, and it made Parsons wonder, as he often did, how a man over twenty could spend all of his time fooling with paints like that.

"What lovely little town is this?" said Webb, and Parsons leaned forward to get a look at it.

"Think it's Upper Darby through here," Parsons said, and peered through the window to get his bearings. The car swerved a little as Webb dodged a woman who was crossing the street.

"Woman hit in Upper Darby," Webb said, soberly, and Parsons was just about to ask him who, when he realized that that was more of the same sort of thing. He was being sarcastic. He didn't think it was a lovely little town at all. The only way to get along with a sharper like that was to keep your mouth shut, and not let him trip you, and Parsons made up his mind that

that was just what he would do. He ran the window down, blew the cigarette smoke out of it. On City Line they went left, then they went right on the road that would take them down to the river. Through the trees, on the horseshoe turns, Parsons could see the morning sun on the water, and the flash of the cars, like so many pocket mirrors, over on the other side. Through an opening he caught sight of a boat with folding chairs on the deck, on the poop he thought they called it, and he knew by its look that it was not a boat at all, but a pleasure craft. All around it were birds wheeling, big water birds, and hearing them honk like they did to each other, the name of the bird, the real name of this bird, rose to his lips. It was always nearly there when the Judge pronounced it, giving the Latin, as he was a real scholar, and Parsons would have given it too if he had been there by himself. *Columbia something*, he said to himself, and right at that moment Webb said aloud—

"Seems hard to realize he's gone, doesn't it?"

Luckily Parsons had his head turned toward the window, and when the whole scene blurred, trees, gulls and shining river, all he really had to do was lean forward, stick his head out the window, and let the wind blow in his face. That was how they went along, nobody talking, until the car swerved sharply again, and Parsons thought Webb must have been dodging a hole in the road. They dipped down, bounced a bit in the gutter, then pulled up to a stop.

"My God!" said Webb, "this been here all the time?"

Parsons turned to see what he saw, and out there on the water he saw a sculler. A single sculler. The water dripped from the oars like it did from the feet of the gulls.

"You like to row?" said Parsons.

"God almighty," said Webb, "Eakins' river."

Parsons had heard the Judge call it City Hall's river, but nothing like that. He wondered if Eakins was the man who discovered it.

"All he needs is a moustache," said Webb, "the drooping moustache and the bandana."

"I don't see him that well," said Parsons, and strained his eyes, but it didn't help him. It occurred to him that a painter needed sharp eyes to paint. Behind the sculler was the bridge, reflected on the water, and the more he looked the more it looked to Parsons like the sculler was like a big water insect, but he didn't say so. He could see the current going along beneath him, the scull resting on top.

"They're raising money to dredge it," he said, as that was something the Judge had a hand in. "Judge had a hand in it," he said.

"Anything he didn't have a hand in?" Webb said.

Parsons had never really thought about it, not in that way, and now he thought and said, "Guess there wasn't much unless you consider the house. Around the house he left it up to the Missus, like he said."

"He said that?" Webb replied.

"Said it was her bailiwick," Parsons said. "Said he'd run the country if the Missus would run the home."

"Well, I'll be goddamned!" said Webb, and leaned forward on the wheel as if he saw something.

"He tip over?" said Parsons, but no, he hadn't tipped over. He was just sitting there, now, wiping his face with a towel.

"Parsons—" said Webb, and then he leaned back as if he wondered how to frame the question. He looked at his hands, and the green paint under the nail of his thumb. "Parsons," he said, "would you say the Judge was a great man?"

Parsons thought he probably was, but he didn't answer that right away. He had the feeling there was some connection between this question and the last one, as when the Doctor asked him about his stool, when it was his head that hurt.

"I suppose you could say he had some human failin's," Parsons said.

"Oh, hell—" said Webb, and Parsons could see that wasn't what he meant.

[85]

"Think he was a great man—for the country," Parsons said.

That seemed to be more like it, as Webb reflected on that.

"Where would you say Mrs. Porter fit into this picture?" Webb asked.

"Mrs. Porter?" said Parsons. Webb nodded. "Mrs. Porter—" began Parsons, and then for some reason he didn't come out and say what he knew to be a fact. He didn't say what a remarkable woman she was. It didn't strike him as the kind of thing that a young man would understand. A railroad train was crossing the bridge, and he waited till it passed before he replied, "Mr. Webb, I've known Mrs. Porter for nearly forty years."

"That's why I thought I'd ask you," he said.

"The Judge had his failings," Parsons went on, as if reviewing scenes from the life of the Judge in his mind, such as the summer afternoons that the Judge sneaked off to eat a *Tin Roof*. That was a chocolate sundae with a lot of salted peanuts sprinkled on the top. Right at a time when he swore he wouldn't eat ice cream, peanuts, or salt. "The Judge had his failings, but Mrs. Porter doesn't," Parsons said.

"Mrs. Porter has no failings?" Webb replied.

"She's got no *human* failings," Parsons said, in order to distinguish between Mrs. Porter and the

Judge. As that sounded a little strange he added, "Mrs. Porter has her rules, and she sticks by 'em,"

"A woman of principle, eh?" said Webb.

"You bet she is," said Parsons. As a matter of fact, that was just what she was, and to illustrate that he added, "If I'm alive right now, and the Judge isn't, you can put it all down to Mrs. Porter."

Webb had started up the car, but when he heard that he let it die again. The point had struck him. Parsons could see that for himself.

"Just how you figure that, Parsons?"

"I don't suppose you noticed," Parsons said, "how she wouldn't let me have both cream and sugar?" No, Webb hadn't. "Well," said Parsons, "in more than thirty years every drop adds up. I got a little diet problem an' she keeps her eye on it."

"You mean she let the Judge have it, Parsons?"

"Not on your life!" Parsons said, "but when he got out of the house, he sneaked off an' took it. He had the cream, and the sugar, an' just about everything she wouldn't let him have." Webb just sat there, and Parsons went on, "Guess I was more around the house than he was. If he'd been around it more he might be alive today."

The Deep Sleep

MRS. PORTER

"Anything, *any*thing to get them out of the house," Katherine said.

On her way from the dining room to the kitchen, the Grandmother had turned up the corners of two throw rugs. "She never fails," Mrs. Porter said, and turned them down. As she stooped for the second corner she turned so that her head faced the front room window, her backside the closed French doors to the rear porch. "She is probably wondering what in the world it was I dropped."

Katherine turned to look for the Grandmother, but she was still in the basement. "Who is wondering, Mother?"

Mrs. Porter straightened her back and gazed through the window at the house across the street. The second floor of that house was on a level with the Porter front porch. The windows were on a line with the living room where Mrs. Porter stood. Mrs. Porter drew her robe closer around her and looked to see what had been left on the dining room table.

"How is Mrs. Erskine?" Katherine said.

Mrs. Porter examined a fresh impression in the table-cloth. It was round. The hot coffee pot had been placed on it. Lifting a corner of the cloth she saw the round pad of lint ironed into the table. "No pad," she said, "hot pot."

"Mother, how is Mrs. Erskine?"

"Dr. Lloyd says if you love your neighbor, just leave your blind up in the morning. Last winter it was her knee, this spring it's her iliac something."

"And Mr. Erskine?" Katherine said.

"When your mother leaves the lights on," said Mrs. Porter, "she calls me up and tells me." She crossed the room to the Webster's dictionary lying open on the dictionary stand. "Il-i-ac—" she said, "I meant to look it up."

"I doubt if that's the right word," Katherine said.

"It's what she thinks she has," said Mrs. Porter, then, reading—"Il-i-um—the topless towers of Il-i-yum." Without turning from the page she said, "She's probably wondering what it is I'm looking up."

"Mother," said Katherine, "if it's as bad as all that, why don't you draw the blind?"

"Your father and I have nothing to hide," Mrs. Porter said. She turned for a moment to check on that, then said, "You think I want to whet her appetite?"

Katherine crossed the room to see what the music on the piano was. Mrs. Porter crossed the room to see how she looked from there. On the table at her side was a picture of the Father, the Mother, and the Grandmother, taken thirty years before in the yard of the Grandmother's house. The Grandmother was holding the infant Katherine. Her eyes were hand-painted blue, and her cheeks were a healthy pink.

"You can bet she's wondering what was in that roaster," Mrs. Porter said.

"I just hope that he's better," Katherine said, and struck a few chords on the piano.

"It very likely needs tuning," Mrs. Porter said. "There's nothing wrong with him that isn't mental."

The telephone rang.

"If it's her, your mother is indisposed," Mrs. Porter said.

Katherine picked up the receiver and said, "Mrs. Erskine? Why how are you? I was just standing here asking Mother how you people were. Last night, late last night, and I'm afraid we—"

"Let me handle her," said Mrs. Porter.

"Here's Mother," Katherine said, and passed the phone to her. She turned to see if the light was on in the Erskine hallway, where *she* should be, but just as she thought, Mrs. Erskine was upstairs.

"Well, I should say," Mrs. Porter said, "but I suppose it's all for the best. Dr. Lloyd, recently, has even been hinting as much. They can do just so much, you know, just so much. For all their sulfa this, their penicillin that, if the rules of health have not— In the drive? Ohhhh, that was probably Mrs. Crowell. Mr. Crowell, you know. Crowell, Loring & Hoff. I suppose you even saw it before we did, we seem to have our hands full over here, and I think it was Paul—no, you haven't met him—Paul went to the door. You can not imagine our surprise when we saw what it was. Twenty, perhaps as much as twenty-five pounds. We will certainly never do justice to it a-lone. If your iliac would permit you, if you thought that you and Mr. Erskine—no, my dear, not a thing, not one little thing. We're saying no to flowers as Mr. Porter himself hated to see them cut, and while my daughter is here we really can't bear them in the house. You know, allergies. Very fashionable right now among the young. It will be very simple, I'm afraid, what the children call an indoor picnic—I suppose around the usual time. Feel free to come over as soon as you see us stirring around. Very good, then."

Mrs. Porter hung up. With her thumbnail she scratched a spot on the front of her robe.

"You didn't *ask* them over?" Katherine said.

A squirrel chattered in the bird box. Mrs. Porter rolled up a section of the paper and slapped it on the screen and the window. The birds left, but the squirrel stayed on top of the box. Seeing the box empty he dropped down inside, his tail snapping.

"If there's one thing they need, it's a really decent

meal for a change," said Mrs. Porter. "Cans. They live out of cans."

The telephone rang again. As Mrs. Porter didn't seem to hear it, Katherine lifted the receiver. "Just a moment, Mrs. Crowell," she said. "It's Mrs. Crowell, Mother."

Taking the receiver, Mrs. Porter sat down on the folding chair. One leg was rocking off the rug, so she arose and put that leg on, then sat down and said, "Lydia, we are completely flabbergasted!" With the paper she held, Mrs. Porter gently fanned her face. "One thing we will not do, Lydia, is grease the palm. Putting money underground is not *in*to it, as Howard said. Dust we are, you know, but *not* in an aluminum casket. No, Howard didn't say it. A simple empirical fact. Fine, just fine. You could never tell a thing by looking at her. She's so used to it, my dear. Everybody. Everybody dying or dead. Reads that column first. Even seems to perk her up to lose someone she knows. Nothing, nothing at all unless you feel like a little G-mother sitting. A full jar of your buckeye honey the last time she was alone! Oh no. No, I was just spoofing. One of the few things they can do. Katherine was just saying, *any*-thing to get them out of the house. Just this morning he says, *What is next on the docket.* On the docket. Sounded so much like Howard it gave me a start. Now as for that surprise, what in the world will we do if you don't come by and help us with it—?"

Spreading her knees, parting the folds of her robe, Mrs. Porter examined the garter rings on her legs, then she drew her knees together, replaced the folds of her robe. While Mrs. Crowell talked she thumbed through her desk calendar. Ahead to August, then clear back to last July. Nothing. A full year out of her life. On the telephone pad, under *Thank You cds.*, she wrote *Turn New Leaf*, and turned it. "Lydia," she said, "I'm going to be perfectly frank. You saw that picture in the *Inquirer* this morning? I didn't recognize it. I mean I didn't even know the man whose picture it was. I know that viewing is a barbarous custom, but if I thought he would look the way I *knew* him, if I thought they could *just* get his hair combed—well, they're going to want to look at him in Finlay, and if the children decide not to look at him here, I'm going to go on ahead and have a quiet little look at him myself. I'm not so modern I can't see the point in something like that. In the entire past year I can't honestly say that I've so much as really looked at him or myself—it would have been too much, it would simply have been the last straw. But I feel perfectly capable if I should want to look at him now." Mrs. Porter stopped there, then said, "Operator, you cut me off."

"Mother," Katherine said, "it's twenty minutes past ten."

"Western Union, please," Mrs. Porter said. When they answered, she said, "Peter Rautzen, R-a-u-t-z-e-n, Finlay, P-a. Howard's service Tuesday two o'clock."

"The service is at three-thirty, Mother."

"Not for *him*," said Mrs. Porter, "for *him* you say two o'clock."

Without rising from the chair she waved the paper in the air and several of the bad birds left the bird box. They *knew*. Their actions were perfectly deliberate.

"Mother—" said Katherine, then she stopped and said, "Why, Mother—who brought this?" Katherine was standing at the far end of the room, facing the coats in the hall. Mrs. Porter crossed the room and stood beside her, where the draft through the door was scented with flowers, and there in the vestibule was a basket of them.

"You can just bet that *she* didn't miss it," Mrs. Porter said.

"Aren't they beautiful?" said Katherine.

"Calla lilies, delphinium, and stock," said Mrs. Porter. A small envelope was pinned to the basket, and Katherine took it off, passed it to Mrs. Porter.

"Deepest sympathy," Mrs. Porter read, "The Dawn Busters."

"Bavardia too, Mother," Katherine said.

"I wonder which Dawn Buster it was?" Mrs. Porter said.

"Mother, you go and get started—" Katherine said, "while I put them in some water."

"A safe place," Mrs. Porter said. "He put it in a safe place."

Katherine thought she meant the flowers and turned and said, "What place do you recommend, Mother?" Mrs. Porter turned slowly and looked around the room. "In front of the fireplace, Mother?"

"A safe place—" she repeated. Katherine went off with the flowers, and Mrs. Porter remembered that it was Mr. Lockwood, dead now, who had given the watch its name. Howard had lost it on the bush, and she had found it; that is to say she had heard it ticking, and then she had turned and seen it gleaming like a golden bird. They had gone out in the woods to see a strange bird and she had found it, she had seen it, and it had certainly been the strangest bird of all. Dr. Campbell had proposed that it be given an appropriate name. Then Dr. Lockwood had put up his hand and said that it should be known as the *Golden Swiss Ticker*, or *tickerus porterii swissicus*. By unanimous vote his proposal was adopted and the bird was listed at the next Dawn meeting as having been *seen and banded* by her. But after that experience he seldom wore it, and when she had finally asked him about it he said that he had put it in *a safe place*. A safe place. He had put it in a safe place.

"Mother," Katherine called from the kitchen, "it's now after ten thirty."

Mrs. Porter closed the door at the front, opened the door on the stairs. Going up she took along the roll of paper she found on the steps. At the top of the stairs, on the nightlight table, she paused to look at the Memo pad, on which, just in passing, she had scratched something. *Clothes* perhaps; if not clothes, *gloves*. Standing there, she called the Mayflower Cleaners and asked the person who answered the phone to *please* rush over whatever it was. The man speaking to her said what a shock the news had been.

"You saw the *Inquirer*?" she said.

"My wife saw it and called me," he said.

She thanked him, and he expressed his sympathy.

"Who was that, Mother?" Katherine said.

"Another one who saw the *Inquirer*," she replied.

"Mother—" Katherine said, "aren't most of the Dawn Busters men?"

"Only men can find time for such things," she said.

"If most of them are men, that probably explains it," Katherine said.

Turning from the telephone, the night stand, Mrs. Porter saw that the guest door was open. On the knob of the door was a pair of soiled, striped men's shorts.

She took them from the door, tried them for size, then saw the word WEBB sewed on to the elastic. With the shorts she crossed the hall into the bathroom, opened the lid to the laundry chute, and putting in her head she was able to detect the smell of the iron. As through a speaking tube, she could hear the Grandmother's choppy stroke.

"Heads up below!" she called, and wadding the shorts into a ball, let them drop down the chute with a swishing noise. The telephone rang, and she stepped into the hall to answer it.

THE GRANDMOTHER

In the cool of the basement, in the corner between the coalbin and the fruit cellar, the Grandmother stood with her back to the light, ironing. Her cane hung from the cold water pipe that passed over her head. Her apron—since she stepped on the strings— was folded over her arm, like a napkin, with the hard-candy pocket where she could get at it easily. On the broad end of the board sat another iron, on a rack for hot irons, although these irons were never hot enough to burn anything. Mrs. Porter had asked her to please stop spitting on them. But for eighty-five years, and maybe longer, the Grandmother had spit on the face of her irons, and what she had done that long she was still inclined to do. So she spit, whether the iron sizzled or not. Then she ironed, whether the iron was hot or not.

When the voice came down the laundry chute, when the wadded shorts fell into the tub, the Grandmother went on with her ironing. She paid it no heed. Water also dripped in the tub, and every now and then, without explanation, the air was strong with the smell of an opossum once trapped in the house. He had come in, it was said, with the wood, then he had been caught in a butterfly net, and if he had died, it was almost certain it had been outside. But the smell of a dead opossum was there in the house.

No light fell on the ironing, but something like smoke seemed to come through the window and tangle like cobwebs in the Grandmother's hair. While she ironed she sang, and the hymn could be heard very well in the bathroom, where the chute was, and over the radiator in the back of the living room. It was like the hissing sound of a phonograph needle without any horn. Now and then, as if a piece of the record was broken, a bark came through. The tap of her foot could be heard on the leg of the wobbly board.

When the shirt had been ironed the Grandmother

would put it on the bent wire hanger, button it at the throat, and then hook the hanger over the edge of the fruit cellar door. She would then take her cane from the pipe overhead. Everybody knew when she had finished the shirt, as the problem of getting her cane from the pipe, getting it unhooked, was like the bird-box racket throughout the house. If it went on too long Mrs. Porter would walk all the way upstairs to the bathroom, put her head in the chute, and ask the Grandmother if something was wrong. The Grandmother never favored her with a reply. The one thing she might do, if she felt like it, was scratch a match. There were plenty of light bulbs in the basement, but if the Grandmother was troubled by the darkness, the only light she was able to see by was a match. In one pocket of her apron she kept a supply. It always got her a little attention, if nothing else. Whoever heard it would hurry down the stairs, their arms full of towels to make her think it was laundry, and they would always find the Grandmother in the same place. She would be in the back of the fruit cellar trying to read, by the light of her match, what the labels on the jelly glasses said. Thirty years before, or maybe forty or fifty, the Grandmother had put up some Damson Plum, but it had all disappeared from her basement before she got a bite of it. She had her suspicions, but she never said anything. But when she got so tired of store applebutter that she thought she would die if she had to eat it, she would scratch a match and look in the cellar for her Damson Plum.

She had never found it, not a jar, but one day, bending over her match, she came on the leg of an ironing board. A new leg, with a rubber tip on the end of it. Then the match went out, and she had to tug, push and pull on the thing in the darkness before she got it out of the closet into the light. It looked like a fine new board when she looked at it. Her own board was so wobbly she could certainly use a board like that, but when she set it up, she could see something was wrong with it. What had looked like a scorch on the pad, just a bad burn where the iron sat, was no scorch at all but an iron shaped hole burned clean through the board. The Grandmother had blamed it on her eyes. She hadn't believed it till she took her cane and waggled it around in the hole. Some of the charred wood had dropped out on the floor, and the smell had been so bad, where she stepped on it, that she had been accused of all but burning the house down with her ironing. And it had been her own son, Howard Porter, who talked to her like that. Sometimes he didn't seem to have the brains he was born with, and the way he talked and acted, once he was married, made her wonder if she hadn't dropped him on his head when he was small. So she had put the ironing board back where she found it, and it wasn't more than a week or so later that it wasn't there, there wasn't hide nor hair of it, when she struck her match, and somebody had come down and put O-Cedar oil over the place.

As she knew it would, the voice in the chute spoke to her again.

"Ohhh, Grandmother?"

"Humphh," she said.

"If we're not back in time for lunch you'll find your fruit in the bowl on the table. We'll butter the bread. If you want spreadings or an oatmeal cookie—" but the Grandmother didn't catch the rest of it, as she had turned, with the iron she held, and let it drop. The house was quiet, then Mrs. Porter called—

"Katherine, would you ask Mrs. Erskine if she would please keep an eye on the house?"

"You want her to come over, Mother?"

There was a pause, then Mrs. Porter said, "She can really see it better from where she's sitting. She has per-spec-tive—isn't that the recommended thing?"

"Mother—"

"Tell her that we're obliged to look into the c-o-double f-i-n problem."

The Grandmother heard a car come up the gravel driveway, heard it honk.

"Here's the taxi, now, Mother!"

"I'd like to know if he honks for Mrs. Crowell like that," Mrs. Porter said.

Over her head, to and fro, the Grandmother heard the steps of Mrs. Porter, loud on the linoleum, quiet on the oriental rug. A window came down, a blind went up, a bolt clicked in a door.

"If we get our feathers wet—" Mrs. Porter was saying, but the screen slammed behind her, the house was quiet, and the Grandmother was alone. Boards that had been pressed down began to push up. The house creaked, and the Grandmother could hear the undesirable birds rifling the bird box and the sound of water dripping in the basement stool. Her eyes had been closed. Now she opened them. She could see the white knob on the end of the chain pull and she remembered the summer that the boy Roger, who was full of mischief, painted it with luminous paint. The Grandmother had wiped what stuck to her hand on to the handle of her cane.

WEBB

"Why don't I just cruise around?" said Webb, "till you show up here on the corner. Take your time. We got plenty time."

Parsons nodded, but his head remained in the door.

"Need a little money?" said Webb, and rocked on the seat to get at his billfold.

"These pants I'm wearin'," Parsons said, "I got no place to keep any money. What money I got I keep in my coat. Forgot to bring my coat."

Webb handed him a five, looked to see what corner he had dropped him off at, then went on down Broad to Chestnut Street. He knew Chestnut. That is, he knew about five blocks of it. From the Wanamaker store to about Eighteenth he knew pretty well. He had never spent a day and a night with the family that the Judge hadn't left him a note in the morning, directing him to come on into town and have lunch with him. That meant Wanamaker's. And after lunch they would walk up Chestnut Street.

Webb had got in the habit, over the years, of looking for that note when he came down in the morning, as it gave him an excuse to get out of the house. It took care of the day, as he wouldn't get back till about five o'clock. A little after ten he would drive to the station, buy himself a morning paper, then take the next Paoli local into town. It was a half-hour ride, but he seldom got the paper read. Webb had lived in several parts of the world, but there was something about the Paoli local, and the people who had grown accustomed to it, that he couldn't seem to put his finger on. It began with the curious *cheep-cheep* of the whistle, like some antique bird. In the summer the aisles would sparkle with the dust and metal filings that came off the wheels, and the air would be full of the groans and sighs of the stops and starts. But Webb could hardly get enough of it. Most of the time he would sit there with the paper in his lap. There were not many types, and what types there were fitted into a fairly narrow compass, mostly professional men, their wives, and a seasoning of domestic help. They read the *Inquirer* going in, the *Evening Bulletin* coming out, and the windows, as a rule, were merely a source of light. The thing that interested Webb, and troubled him, was that the local seemed to be a passage, a more or less blind passage, between their public and their private lives. The connection, if there was a connection, was hard to pin down.

It was just ninety miles from New York to Philadelphia, but several thousand miles, perhaps even further, from the Times Square subway to the Broad Street Suburban station. Webb had remarked that change himself. Fighting his way on and off a subway, the taste of the battle still in his mouth, he had calmly boarded, less than two hours later, the west-bound Paoli local. *Boarded.* The word summed it up. After a five-minute spin through the railroad yards, and one or two depressing glimpses of the city, one arrived, one had been transported to the Main Line. The Main Line began, Webb had observed, where the first mass but orderly unboarding of the passengers took place. The train stood. The passengers moved slowly down the aisles. Out the windows there were trees, rows of comfortable homes, brief glimpses of troubled estates, and, of course, a right and wrong side to the tracks. Out the window, that is, was what the Judge had described, in a much-quoted paper, as the untamed station wagon country. Just what did he mean? He did not elaborate. The Judge, whatever he meant, was part of it.

The Judge had not been born to the purple, a phrase he often used himself, but he had acquired a certain taste for it. Not for its show, not for the pretensions that he hardly troubled to puncture, but for the very thing that Webb found it hard to put a finger on. The world that began, really began, when he bought his *Inquirer* in the morning, and ended when he left his *Bulletin*, folded up tightly, in the empty seat. The Paoli local, in one way or another, summed it all up. The big antique cars, holding off progress like the customs of the natives, and the stations that evoked the pastoral Welsh countryside: Narberth, Wynnewood, Haverford and Bryn Mawr. It was more than a joke. It had more than a faded charm. When he lay awake at night Webb could often hear the shrill cheep-cheep of the whistle, and he never heard it without a bemused wagging of the head. There had been a time when he made that noise around the Porter house. Mrs. Porter had made no comment, but Webb had been amazed to find that the Judge, when he heard the imitation, even bridled a bit. Webb had once thought it showed a hidden stuffy streak in him. He didn't think it anymore, as the ridiculous whistle, like the tinny chords on a toy piano, seemed to serve as a link, a missing link perhaps, in the Judge's life. It served as some sort of connection, like the train itself, between worlds that were strangely divided, and linked an uncertain present with an anchored past.

A big man, the Judge only looked right in some place like Wanamaker's, where he liked to sit with four or five big men on each side of him. Wanamaker's, as it turned out, was just the eastern end of the Paoli local, as an underground passage connected it with the Main Line. It was not necessary to mix with the traffic at all. On sultry days, or the very cold ones, the Judge would walk him from the Suburban station right to the Wanamaker store without ever coming out on the street. There they would take the elevator to the restaurant, where the hostess had known the Judge for twelve years, and be led to a table where the waitress had known him for twenty-three. But it might be an hour or more before they got around to eat. Everybody knew the Judge, he knew everybody, and Webb spent most of his time getting up and sitting down, or stooping for the napkin he had dropped. Then they would finally eat, and after eating Webb would smoke one of the Upmann cigars the Judge had bought him, and sit trying to think of some further use for the aluminum tube. Right up to the last there would be four or five of the old men around.

They were inclined, Webb found, to accept the Judge's opinion of him. At one time Webb had thought he was being bored, passing the time with these old fogies, then he found he looked forward to these luncheons with the Judge. Just sitting there with these older men made him feel a good deal younger, for one thing, as the world still lay before him, in their eyes, and he liked that. As a matter of fact, he *needed* that. He sometimes had the feeling that the world was slipping away. They were mostly pensive, troubled men, with their own lights, as the Judge described it, and Webb had come to see that these lights were not at all bad. They had come to feel that a man might paint, and not be a damn fool. One old man went so far as to say that he remarked, in Webb, certain traits of the Porters, and another had assumed, he said, that they were father and son. Into his Wana-

maker napkin, when he heard that remark, the Judge
had blown his nose. That day, as they walked up
Chestnut, the Judge had introduced him to Mike Garcia, a traffic cop on that corner for twenty-seven
years. The name of *A. Garcia*, his son, Attorney at
Law, could be seen on one of the fourth floor windows, where he put into practice what the Judge had
taught him. Shaking Webb's hand, Mike Garcia had
said, "Well, I've been hearin' a lot about you," and
it was clear that he had heard nothing but good. Just
a block from that corner, over Florsheim shoes, a man
named Kaufman was usually at the window, rain or
shine, when he and the Judge went by. The Judge
had had Mr. Kaufman at night school, *he* had put
all four of his sons through the Law School, and he
now had a new generation of Kaufmans coming up.
Mr. Kaufman had come to the Judge when he needed
money, when he donated money, and when he wanted
advice about the marriage of his sons. That day they
had stood there in the street—the Judge had made
it clear that Webb was one of the family—while Mr.
Kaufman read a letter from one of his boys on Saipan.
Say hello to the Judge, was how the letter closed, not
added on to the bottom, as though he had thought it
over, but right there in the letter with the kisses for his
mother and the stamps for his child.

"See he's learned to dot his i's," the Judge had

said, looking at the holes he had poked through the paper, "guess the army's teachin' him more at quite a bit less." Mr. Kaufman had just smiled, he closed his wide mouth on a great pronouncement, then placed one of his hands on the Judge, and the other on Webb. Seeing the time on the clock across the street, he had turned and walked off.

Webb stopped at a light, then turned up Broad Street and idled along with the traffic, till he saw, up ahead, someone waving at him. It was Parsons, with a stack of papers under each arm. Getting into the car Parsons said, "Guess he's going to be in the *Bulletin* too. But he won't be out on the streets for a while yet." He grinned and said, "Really too bad he has to miss that."

KATHERINE

"You see—" Mrs. Porter said, peering into her handbag, "You see, what did I tell you?"

Katherine leaned forward to see what it was that had spilled, what had been lost, or what had been forgotten.

"O-u-t the window," Mrs. Porter said, and took a

quick sniff through her nose. Katherine turned just in time to see Mrs. Erskine, in a faded sunsuit, her rickshaw straw hat on her head, throw open the wide front door and stare after them. In her right hand, drooping, she held an antique copper watering can. In the yard, flanking the flagstone walk, were the concrete urns made in Hoboken, and known to have been crated and shipped from somewhere in France. In the bowl of each urn were a few sprigs of dead weeds.

"Pure camouflage," Mrs. Porter said, "I happen to know it won't hold water."

Whether she saw Katherine or not, Mrs. Erskine threw her huge right arm in the air, the one with the can, and verified what Mrs. Porter had said. Four or five playing cards spilled out of it. The copper bottom of the can reflected the light, throwing it around the yard like a beacon, and Katherine, her own gloved hand at the window, managed to waggle it. Then the taxi made the turn and a wild privet hedge cut off the view.

"I can see you've been away for quite some time," her mother observed. From her own handbag she took a plastic shoe horn, handed it to Katherine and said, "If you're going to wear pumps, you better rest your feet."

"I decided not to wear pumps," Katherine said.

Her mother leaned forward to see what it was she

had put on. "Ohhhh!" she said, slipped the shoe horn into her bag, closed it with a snap, then added, "Brown with black. An unholy alliance."

"It's a very dark brown," Katherine said, "and after what you were saying about pumps—" Her mother placed her right hand on her arm, and with the other pointed out the window. Several birds, black birds, winged into, then out of, the light.

"Grackles?" Katherine said.

"You missed it," said her mother. She wagged her head, then added, "You missed the iridescence."

Always something, Katherine thought: the iridescence of the black bird, the unholy alliance, the reason for preferring soya bean flour, the meteor shower, the aurora borealis, the turning point in history, the boiling point of taffy, and the dripping point of fudge. They always missed it. Or they failed to grasp it soon enough. When they combed their hair, they missed the part. When they were sick, they were slow to recover. When they were well, whatever they were doing would make them sick. They were said to be bright, attractive children from an outsider's point of view, but nothing they ever did on the inside was good enough. And they had both reached that conclusion at the same time. Under the front porch, sitting in the deep dust or on her brother's Flexible Flyer, they came to the conclusion that they were both orphans of the storm. That Mrs. Porter, a civic-minded person, had adopted them. Mr. Porter might or might not be their father, but the reason he did so little about it was that fathers had little or nothing to do with the inside of a house. But *they* did. So they were Mrs. Porter's property.

"Butter and egg," her mother said, lowering the window, "a single lovely stalk."

So they thought they were orphans until Mrs. Erskine came home from her long honeymoon in France, and moved into the mansion Mr. Erskine had built right across the street. The Erskine house sat so close to the road they could stand on the curb and look into the windows, and Mrs. Erskine had thrown open one of the windows and called to them. "Why, you lovers!" she had cried, waving them over, "why, you little lovers, you're cute as cotton!" and when her brother heard that he was almost beside himself. He ran around and around the house, firing his toy gun. So they were her lovers, they were cute as cotton: she couldn't love them enough, she couldn't see them enough, and there was only one way to explain something like that. Only a loving mother, as they had read in their books, would ever treat a pair of orphans like that, and they could see for themselves she didn't have any cute-as-cotton lovers of her own.

Rosa Bloom had been the hostess at the Covered

Wagon when Newcomb Erskine first set eyes on her. He had been in his fifties, twice married but childless, and Rosa Bloom had been in her thirties, a full-blown, and, as Mrs. Porter described her, earthy type. As two proper marriages had brought him no heirs, Newcomb Erskine had more or less hinted that only an improper union would take care of that. That had been in the twenties, right after the war, and while their new place went up, right across from the Porters, Newcomb Erskine had taken his bride to France. Every week or so something crated arrived from Europe. Tiles for the kitchen, panelling for the study, an Empire bed that some great lover had died in, and concrete statues of such generous proportions they were said to resemble Rosa Erskine. From Italy came a gardener, and from somewhere else, complete with everything but the children, a miniature Villa that they would have all to themselves.

They were gone for two years, people speculated on the language they were teaching the children, and then one day in the summer, in the middle of the summer, Rosa Erskine arrived. A Philadelphia taxicab had driven her out from 30th Street. A clipped French poodle, but no child, was in her arms. She had also lost the key to her new house, and the taxi driver had to pry up a window, crawl through it, and then find a door where he could let her in. Newcomb Erskine came along several weeks later, coming out from town on the 5:08 local, a *Bulletin* under his arm, as if he had never been away. In the rooms over the garage, intended for the servants, he put his miniature electric trains, and when the windows were open, on the warm summer nights, you could hear them run. Some of the engines whistled, and at dangerous crossings there were crossing bells. Some people said the trains were intended for the children, but other people, like her mother, felt that Newcomb Erskine had never really grown up. Rosa Bloom had married him, everybody said, because he was old and would soon leave her his money, but old as he was, he seemed to want her to himself. In the twenty years of their married life he had refused to die and leave his wife to anybody else. He had lost what brains he had, if he ever had any, but his health, for a man in his late seventies, was good.

"Dr. Barr," her mother said, as they went past the church, "has a new assistant. Amherst, I think. Field experience in the Orient. No white men, as I remember, permitted in Nepal."

So the strange Erskine dogs would cross the road as if they wanted to live with the Porters, and the strange Porter children would go over to live with the Erskine dogs. That was how her father used to speak of it. He often did. It was always good, as her brother pointed out, for a laugh. It seemed to explain the

strange Porter children to the people who gathered on
the Porter porch and saw them playing in the narrow,
seedy Erskine yard. It was typical of dogs and kids,
they seemed to think, to behave like that. While they
were playing they would often hear the visitors laugh.
They always played out in front, where Mrs. Porter
could see them, swinging by the hour in the old rubber
tire that hung by a rope from the only tree. It made
the yard something of an eyesore, and the Erskine
mansion, from the Porter yard, looked like the fine
homes with a used-car lot right out in back. Mrs.
Erskine, however, didn't seem to mind. Nobody
seemed to know, or to care, what Mr. Erskine thought.
When the Porter children stopped swinging in the
tire it just hung there, like an old horse collar, till the
rope rotted and broke, and then it just lay there in
the yard. A hollow had been worn where their feet
had dragged and after a rain the water would stand
there, but neither grass nor weeds ever grew in that
spot again. A piece of raddled rope, about a foot or
two long, still dangled from the tree.

"Capital—" said her mother, "three million and
seven hundred and fifty thousand dollars. Surplus, one
million and four hundred thousand." The taxi had
stopped so they faced the bank window across the
street. "I'm just a plain housewife," her mother said,
and lidded her eyes.

The Deep Sleep

The Erskines never did have any children of their own, only dogs and cats. The dogs were soon run over, or died because they weren't properly fed. The cats went wild and lived in the jungle behind the house. At one time a Dachshund, Himmel by name, would come back at night and bark at it, but he even did that from the Porter yard across the street. They were still lovers, they were still cute as cotton, but they began to worry about Mrs. Erskine, as she didn't seem to know how to worry or to take care of herself. She was sometimes very careless about her dress, and would walk around the house in just her corset, looking like the ladies in her French magazines. Twice in one week she fed them cream puffs that had spoiled. They went off to be sick in one of her extra bathrooms, but Mrs. Erskine, who believed in mind over matter, nearly died in her own bedroom. She turned a skimmed milk color and they couldn't understand a word she said. To keep them from going for the doctor she locked them right there in the bedroom with her, where they sat on chairs and watched her dying in her Empire bed. She didn't die. After a while she felt better and gave them a silver dollar apiece to keep their pretty little cute-as-cotton traps shut. And they did, they didn't say a word, nor did they object when Mrs. Porter, their mother, said that as a person Mrs. Erskine left something to be desired. That was true. It seemed to be true of everyone.

The next summer they were sent off to camp and they saw no more of Mrs. Erskine, between camp and school, than what they could see through the window when their father drove them past her house. Years later, when Katherine was in England, Mrs. Erskine had asked her for English safety matches, as Newcomb, her husband, had got around to collecting them. He collected, sooner or later, nearly everything. And then during the war, when she was shopping with Mr. Parsons, she saw a little withered man in the new Acme market who was buying nothing but rolls of toilet paper. He would buy the ration limit, which was three rolls, and then go off with them. Ten minutes later, in a different hat or coat, he would be back. Katherine had been curious enough about him to peer through the window to see where he was going, and there he sat, big as life, in a new car parked at the curb. Sitting right there beside him was Mrs. Erskine with a small, frail child in her lap, a little war orphan, as it turned out, from somewhere in France. As she learned later, the child hadn't done any better than the dogs and cats. Too much love seemed to be just as deadly as not enough. She kept running away, she kept being sick, until they finally shipped her back to France, and that had been the last of Mrs. Erskine, as far as Katherine was concerned, until the door flung open and she waved the copper watering can over her head.

"Here we are," her mother said, "here we are—" and the taxi swung into the drive of Clough & Bayard, Funeral Directors. "Mr. Bayard knew your father, you know," her mother said, and got out the left side of the car. Katherine got out on the right, where the driver held the door. He removed his chauffeur's cap and said—

"We're all going to miss him, Miss Porter," and Katherine wondered if this old man had known her as a child. He took a kerchief from his pocket, wiped the sweat from his head.

"You're very kind to say so," she said, paid him, then looked around for her mother. The taxi door stood open, but Mrs. Porter was not in sight. She was neither down the drive, nor on the Greek columned porch. The taxi driver stooped and took a quick look under his cab.

"Oh, Mother!" Katherine said, and walked to where she could look down the drive. A gardener working at the edge of a bed of flowers took off his cap. With the trowel he was holding he pointed across the manicured lawn. In the pachysandra bed at the edge of the lawn, in the shade of several flowering dogwoods, Mrs. Porter stood with her back to the drive.

"Oh, Mother!" Katherine called.

"Why, here's a *May* apple," her mother said, and crouched to lift the wide leaf, peer at the flower. "The twenty-second of June," she said, "imagine that!"

PARSONS

Parsons held the paper out before him, tipped it to catch the light, then said, "If it didn't say so, don't think I'd know it was him."

Webb turned to glance at the picture, nodded his head. "He'd lost a lot of weight," he said.

Parsons was wondering if the Judge hadn't lost even more than that. Seeing the picture was a good deal different from seeing the Judge. In the picture, about all you saw was what he had lost. For four months, maybe it was five, Parsons had seen him face to face every morning, at a time in the morning when nobody ought to be seen. When there was just enough light in the room to turn him green. The night light would be on, and the Judge would be lying there, his eyes open, staring at whatever it was that had scared him to death. Parsons sometimes felt it right there in the room, a third person that was right there with them, like he felt that the empty bed near the door was occupied. Mrs. Porter, of course, had stopped using it. To get any rest at all she had to sleep somewhere else. But her shape was there in the bed as if she had never turned on the mattress, but just lay there, without moving, all through the night. Thinking her thoughts, if thoughts were what she had. The spread had been taken from the bed, as the Doctor himself sometimes sat there, and he was covered with the hair from the long-haired dog that rode around in his car. At the start, Mrs. Porter spread a newspaper on top of the spread to protect it, and one on the floor to catch the ashes from his cigar. After he had come and gone she would take them up. But Doctor Lloyd didn't seem to like the sound of the papers, when he sat on them, and he would give them a backhanded swipe that would send them to the floor. Those on the floor, he would kick under the bed. So Mrs. Porter had been obliged to remove the spread, rather than ruin it, and take the rug between the beds off the floor. The bed, without the spread on it, looked occupied.

"Born in eighty-one," Parsons read, then he added, "that makes him just sixty-eight years old."

Webb didn't bite at that.

The Deep Sleep

Parsons wondered why it was that the bed, without anybody in it, troubled him even more than the Judge lying there gasping for breath. He really looked a sight, as his hair was wild and up around his head like a halo, and there was an egg-shaped bald spot at the back because he tossed so much. But the empty bed was worse. It troubled him more than raising the blinds and letting the winter light into the sick room, where it would crawl up the legs of the bed to the face of the Judge. It troubled him more than the understanding, if that was what you could call it, that the Judge really didn't want him around; no, he really didn't, but he couldn't stand to be alone. It was easier for the Judge to know that Parsons was just sitting there, watching him dying, than to know that he was lying there in that bed and dying alone. It had been a pretty awful truth for Parsons to bear. If this great man, this pillar of state, was afraid to lie alone and die in his sick room, what would Carl Weber Parsons do when his own number popped up? A *really* lonely man, without a Carl Parsons to wait on him. Without a Mrs. Porter to come in at night and clean up his mess. It was almost more than Parsons could bear to sit there in the room and watch himself dying, but it was not so troubling, terrible as it was, as the empty bed. The sheet spread out smooth over the shape that had been pressed on it.

But Parsons didn't mean by that what you might think. If that was all he meant, it wouldn't have been so troubling. As attractive as Mrs. Porter was, and for a woman of her age she was very attractive, there was nothing you might call sexy about her. A very strange thing, too. A remarkable thing, in fact. Many years ago, before he knew her better, he thought he had detected something like that, but he had been wrong. He had only detected it in himself. She had this habit of reading off the floor all the time. But she seemed to have no idea at all what it meant to a man. Out in the yard, especially in the summer, Parsons had often stood beside the Judge and watched Mrs. Porter go around the yard picking up twigs. Years ago that had been hard for him to do. Parsons had the feeling that it had also been hard on the Judge. But they had come to an understanding, and the understanding was that Mrs. Porter had never in her life had such an idea in mind. They knew it. There was never any doubt about *that*.

That was why it was so hard to understand why a bed, especially Mrs. Porter's, once the spread was taken off, seemed to trouble him the way it did. Mrs. Porter's shape was there, but *that* wasn't it. Something was there that he found it hard to put his finger on. He had no idea at all what it was till the day that the Judge, as though suddenly speechless, made a circling motion in the air with one of his hands. Parsons had come forward to see what troubled him. The Judge had closed his eyes, he had sealed tight his lips, but with his right hand he made this gesture, strange as it was, which Parsons found unmistakeable. He wanted the bed, the other bed, drawn up alongside. He wanted it where he could reach and touch it with his hand. That proved to be quite a little problem, as Mrs. Porter would notice any tampering like that, and they both knew that something like that would embarrass her. So they left her bed right where it was, and eased over the Judge. It almost killed Parsons as he had to do it by himself. He got him over just enough so the Judge could rest his hand on the mattress, or hook one of his fingers in the mattress loop along one side. When Parsons thought it over, and he often did, he wondered if any other man in the world would understand, and not misunderstand, what that meant. He only understood part of it himself. But just as movie stars put their footprints in sidewalks, or mothers make bronze casts of soft baby shoes, Mrs. Porter had left her permanent print on that bed. She wasn't in it anymore, but the Judge didn't want to be alone.

Now the strange thing was that Parsons felt that too. Sometimes he dozed off, while the Judge was sleeping, but sure as he did he would wake up thinking that he had heard a voice in the room. Not speaking to him, nor to the Judge, but just a calm voice speaking to the world in general, and more than likely reading from a newspaper spread out on the floor. A presence, perhaps that was the word for it. That was what they had, both of them, in the empty bed.

"Parsons—" Webb said suddenly, "you know, he was losing more than weight," but Parsons, who had been thinking just that, pretended not to hear. He kept his eyes on the newspaper, on the strange but familiar face of the Judge, the jaw uncertainly clamped on what had been a new set of teeth. They had tried everything. They had all done what they could.

"He was a bit too heavy," said Parsons, "but I guess he lost some of it too fast."

As if he hadn't heard that, Webb said, "Bygod, it must have driven him crazy!"

Parsons gazed through the windshield as if he might see what this thing was.

"Jesus Christ," Webb went on, "just imagine how he felt. Imagine lying there, wheezing for air, and all that time—" he waved his hand in the air as if to grab the right word out of it, "all that time that damn rock of ages around the house. Getting stronger, bygod, right when he was getting worse. Hanging on like she never heard of dying, or anything else."

The Deep Sleep

Parsons turned his head away, closed his eyes, as if it had long been his custom not to see, to hear, nor to speak of an evil like that. Nevertheless he said, "You mean his mother?"

"Uhuh," said Webb, "I mean his mother."

"Hmmmm," Parsons said.

"You can't do too much for your mother, Parsons, but if you kill yourself trying there's a pretty good chance the old girl will outlive you. There ought to be a black rose these mothers could wear for such loving sons. Or a satin pillow case, with blue and gold tatting, and in the mother's own loving stitch the motto— *He Didn't Make It, But He Died Trying.* No man can do enough for his mother, but he can always die."

Parsons was wondering what the Judge would think of talk like that. More than likely he had never heard it, as youngsters didn't talk to the Judge like that, but if he *had* heard it, what would he have said? Parsons often asked himself questions like that. What would the Judge have said? What would the Judge have done? Ordinarily he had a quick answer, as the Judge was quick to speak his mind, but now, strange to say, the voice of the Judge said nothing. The jaw in the newspaper picture remained clamped shut. Gazing at the picture Parsons was reminded how much he had grown to look like his mother. But what a strange sort of loving son he had been. Not that there were very many people who realized that. It might be that nobody realized it as Parsons did. The Judge was certainly proud of his mother, and knew what a remarkable woman she was, as he never got tired of bringing people out to chat with her. He never tired of hearing what other people thought of her. But Parsons often wondered if anybody else—and that even included Mrs. Porter—ever noticed what Parsons had observed to be a fact. The Judge himself never spoke to her. Not a word. He always spoke it to somebody else.

"Parsons," he would say, "ask Grandmother if she wants anything."

So Parsons would ask her, although they would be right there in the same room together, and the Judge had an even stronger voice than Parsons had. He would do the same thing with Mrs. Porter a good deal of the time. "Mother?" he would say, "you think Grandmother wants anything?"

For maybe five or ten years Parsons had thought that was just a habit the Judge had, growing out of the fact that he was getting pretty heavy to get around. He was also in the habit of telling other people what to do. Parsons particularly. Parsons didn't resent that very much as he and the Judge had a certain understanding, and the Judge seldom asked him to do what he was able to do himself. He was a big man. People liked to do things for him. The Grandmother business had been hard to figure because the Judge gave you the feeling that it was just a special way of showing his mother off. A way of getting strangers to feel right at home with her. So and so, he would say, to whoever it was, you want to bring her that shoebox full of letters?—and the stranger would think it was a sort of special honor for both of them. It was the same with Katherine, and then with Webb, once she had married him. When the Judge spoke to the Grandmother at all, it was *through* one of them. Parsons didn't come to see the truth of that until the Judge was in his own room, flat on his back, and the Grandmother was in the boy's room across the hall. Along about daylight, which was when she got up, she had to make her way past the Judge's door, which was always left open to pick up the breeze that came down the hall. Parsons would be sitting there at the foot of the Judge's bed. When his breathing got too bad, he would take him by the arm and pull him up. The Grandmother would always crane her head around and peer into the bedroom as she passed it, but she never spoke unless she knew Parsons was there. And that was strange, as she never spoke to Parsons himself.

"Howard—" she would say, "you still poorly?"

And the Judge would say, "You tell her, Parsons," and Parsons would tell her that the Judge was looking better, or about the same. That was back when the Judge thought so himself. When he used to think that a week in bed would put him back on his feet. Then the time came when he didn't think so, or if he thought so he didn't believe it, as he could throw the covers off and look at the feet himself. They were not really feet, they were more like a pair of boots. Nearly heavy enough, they looked, to prop a man up. So the Judge didn't believe it, but toward the end, every last morning, the Grandmother would stop there in the door, crane her head around, and then ask how he was. "You still poorly, Howard?" she would say.

It got so it was nearly more than the Judge could stand. Parsons couldn't stand it either, and he tried closing the door, but if he did that the old lady would hammer on it with her cane.

"Howard!" she would croak, "Howard, you all right?"

That's what she did on the morning that they all figured they were going to lose him, and Parsons had gone downstairs to heat up some coffee, when he heard her hammering on the Judge's door with her cane. Parsons ran for the stairs, but before he made it, before he got any farther than the downstairs landing, he heard a voice that was and wasn't the voice of the Judge.

"In the name of God," this voice cried, "will you let me die?"

"You dyin', Howard?" the old lady replied.

If it hadn't been for that, Parsons was sure he *would* have died. But the Judge was a strange man, and hearing that he said, "No, Mother, never felt—better—in—my—life."

It was the first and the last time, Parsons heard him speak to her. Three months later, and that was just yesterday morning, he was dead.

"What is she now—" said Webb, "she a century yet?"

Shaking out the paper, Parsons read, "Judge Porter is survived by his wife, Mrs. Millicent Ordway Porter, a daughter, Katherine Porter Webb, and his mother, Mrs. Angela Rautzen Porter. Mrs. Angela Porter, the mother of the Judge, was born in Finlay in 1849, and is one of the few living people who ever set eyes upon the Great Emancipator. She will be one hundred years old on the 3rd of October of this year."

"She'll probably live to bury the whole damn family," said Webb.

Parsons wondered why a young man should think of something like that. He thought of it himself because he was five years older than the Judge, and the Grandmother naturally made an older person think of it. She didn't change. She had looked about the same for thirty years. Wrinkled and old as she was, there was something permanent about her, and something more or less unpermanent—if there was such a word—about everybody else. They changed. They grew up, they grew old, and one day they died. But the Grandmother merely added another clipping to the collection in her shoebox file. Her sight was nearly gone, but her mind seemed as sharp as it ever was. That always impressed him, so he said—

"I'd·say her mind is just about as good as ever."

Webb smiled.

"What you see funny in that?" Parsons said.

"If you start with a good third-class set of brains, and if you live long enough and manage not to use them, one day they'll point out that your third-class noggin is in first-class shape."

"All I know is, she never misses a trick," Parsons said. He was wondering if these smart young fellows like Webb really believed anything. If they ever got farther than seeing what was wrong with everybody else.

"You know, Parsons—" said Webb, and the funny

thing was that Parsons *didn't* want to know it. He even flinched a bit, as if Webb had made a pass at him.

"You make a left up ahead there," he said, hoping to cut him off.

"You want to know the truth, Parsons?"

Parsons did not. He didn't want to know the truth at all. *If* that was what these young people had, why then he would willingly do without it. So he shook his head. But Webb was not looking at him.

"Everything I am or hope to be," said Webb, in the voice of a radio announcer, "I owe to my mother—I owe to the fact that she died when I was very young."

Parsons raised his hand to his face, as if to ward off the blow.

In a different voice Webb went on, "She was a very beautiful woman, Parsons. I'd have never had a chance. No doubt about that."

It crossed Parsons' mind, just crossed it, that he might be a little tight. Whatever he was saying, anyhow, didn't make a bit of sense. "Turn here," he said, raising his voice a notch, as it made so little sense he didn't find it frightening, and he might have said so if they hadn't been passing the Erskine house. Mr. Erskine, looking just like a mummy, was out in the yard. He had a blanket on his legs, and a green tennis visor shading his face. There were holes in the visor, and Parsons could see the thin ribbons of smoke that were rising through them, and the pack of cigarettes that lay beside him in the grass.

"Who in the hell is that?" said Webb.

"That's old Erskine," Parsons said, although he himself was four years older. But he was *not* senile. He didn't pat his head like a patty-cake. "He collects old razors," Parsons said, although he really didn't mean to say so. What did it really matter if a dying old man collected razors or not. Not much, but what did matter was that Newcomb Erskine, just the day before, had offered Carl Parsons twenty-five dollars cash for the one belonging to the Judge. Parsons had it. He not only had it, but he had shaved with it. It just so happened that he liked an old razor himself.

"Looks like the women are gone," said Webb, and as the car went up the drive, Parsons could see that the window box was full of grackles and squirrels.

MRS. PORTER

"You needn't tell me," Mr. Bayard said, and stepped behind the door he had just opened, "you needn't tell me," he said, from behind the door, then closed it and smiled at Katherine.

"I am Katherine Webb," her daughter said.

"You are Katherine *Porter* Webb," corrected Mr. Bayard.

"You've redecorated," Mrs. Porter said, and turned to gaze at the room. Mr. Bayard moved around to one side to get out of her view.

"I'm afraid it was about time, Mrs. Porter," he said.

"I was here with Mrs. Logsdon," she said, "when it was not air-cooled."

"In times like these," Mr. Bayard said, drawing up chairs for them to sit on, "the least we can do is try to make the ordeal comfortable." He looked at Mrs. Porter, and she looked at his tie. He fingered his tie, looked at Katherine, then said, "Mrs. Webb, I knew your father. We were always frank with each other. We often discussed why society makes this such an ordeal."

"My husband certainly thinks so," Katherine said.

Mr. Bayard smiled with understanding, then said, "A man usually prefers something simple."

"I was wondering when you would go modern, Mr. Bayard," Mrs. Porter said.

Mr. Bayard looked around. He looked skeptical.

"Your type of business calls for it, I would think," she said.

Mr. Bayard took the pen from the holder on his desk, fingered the point, and saw that it was dry. He put it back into the holder, then said, "We hoped to brighten it up a little, it was a trifle dark, as you may remember, but I really wouldn't say that we had modern in mind."

"I thought the empty look was modern," she said. "I see only one chair."

"We have more," said Mr. Bayard, hastily. "We have them stored in the closet here on my right. Idea was to keep the room uncluttered. Seems cooler that way."

"I didn't know *that* was modern," Mrs. Porter said. Mr. Bayard and Katherine turned to see what it was she saw. A large photograph of a shrouded figure, one hand raised to the face, one thrust forward, hung in a simple frame on the wall.

"Don't think it is," Mr. Bayard said, "just something I happened to have grown a little fond of. Hung right there. Thought I might as well make use of it."

"It certainly isn't *my* idea of modern," she said.

"I don't mean to infer it is," said Mr. Bayard, looking at Katherine. "Nail was still there. Just thought I might as well use it."

"Mother," Katherine said, "Mr. Bayard also thinks it should be simple."

"A simple rule of thumb," said Mr. Bayard, leaning forward to put his thumb up, "is the simpler the Service, the bigger the man."

The Deep Sleep

"It is a problem, isn't it?" Mrs. Porter said.

"It is indeed," said Mr. Bayard. "Bodies—" he began, then coughed and said, "people die, and they have to be buried. If you make it simple, along comes a woman who wants it elaborate. We are in business. We have to give people what they want."

"Supply and demand," she said.

"Ex-act-ly," Mr. Bayard replied.

"But I suppose the demand is mostly for modern," she said.

"Mother," Katherine said, "modern *is* simple."

"You may have heard him say it, Mr. Bayard," she said, "money underground is not money in it."

Mr. Bayard gazed at the memo on top of his desk. "There's just one thing," he said, "that I'd like to suggest. There have been calls all morning concerning the viewing, and—"

"Oh, no—!" said Katherine.

"You don't plan a viewing?"

"Oh noooo!" Katherine replied.

Mr. Bayard spread his arms and put his hands flat on his desk. He looked at Mrs. Porter who said, "I don't think viewing is a modern custom."

"We simply do *not* want a viewing," Katherine said.

"Mrs. Webb," said Mr. Bayard, "I know how you feel. I have felt that way myself." He paused, then

[135]

said, "You may not know it as I do, Mrs. Webb, but your father had a second family. He has been a friend and a father to hundreds of young men. He belongs to you, but he also belongs to them. Seeing his picture in the paper this morning—" Mr. Bayard looked around as if he might see it, "I was suddenly reminded how long it has been. I hardly knew him. Many old friends—"

"But who—" Katherine said, "wants to see him—dead?"

Mr. Bayard removed the glasses from his nose, peered through them at an ink spot on his blotter.

"Mrs. Webb," he said, "I'm afraid that many old friends do. I did myself. When I saw the picture in the paper this morning, I said to myself, this is not Judge Porter."

"I know—" said Katherine, "but—"

"During a long illness," said Mr. Bayard, "all we see in a man is his struggle with the illness. After it is over he looks more like himself."

"Then why can't we leave him in peace?" her daughter said.

"If that is Mrs. Porter's wish," said Mr. Bayard, and turned to look at her. When she said nothing, he said, "Here in this building, Mrs. Porter, I have often passed long hours with the Judge. We both, in the last few years, lost many close friends."

"I often wondered where your father went off to," Mrs. Porter said.

"Let me suggest," said Mr. Bayard, "a compromise. Not a public viewing, but perhaps a small, private viewing in the home."

"Ohhh, Mother—!" her daughter said.

"Mrs. Webb," said Mr. Bayard, "I fully respect your sentiments, but the sentiments of others also merit your respect." Mr. Bayard tapped the point of his letter opener on his palm.

"We all admit it's barbarous," Katherine said, "and then we—"

"Mrs. Webb," said Mr. Bayard, "when did you see your father last?"

"About three months ago."

"And before that?" Katherine did not reply. "With all respect to your feelings," said Mr. Bayard, "I think we can sometimes get too squeamish. I should think it would be helpful to his memory to see how he really looks."

"Thank you," her daughter said, and stood up.

"I am very sorry," said Mr. Bayard, "and it is certainly poor business ethics, but your father's passing is more than a small private event. He was a well-loved man. He was a father to many of us."

"I always have to remind myself," Mrs. Porter said.

"It is not," her daughter said, "a public event."

Mrs. Porter looked at her daughter and said, "I just wonder if we'll have the room for it."

"Since my opinion isn't needed any further," her daughter said, "will you please excuse me?"

Mr. Bayard rose from his desk and started for the door. He opened it for Katherine, then said, "Mrs. Webb, permit me one more word." He took his glasses from his face, and rubbed the bruised spot on his nose. "Young woman," he said, "as a friend of your father, as a father with five grandchildren, perhaps you will permit me a word of advice?" Katherine waited. "I don't like everything I hear, or everything I know about the undertaker's business, but I'm not afraid to look a dead man in the face." When Katherine turned away he said, "Good day, Mrs. Webb," and opened the door.

Coming up from behind, Mrs. Porter said, "I'm just hoping his family isn't too large—"

"We will try to keep it small," said Mr. Bayard, "We will say as much."

"We have a twenty pound bird, Mr. Bayard," she said, "thanks to Mr. and Mrs. Crowell—"

"Mother!" Katherine said, "for heaven's *sake!*"

"Mrs. Porter," he said, "there is just one little detail. I'm afraid that Mr. Porter arrived with a minimum of clothes. If you can furnish me with a suit, one that he was accustomed to wear, and perhaps a shirt and a tie that he usually wore."

Her daughter left the porch and walked down the flagstone steps to the drive.

"He lost so much weight," she said, "I hardly know what will fit him."

"You can leave that to us, Mrs. Porter," he said.

She stepped through the door, then she turned and said, "Shoes? I hope you don't need shoes?"

"I'm afraid we will need a pair," he said.

"Why, I think I gave them all away, Mr. Bayard," she said. "It's been so long since he wore them, and—"

"Mother!" cried Katherine.

"I don't suppose slippers would do?" she said.

"I'm afraid—" said Mr. Bayard, but the phone began to ring on his desk. He left the door open as he went back to answer it. "Mrs. Porter was just here," said Mr. Bayard, "and there will be a small, private viewing. Yes. Yes, at the Porter home." He hung the phone up and came back to the door.

"Now who would that be, Mr. Bayard?" she said.

"Mrs. Newcomb Erskine," said Mr. Bayard.

She left him there and came down the steps and entered the cab. Mr. Bayard waved, she waved, and as they moved into the street she said, "I just knew it. I could tell the way it rang."

The Deep Sleep

As he entered the house Webb called out, "Anybody here?" then waited for the answer that did not come. A loose board twanged in the floor where he stood. The electric clock over the sink made a rasping noise. "Anybody home?" he repeated, then dropped the load of papers on the kitchen table, and walked around the table into the dining room. A note had been left on the telephone pad. He picked it up and read—

> Grandmother in Basement
> Dry Cleaning in hallway.

He left the pad on the table and came back through the kitchen to the basement stairs. "Oh, Grandmother!" he said. No reply. He could hear water dripping into one of the tubs. He switched on the basement light and went down to where he could see the furnace, and the ironing board with the two irons on one end of it. The door to the fruit cellar was open, but he could not make out if the room was empty. He walked to the door, then said "Oh, Grandmother?" before he looked in. Nobody there. He stepped inside and looked at the shelves. The smell of the place reminded him that he needed food. He

[140]

looked at the jars on the shelf above him, the one next to the ceiling, and thought he saw a familiar label on a jar at the back. He moved the jar at the front to one side, struck one of his safety matches, and gazed at the label on a full bottle of Old Grand-Dad.

"Well, I'll be damned," he said softly, and saw that the seal had been broken. A jigger, perhaps two jiggers, had been taken out. The cork was down, but he was able to work it loose. He sniffed the whiskey, passed the palm of his hand over the mouth of the bottle, then he had the bottle raised to his lips when he remembered the light. He switched it off, and there, in the dark, he had himself a good swallow. It brought tears to his eyes, blood to his head, and standing there he said, "Ohhhh, *Grand*mother!" Then he returned the bottle to the shelf, far to the back, and placed the jar of beets before it. He left the fruit cellar and stepped into the basement, facing the stairs. Right there before him, under the stairs, were three or four cartons of the Judge's notebooks, and on one of the cartons was written, in crayon, the word LAW. It struck him as quite a joke. The law hiding under the basement stairs, and the whiskey hiding in the fruit cellar. It also reminded him of something else.

In the Judge's office, down at the school, in a metal cash box that had his Will and other papers, the Judge had a bottle with a liniment label pasted on it. It was whiskey. Cheap moonshine of some kind. It had been in the bottle, and the bottle in the drawer, since Prohibition days. But the level of the liquid was always the same. The Judge didn't drink it, he didn't like it, but just so long as he had it he knew he could pass for one of the boys. He could open his drawer and show he was as wild as the best of them.

"Lin-i-ment—" the Judge would say, then chuckle, just to make sure you got it, and if his secretary came into the room he would make quite a fuss. He would blush like a first-class celluloid Babbitt caught in the act.

It had taken Webb fifteen years to see that a man like the Judge could behave like that, actually be like that, and still be as big a man as the Judge. If you could understand something like that, you could understand something about America, and if you couldn't understand it there was nothing to do but give it all up.

Webb could. He didn't have to look farther than himself. He didn't have a liniment bottle in his car, or stuck in the back of the medicine cabinet, but before he took a swig of the Old Grand-Dad he had switched off the light. There you had it. There you had a picture of a really screwed up American. Paul Graham Webb, bohemian and artist, free thinker, free-liver, and man about town, switching off the fruit cellar light before he took a little nip. It said OLD GRAND-DAD on the label, but what he had in his hand was the liniment bottle, the forbidden fire water, the middle-aged man's fountain of youth.

"Oh, Grandmother!" he said, and gave a tug on the light cord that pulled it off. As he lowered his arm he felt it swishing on the leg of his pants. So calmly it surprised him, in a voice as deliberate as Mrs. Porter's, he said aloud—

"It's the house. It's the goddam house."

The cuckoo clock, in the Grandmother's room, cuckoo'd one o'clock.

"OHHhhhh GRANDMOTHER!" he bellowed.

No reply.

It crossed his mind that something might be wrong. Not that it worried him, merely crossed his mind. For many years they had been hoping, as some wag had said, for the best.

He went up the basement stairs to the kitchen, then up the hall stairs to the landing, where two of the bedroom doors stood open—but not the Grandmother's. Tapping on it gently, he said—

"Oh, Grandmother?"

Not a sound. He gave the knob a turn, opened the door, and put in his head. The curtain flapped in the draft he had stirred up, but that was all. The bed was empty, but it had been made. The Grandmother had

been the one to make it as the covers were nicely
smoothed at the front, but at the back, where she
couldn't reach them, they were still in a wad. Her pair
of black Sunday shoes were on the floor. Each shoe
lay tipped on its side, as both the heels were rounded,
and the tips were as scuffed as the point of a cane. At
the head of the bed, where she could get at it, was a
black fiber bag full of pot holders, heating pads, and
afghans of all sizes, waiting for Mrs. Porter to make
a selection at Christmas time. Every member of the
family, and there were dozens, had more afghans than
they could use, but they always received one more
from Santa Claus. The selection was made in terms
of the wool, and the colors that matched. The Grandmother could no longer tell what some colors really
were. On the closet door, from a wire hanger, hung
the Grandmother's party dress, of a dull black material, with the brittle-looking lace at the throat and
cuffs. Two other dresses hung *in* the closet, one for
travelling on the Pennsylvania Railroad, and one for
the summer when she just might appear on the front
porch. It was spotted with flowers, and known as her
summer frock. That was all the room contained, since
all the Grandmother did in it was sleep, and what was
not there she put on when she got up. It went out
of the room with her when she left. All her valuables
were in the shoe box on the window seat. She owned

one ring, and it had never been taken off. Although it was summer the windows were down and the room was hot and stuffy, as the Grandmother refused to breathe the night air. During the day it was up to somebody to open them. Not Webb, as he had the feeling, whatever he thought of the Grandmother, that she was the last hope of the world for privacy. The world no longer chose to put up with it. But here in this room, and in this old woman, there was something that Webb considered to be holy, and it was not his business, nor that of the world, to tamper with it.

Through the bathroom window, which he faced, Webb could see the car, the stretch of unkempt yard, and the figure of a man who was walking toward the back of it. Parsons. He had just stepped out of the garage. He held in one hand a rake, and the other arm hung at his side. Webb was in the habit of observing people, and something about the way Parsons walked, something about the arm, seemed a little stiff and half paralyzed. He wondered if he had missed that all this time. The arm at his side did not swing free. Neither did it hang. It was drawn in to his body, his groin, as if he might be in pain. Webb stepped to the window, he almost cried out, "Oh, Parsons, having any trouble?" when the trouble he was having dropped out of the leg of his pants. The right leg. The pants leg on that side. And the trouble he was having took on the shape of a garden tool. And right at that moment, at that *exact* moment, just as if he had heard Webb holler at him, Parsons craned his head around and looked directly into Webb's face. Right at him, right straight at him, and on the old man's face there appeared a smile that Webb found indescribable. As if a grown man, out in public somewhere, had wet his pants. A smile of shame and implicit understanding at the same time. Webb had been too paralyzed to move, he had just stood there, his face at the window, until Parsons had leaned on the rake, bent over, and picked up the tool. Then Webb had bellowed,

"Oh, Parsons! Haven't seen Grandmother, have you?" as if *that* had brought him to the window, explained why he was there. Very slowly, as if it hurt him, Parsons wagged his head. Something about it, God knows what, made Webb realize that Parsons, Parsons, the thief in the case, had come out with the best of it. He had been caught, but he had *not* turned around and lied. He had *not* screamed some silly nonsense to cover himself up.

"OH—Grandmother!" Webb bellowed again, more in pain than anything else, then turned from the window and crossed the room to the laundry chute. As if he might hide there, he raised the lid, put in his head. The draft from the basement smelled of the whiskey on his own breath. That's where he was when the telephone rang, and he left the bathroom, went down the stairs, and then around through the living room to the phone. Facing the wall, he picked up the phone, and hearing Mrs. Porter's calm voice at the other end, he turned around to face the bird-box window and the light. The Grandmother was sitting there in her rocker, her cane in her lap. She was gazing at the riot the squirrels were having in the window box. Her jaw was set, and seen against the light, her chin and her nose hob-nobbing, she looked more than ever like a sleeping lizard sunning on a rock.

"Oh Paul," Mrs. Porter was saying, "are you there, Paul—?" but Webb just stood there, the receiver at his ear, mulling over whether the Grandmother was dead, playing possum, or just asleep. "Paul—?" said Mrs. Porter, "Oh, Paul—" but he didn't hear the rest of it, as the Grandmother had put her cane into the bird box, waggled it. "Why, I can hear that clear in here!" Mrs. Porter said.

"Is that you, Mother?" said Webb, and with the hand that had the smell of whiskey on it, he wiped the sweat from his forehead, and then dragged it down his face. Mrs. Porter was saying that she wanted him to find the Judge's herringbone suit. Find the herringbone suit, the white shirt, the wool tie, and meet them in an hour at the Hot Potato.

"Yes, Mother—" Webb had said, but she had already hung up.

KATHERINE

From the counter of the drugstore in Suburban Square, Katherine could see her mother seated in the phone booth, her bag open in her lap, while she fumbled for a coin. The glass doors of the booth were closed, overhead the dim booth light was on, and her mother appeared to be in a private, undisturbed world of her own. The life of the drugstore did not penetrate to her. While she sat searching for the coin her lips carefully formed what she was saying, as if the silence was intended and she was speaking in pantomime. Her mother faced the glass doors—she never faced the telephone or anyone else to whom she was speaking— so it was sometimes hard to understand what she said. People were often uncertain to whom her mother was speaking. At an early age Katherine had discovered that she was *not* really talking to people, but while they were present she talked to herself, aloud. In the company of people her own thoughts seemed to form. As they did she would state them, *state* perhaps being the word for her mother's sober, undistracted monologue. If somebody answered she might incorporate the answer in what she knew. She heard a good deal more than some people were inclined to think. She was like a cat, in that she heard only what was useful to her. In a room full of loud talk and noises she would hear a glass scrape on her cherry wood table, or the silliest remark on the care and feeding of birds. It had certainly kept her from becoming rattlebrained.

But her mother had lived all of her life, it seemed to Katherine, in a kind of phone booth, cut off from her family, but thanks to the phone she kept in touch with them. She had been like a hermetically sealed unit, a term that had meant a great deal to her, and had been on her tongue when she finally decided, in preference to other makes, to buy the Frigidaire. As a child it had been more than Katherine could stand, and when the kittens were born in the carton in the basement, each one of them wrapped in a cellophane wrapper, she had thought of her mother and had just stood there and cried. And then later, when she was taken by her father to hear the naturalist, Dr. Beebe, she had been terrified by the underwater pictures of his diving bell. Her mother also, she had felt sure, had been trapped down there. Anything that was bottled up and sealed off from the others, like the

insects in amber that her father brought her, made
Katherine first think of her mother then of herself.
Which one was it? In her dreams it had always been
herself. She would dream she was suffocating and have
horrible nightmares. Other times she would dream she
was the fairy princess living in the castle that came
along with the goldfish, cut off from everything in the
world but the fish. It had been too much for a child
to comprehend, but the longer she lived the more she
seemed to understand. That was not saying she
thought her mother was right, or that a human being
should be trapped in a phone booth, but it seemed to
suit her mother, and if you looked around and saw
what life did to people, there was something to be said
for what her mother had worked out. She lost touch
with her family, but she seemed to keep in touch with
something else. God only knew what it was, but it was
certainly there. All she had to do was lift the receiver,
speak into the phone. But it was not a pipeline to God,
as Paul described it, and if there was a pipeline Katherine felt that both God and her mother had to share
it equally. Like the Grandmother, her mother was not
beholden to *any*one.

"I simply try to live up to the rules," was all she
said.

When she stepped from the phone booth her mother
left one black glove looped over the mouthpiece,

where she had placed it while looking for the coin. Wearing one glove, carrying a gaping purse, she came toward Katherine who said, "Your purse, Mother," and when the purse was taken care of, "Mother, your glove?"

She saw that it was missing.

"We had quite a little discussion," her mother said.

"You left it in the phone booth, Mother."

"I have *more* single gloves," her mother replied, and Katherine left her at the counter and crossed the room to the booth. A man was in it, smoking, and the cloud of smoke made it hard to see. But he saw her, and opening the doors he said—

"Something, Miss?"

"Is there a glove—?" she said, and the man saw it, passed it out to her. Then he looked around behind him, he spread his legs and looked at the floor. It was clear that he was married, Katherine was thinking, and with the glove she came back to the counter where her mother held the menu at arm's length before her, her head tipped away from it. She did not wear her glasses, as a rule, when she left the house. Her eyes were large, rather dark, and when seen without her glasses few people ever wondered why the Judge had married her. They were calm, they were unblinking, and when actually focused on something they gave an impression of serenity and depth. In public, as Katherine had observed, Paul found it convenient to stand beside her mother, refer to her *as* mother, and take her arm as they crossed the street. Now there were dark rings under her eyes, but they merely seemed to call attention, like some theatrical eye lotion, to what large, serene womanly eyes they were. The middle-aged soda clerk, Katherine noticed, had a look at Mrs. Porter when he turned to face the mirror, and she could see him speculating on her mother's age. The mirror that they faced was full of women's faces, the faces of the sun-tanned horsey set with their wind-blown dyed hair and the distracted smoke-screened gaze. What Paul called the suburban huntresses, the killers of the untamed station wagon country, and in this row of faces, that of Mrs. Porter's seemed very strange. Part of this, as Katherine knew from experience, was merely that her mother couldn't see without her glasses, and the large, dark eyes turned in when they could not see out. That was part, certainly, but not all of it. For her mother, seated there at the counter, had her hermetically sealed unit right along with her, the phone booth that sealed out the life that distracted everybody else.

"I shall have a dish of coffee ice cream," she said. "Small."

"Where did you tell Paul to meet us?" Katherine said.

"Twenty cents," said her mother, "the last time it was fifteen."

She returned the menu to the slot between the sugar bowl and the napkins, took another napkin, and cleaned the finger tips of her ungloved hand. As if it reminded her of something, she said, "The Hot Potato."

"The what, Mother?"

"We will meet him there," said her mother. "They serve hot potatoes." She took a spoonful of her coffee ice cream.

"The Hot Potato is a lunch room, Mother?"

"Men go there," she replied. "They serve hot potatoes."

Katherine gave the froth on her soda a stir and looked at the street. Three women in sunsuits, looking like a single beetle with assorted spots on its back, came out of Strawbridge & Clothier and waited for a car at the curb. They each held a large Strawbridge & Clothier shopping bag. Paul was not with her, but she heard his voice say, "Just look at the goddam biddies, off spending the old man's money!" It made her ashamed what living with him had done to her. She even saw women through his eyes. She laughed at them as he did himself. She sometimes wondered if she had any eyes of her own. "Think of the poor bastard," he would go on, "padding around somewhere with his monogrammed brief case, his ulcers, and his high blood pressure, trying to turn a nickel while the old battle-axe is spending a dime." It made her so mad she could hardly speak. What were the old battle-axes supposed to do? Sit around watching ball games? And yet, when she saw these women, it was through *his* eyes. She felt his indignation, his disgust, in spite of herself.

"What size does he wear?" her mother said.

"Daddy?" she said, since they *were* buying him shoes.

"Paul," her mother said, "he will have to have a white shirt."

"He won't wear it, Mother. He will refuse to wear a white shirt."

"How well I remember your father," her mother said.

"It simply won't work, Mother, trying to force him to wear something."

"A tie, too," her mother said. "He won't like your father's ties."

A new station wagon, with the words ALMOSTA FARM printed on the woodwork, drew up to the curb and two of the sunsuit biddies climbed in. The woman at the wheel had long brown arms, a tight-fitting jockey cap without a crown, and the habit of glancing over her shoulder at the back seats. It was empty now, but the children were usually there. Going to school, coming from school, going to the dentist, going to the game, going to the dance, going to the movies, and as Paul liked to say, really going to the dogs. Mother was the chauffeur, now, and they were all going to the dogs.

"I don't think they're using real cream any more," her mother said. Katherine turned and saw her mother, her eyes softly closed, testing the ice cream. It sharpened the senses, her mother believed, to close down on some of them.

"When did you say we'd meet him, Mother?"

Mrs. Porter did not answer. She took another spoonful of the ice cream, let it dissolve away. "I don't know whether I mentioned it or not," she said.

"Mother," she said, "how are we to know—"

"I was looking for the nickel," her mother went on, "the operator was saying would I please drop a nickel."

"It's one-thirty now, Mother."

"If I just sat quiet, your father would always find me," she said.

"Paul is *not* Daddy," Katherine said, "if he goes there and we're not waiting—"

"It's air-cooled," her mother said. "It's a comfortable place to wait."

Katherine picked up the checks, looked in her

purse for money, and left a tip on the counter.

"I refuse to accept the principle," her mother said.

"Where is the Hot Potato, Mother?"

"Shoes first," her mother said, "your father was very particular about his shoes." From the bowl on the counter, so absently Katherine wondered if she really knew what she was doing, her mother's right hand took five pieces of lump sugar, dropped them in her purse. As they stepped into the street a newsboy stood there, holding up before them an evening paper, and her mother stopped to look at it.

"*Bulletin*, ma'am?" the boy said, and Mrs. Porter moved forward a step, then backward, before she got the distance on the headlines just right. Once she had it, she began to read.

"Mother!" said Katherine, "he wants to sell it!"

"Why, look here," her mother said. "Why look here, he's in the *Bulletin*." Katherine came back and gave the boy a nickel, and her mother took the paper. "On the front with General Eisenhower," her mother said.

"Come, Mother—" Katherine said, but a line of cars kept them from crossing. They stood on the curb waiting for the signal from the traffic man. "Do we go to Strawbridge's for shoes, Mother?"

"Eisenhower," her mother said. "General Eisenhower. Now he would approve of *that*."

The Deep Sleep

PARSONS

Carl Parsons' father, Earl Parsons, had devoted his life to the proposition that all men wanted to build their own homes with their own bricks. He had invented a portable mould to make this possible. All that men needed was the Parsons Mould, and the Parsons Mix. Earl Parsons had also wanted privacy, a rustic, unspoiled life in the woods, so he had built his house far back from the road, in a grove of trees. The stream that wound across it had supplied water for his bricks. In the spring and summer a dense growth of foliage concealed the house from view. Half of the Parsons house, the front half, had been erected with the Parsons bricks, and resembled a garage to which a square frame house had been attached. Some people had thought he was building a mill, but when it was discovered to be a house the neighboring property fell off in value, which was why Judge Porter, a young man at the time, had bought a big piece of it. The Porter house, of course, faced the road, and from early spring until after Thanksgiving, the Parsons monster, as some people described it, could not be seen. It stood far to the rear, and was even thought to be unoccupied. Vines had been trained to cling to the bricks, the wood frame of the house had never been painted, and neither lights nor fires were ever seen at night. Lights were often on, fires were usually going, but there were not many windows in the Parsons house. They were just one of the things that did not come along with the bricks.

The front of the house faced the woods in the summer, but in the winter, when the trees were bare, the land fell away to where the Schuylkill cut a deep gap. It was not possible to see the river, but the gap was full of the idea of it, and one could see, on a clear winter day, nearly forty miles. All along the river were the smoking manufacturing towns. Industrial eyesores, Mrs. Porter called them, but seen through an Indian summer haze the far blue hills seemed to be an inviting place. Full of better people, that is, than Parsons just happened to know. Off to the west was Valley Forge, where the nation itself had been manufactured, and the lines of a new super-highway could be seen taking shape.

That was the view over the winter, and it was why Earl Parsons had built his house there, but his son, Carl, had not looked at it for many years. He lived in two rooms at the back of the house. In nearly thirty years, since the day that the Judge had asked Carl Parsons to lend him a hand, Parsons had seldom been around to the front of his place. He entered, and he left, through the door at the back. He slept in a room where the window looked out on the Porter yard. On the hot humid days of the summer, when the bricks sweated like a glass of cold water, he would open the door at the front to stir up a draft. To air the rugs, and the furniture, damp and green with mold. But he never stepped through this door, as nothing was there. The wide porch his father had planned had never been built. The piece of etched plate glass in the door reflected the jungle out in front, where streamers of honeysuckle hung from the trees like drying nets.

The front of the house, the fine winter view and the dense summer foliage, brought nothing to Parsons' mind that he had not spent his life trying to forget. His life, such as it was, was lived at the rear. There had been very little life in it to speak of until that day, just forty years ago, when he saw the young couple looking over the lot next door. They had bought the ten acres, and built a house on it facing the other way. While this house was a-building Parsons sat by the hour at the window by his kitchen table, or he would go upstairs where the bedroom window was level with the floor. He would lie there by the hour, watching this house go up. He knew it far better than the Porters knew it themselves. Here and there he might have given them some sound practical advice. But who would listen to the son of a man who had built a house with his own hands, but forgot to connect, by any means whatsoever, the upstairs with the down? Who had been *up*stairs when the last floor board had been nailed down. Who had had to let himself out through a window and drop to the ground. Whose son had lived in such a house for twenty-five years, and went to bed every night, if the truth were known, through a hole that had been sawed in the ceiling, like the entrance to a hayloft, and then dragged the ladder up after him. He was afraid somebody he knew might set eyes on it. No sensible man could be asked to believe that another man had built such a house, and he would certainly not turn to that man's son for advice. But it had made that son fairly tolerant of other people's mistakes. There was just no limit to what a human being might do.

Until the Porters came, Carl Parsons would walk into town for what he needed, and then ride back with the boy who made the local deliveries. He seemed to have enough, as he told the Judge, to keep heel and sole together, and he gave no indication that he had ever wanted much more. When the Porters came, he did the handy work. It crept up on him, and it was soon a full-time job. It crossed his mind that he was being exploited, and to put an end to that without any hard feelings, he went into town and took a full-time position helping with the mail. But all day long he found he had the Porter place in mind. He could hardly stand to see what the new hired man was doing to it. After a full day delivering mail he would come home, gulp down his supper, then go over and put in two or three hours on the Porter yard. It wasn't his, but he felt responsible for it. He didn't accomplish a thing in the sense that the Judge didn't offer him any more money, but it cleared up the fact that where he really lived was the Porter place. He had to look after it, whether he was paid for it or not. So he told the Judge that his sacro-iliac wouldn't let him rise as a mail carrier. It was just in time, because it was over that winter that the Judge began to slip. Parsons noticed it long before anybody else. Not that it was a mystery; it was just that Parsons noticed how many more things *he* seemed to be doing, which the Judge had once managed to do himself. Every week or so the Judge would say—

"Parsons, if you get the time—" and that always meant that he had to find the time for something new. Something the Judge could no longer do himself. Empty the ashes, or carry in the log that sat in the fire place all winter, then carry it out and carry in the dried arrangement that took its place. Little things, piddling things, but they soon added up. And in the summer, when it began to get hot, the Judge would drop down in the canvas sling chair, the garden gloves

limp on his hands, and just point out the things that he
wanted Parsons to do. So *he* knew it, the Judge knew
it, and it was just one of the many things between
them, since nobody else seemed to have any knowledge
of it.

Then the war came along, the Judge helped to run
it, and though nobody else seemed to realize it, Carl
Parsons was really the man around the Porter house.
He ate there, he read letters to the Grandmother, he
did the shopping, he opened the drains, and he listened
by the hour to Mrs. Porter talk. But there was no
indication that Mrs. Porter knew it herself. It was
nearly always the Judge, and his affairs, they talked
about. So the Judge was there; in a curious way he
seemed to be there more than ever, since when he was
not around Mrs. Porter was inclined to talk about
him. When he was in the house, she never seemed to
have much to say. She didn't want him to be getting
"a head too big for his hats," as she liked to say.

On the other hand, a man in Mrs. Porter's house
was still not much. After five years of it, Parsons
had been able to see that. *Around the house, the Judge
had said to him, I leave it up to the Missus.* So did Parsons. It was *her* bailiwick. Parsons' bailiwick wasn't
so much the Porter house as the Porter garage. He
stood there in the rain, he went there when he had
nothing better to do. There was a keg he could sit on,

and there was always a blade that needed an edge. One day the Judge had found him there and said—

"Parsons, what you have in mind, right of domain?" which was a joke, of course, but there was a certain truth in it. The Judge had stocked it, but the stuff really *belonged* to him. He used it. He oiled and repaired it. He had right of domain. So when Webb had let him out of the car, Parsons had headed for the garage like a dog for its kennel, and there in the garage he stood wondering what he should do next. It wouldn't be much. He was tired, and the weather was hot. He had the feeling that something was slipping away, as if the floor of the garage itself was moving, and it had led him to turn and pass his eyes over the walls. On a shelf at the back, where he had overlooked it, was a stainless steel trowel. He walked to the back, took it from the shelf, and chipped the dirt off it. Mrs. Porter had given it to the Judge. She was always buying things, and giving him things, he could no longer use. There were big holes in both of Parsons' pockets, but he figured he could hold it there with his arm, and on his way out of the garage, as he planned to do some weeding, he picked up the rake. Then he crossed the yard toward his own place, and he had no warning whatsoever until he felt the trowel cold on his leg. It slid down the chute of his right pants leg, and spilled out on the ground. As it did, without stooping, Parsons had craned around to look at the window where the Judge, if anybody, might be looking at him. The Judge liked to shave with his mirror propped there on the sill. A face was there, and just for a moment Parsons thought his heart would stop beating—then he saw that the face was Webb, and not the Judge.

"OHhhh, Grandmother!" Webb had shouted, and Parsons realized that though *he* had been caught, Webb seemed to have the guilty conscience. Yelling like that, he was showing more shame than Parsons felt. There was nothing for Parsons to do about it but pick up the tool, cross the yard, and try to get out of sight before he yelled again. So he had his back to the yard when he heard the Porter telephone ringing. But he kept going for his own place, and he was right there at the door, on the steps at the back, when his own phone went off. He had had one put in when the Judge took sick. He still had the trowel in his hand when he crossed the kitchen and lifted the receiver—

"Hello?" he had said.

"Parsons, this is Webb."

Parsons couldn't think of a thing to say. Not a thing.

"Mrs. Porter just called," Webb said, "and I've got to run off on an errand. She wondered if you'd come over and sit with Grandmother?"

"Why, yes," Parsons said, "why, sure."

"I hate to ask you," said Webb, "but hell, I've got to leave the house."

"That's perfectly all right," Parsons said.

"I just want to tell you," said Webb, "that I consider you a part of this family, and that in my opinion you have a right to anything on the place. I mean that. I'm sure Katherine feels the same way."

Parsons did not reply.

"Well, I got to beat it," said Webb. "I got to take his suit down to the undertaker's."

"I'll be right over," Parsons said, and Webb hung up. On the chair pulled out from the table, Parsons sat down. He was there when Webb came out of the house, let the screen slam behind him, and went up the drive with the Judge's light gray suit on his arm. Parsons recognized it. He wore it on Sundays, and when he went out with Mrs. Porter. Webb threw the suit into the car, then he backed the car around and headed down the driveway, giving the horn a toot as he swung into the street.

THE GRANDMOTHER

The top of the roaster she held before her, like a shield. Over the slippery skin of the breast she passed her hand to the legs, then between the legs to the skewers, where the bird was laced like a corset to hold the stuffing in. Working with one bony finger she found a slit, forced an opening, and, crooking that finger like a hook, drew it out. The grease was cool on her lips and the smell of the sage went up her nose. The finger popped like a cork when she drew it out of her mouth.

"Humphh," she said, but nevertheless, had another sampling. She peeled a strip of the skin from the flesh around the neck. The finger she wiped on the front of her apron, honing it like a blade. Peering through the open kitchen door she saw the blurred cloudy yard, but in the green at the back of the yard a moving spot. Raising her cane, she thumped it soundly on the lid.

"Oh, Grandmother!" she said, with a croaking noise, "your Uncle Billie's britches!" That pleased her so much she hoisted the cane, wagged it like a sword, and then rapped her knuckles on the roaster lid. But she was in the rocker by the window box when Parsons entered the house.

"May I come in?" he said, stopping at the dining room door.

"You're already in," she said.

He came through the door into the room, and she saw that he got to the table, farther than usual, before taking off his hat.

The Deep Sleep

"Scared the squirrels'll get it?" she said.

Parsons took off his hat, set it on the table. He drew up a chair and she waited for him to speak.

"Cat got your tongue?" she said.

"It's too hot to talk," he replied.

He was a fool but she liked him. A gentleman.

"The *Nonpareil* come this morning?" he said.

"It's printed on Monday," she said, "and it *comes* on Tuesday." That was all. But Parsons understood what she meant. The Grandmother had never forgotten the Friday that her son, Howard Porter, had brought into the house the newspaper for the following Sunday. A city paper. Heathens put it out. Leaning forward, leaning over the table where her new afghan was folded, he took the paper from her shoe box, settled back.

"June the 17th," he said, "that it?"

She didn't answer. He could see that for himself. She sat waiting while he looked it over himself. She had already read the headlines, the weather they were having, and she had puzzled out the photograph on the front. *Niagara Falls.*

"Where young Brides go," Parsons said, "you see that?"

Tipping back her head the Grandmother said, "Nigh-gra Falls, Buflo New York, Falls on American an' Canadian side. American falls fourteen hundred feet wide. Cave of winds under falls on American side." There she stopped.

"Canadian Falls twenty-two hundred feet wide," Parsons said.

She let it pass. She waited for him to turn the page. The Grandmother didn't really give a hoot how high or wide the Canadian falls were, but if she didn't use her mind she would lose her wits. She had said as much. So she memorized what she thought was important enough to read.

"*Thought for the Week*?" said Parsons, "you get it?"

"He who does not advance recedes," she said.

"Who said that?" said Parsons.

"It don't say who said it."

"I was just wonderin'—" he said. He folded the paper, drew his fingers along the fold.

"Here's the *Church in Action*," he said. The Grandmother waited for him to go on. There was usually so much action in the church that it had to be printed in fine print. So she missed it. "The Bowery," Parsons said, "New York. Instead of rescuing the perishing the Church in Action now endeavors to assist in the home so that there will be less who need rescuing."

"Humphhh," the Grandmother said. Of all she'd heard of New York, she didn't believe a word of it.

"The rest's about China—" Parsons said, and turned

to the other side of the page, as the Grandmother would not hear a word about the Chinese. They ate with sticks. They spit on your own shirts when they ironed them.

"How to make $50 grow into $1,000,000," he said. He chuckled. He didn't have to ask her what she thought of *that*.

"*Laugh for the Day*," he said, then wet his lips before he read it. "Have you any invisible hairnets? the man said. Yes ma'am, said the clerk. Said the man, Let me see one."

There was no change in the Grandmother's face, if that was where you looked. But Parsons didn't, he saw her right foot lift an inch or so off the floor, then he heard the round heel of that shoe come down with a faint click. The Grandmother was laughing. She was laughing nearly to split.

"See here, said the Farmer—" Parsons went on, "see here, young feller, what you doin' in that tree? One of your apples fell off, said the boy, an' I'm putting it back."

Not so good. The Grandmother's foot remained on the floor. Parsons turned that sheet and looked at the next page. He sized it up briefly, then said, "Schu-mann-Rindsfoos nuptials?"

The Grandmother wagged her head.

"Well, now let's see," Parsons said, as the report

ran a full column. He got the gist of it, then began, "A leading social event of the season was marriage of Pearl Schumann of Finlay, with Heinrich Rindsfoos of Sedalia. The event took place at the home of the bride on Clinton Street—"

"Why, they moved," the Grandmother said.

"—to the strains of the Lohengrin Wedding March played on the harp by Peter Klinger, of Mercer. The ring bearer, Master Andrew Cable, approached bearing ring on white satin pillow followed by bride on arm of her father, Emil Schumann." Parsons looked up, then went on, "The bride was very beautifully attired in a gown of white crepe meteor, court train, and trimmed with real point lace. The Schumann home was tastefully decorated with cannas and asparagus, the color scheme of pink and white being carried out in all its appointments. The bride and groom left for Dayton on the nine-twenty-nine, and from Dayton, at eight past midnight, they went to Detroit, and thence to Ann Arbor, the home of the groom."

"A Rindsfoos is a Locher," the Grandmother said, "and a Locher is a Rautzen. Had seven children but five of them girls, Link, he never married, Ida married, a Locher, issue from that union was all of them Rautzens. Clara married a Rindsfoos but the boy is a Rautzen."

"Biggs-Oberholzer nuptials," Parsons said.

"Biggs?" said the Grandmother. "That a man's name?"

"Ewing Biggs of Ottawa, Ohio," said Parsons.

"What will they think of next?" the Grandmother said.

Parsons rattled the paper, folded it, and said, "Editorial. The 4th as It Was."

"Biggs!" said the Grandmother, and wagged her head.

"Time was—" began Parsons, raising his voice, "when the small boy with the firecracker was the only patriot on a Finlay street. Everybody left town for Mercer, Piqua, and points east. The band went to Leipsic, and the baseball team went to Webster. Some citizens took their guns and advantage of the squirrel law to hunt squirrels. They reported the hunting excellent, but no squirrels. Others picnicked on the oleaginous O-h-i-o and saw the blinking turtle in the basking sun, the basso-profundo bull frog sang 'Rocked in the Cradle of the Deep,' and the fleecy lambkin with the twinkling tail bunted his mother for sustenance in the sere and yellow pasture. Everybody had a wonderful time and came home tired to death. How many of us yearn for the good old Fourth of July as it was!"

The Grandmother didn't, but she held her peace. Her only son, Howard Porter, had never been to

Mercer or shot a squirrel, but he had twice burned the eyebrows right off his face.

"Where they going to take him?" she said.

"Take who?" said Parsons.

"Howard!" she said, and she saw him jump like she'd stuck him with a hat pin.

Parsons didn't answer, then he said, "Mrs. Porter, I don't really know."

Well, maybe he didn't. She liked him, but he was an awful fool.

"*The Power of Women,*" Parsons read. "Such is the transforming power of a woman that last night the Chamber of Commerce Hall was transformed into a place of homelike beauty by a woman's hand. Neat white tables were everywhere seen, and easy seats, with comfy pillows, sprang up like magic as if from a Wizard's touch. Palms and ferns added their rustic touch to the scene. The Misses Hokinson, Weintraub, Oberholzer, and Seidel stood in line to receive their many friends and guests, and after felicitations indulged in games of 500 and Flinch. When scores had been reckoned it was found that Miss Stonecipher had won. She received a pair of sports, and Miss Prouty a half sports, respectively. At Flinch, the Misses Stroud and Oberholzer received a pair of quarter sports. Don't you know what sports are? For shame! Throughout the event delightful music was played by the Ladies

String Quartet, led by Miss Olive Henninger. Near the close of the function refreshments were served by Sandersons Caterers."

From the glass saucer on the window sill the Grandmother took a piece of hoarhound, slipped it into her mouth, then licked the sugar from her finger tips.

"*Local Gossip*," Parsons said, wetting his finger, and folded the page. "Minton—" he went on, "has a new Masonic Hall."

"Hmmmm—" she said.

"Clarence Anglemeyer was in Pittsburgh last Saturday. The platform scales that have stood near the corner of Beach's barn, for so many years, have been sold to Jake Courtright and moved to Clover & Gills, near Third and Spring. Mr. Courtright invites all and sundry to come and be weighed."

"Court who—" the Grandmother said, but not like she cared.

"If you haven't seen the Redbirds in their new uniforms, supplied by Cutler's Pharmacy, there are some things about the National Pastime that you may have missed."

"Mamie Cutler married Charlie Fry and blessed him with two sons."

"A young man, seventeen years of age, giving the name of Albert Wilkinson, was arrested on the outskirts of Finlay last Saturday, by Detective Ringold.

He had stolen forty-five dollars in money and a pair of pants valued at ten dollars from Frank Anson, who gave the alarm. Wilkinson is bound over to the next term of the court, and is now boarding with Sheriff Burgess."

"Burgess is a Porter," she said, "twice removed."

"Mrs. Frank Blackman lies very low in her home on Sixth Street. Last January Mrs. Blackman had some teeth drawn which were badly ulcerated and she has been troubled ever since. It is feared that her jawbone is infected and her condition is very serious."

"Three-six-nine West Sixth Street," the Grandmother said.

"The home of Mr. and Mrs. John F. Leahy was shrouded in gloom last Wednesday, when the light and sunshine of the home, little Martha Leahy, was taken from them by the dark hand of death. Funeral services were held at the residence, and Reverend J. Werner chose the touching text, 'My Beloved is Gone Down Into the Valley to Gather the Lilies.' The music was afforded by Misses MacDowell, Oberholzer and Rautzen, and was very nicely rendered."

The Grandmother did not respond.

"The music was nicely rendered—" Parsons repeated, "by the Misses MacDowell, Oberholzer, *and Rau-tzen.*"

The Grandmother's face was turned toward the

bird box. Her eyes were closed. But her cheeks puffed in and out as she worked over the hoarhound.

"Which Rautzen would that be?" he said, to see if she got it.

"Gerchude—" she replied, to show that she did.

"Here's a picture of Ethel Baumann," Parsons said. No reply. "Annual Heart and Heart Frolic to be Mardi Gras in conception."

No reply.

"Marriage cheap in Melbourne," Parsons said, picking up a note at the bottom of the page. "A man can be married cheaper in Melbourne than in any other part of the world."

The clacking of the hoarhound, the creaking sound of the rocker, had stopped. Parsons raised his eyes and saw that her head was bobbing down. While he sat there waiting he finished reading a piece himself. When he looked up again her head was down, but the rocker was still moving, as if something had given the house a jolt. He folded the paper, sat for a moment resting his eyes. When he looked up again the Grandmother was asleep. A blackbird, with yellow hatpin eyes, sat on the near rim of the bird box, but he waited a moment before playing his hand. Then he dropped into the box, hammered at a seed, and when the Grandmother did not stir, Parsons folded the *Nonpareil*, returned it to her box. He watched the jay chase away the blackbird, then the squirrel chase the jay. Then came the pigeons, the sparrows and the catbirds, then came the host of unwanted Friends, and finally, when they had come and gone, the cardinal came. But Parsons missed him. He was asleep himself.

MRS. PORTER

On the Mezzanine, in Strawbridge & Clothier, in the air-conditioned draft that blew from the powder room toward the annex, Mrs. Porter took a seat at the writing desk on the rail. The beige shade on the lamp cast a friendly glow on the terra cotta pad. The black and gold pen in the onyx-type holder had a translucent cap in which a four-leaf clover was embedded at the tip. The yellow light from the lamp cast a four-leaf shadow on the aztec brown paper, with the words *Lucky for You* in a written-on-water effect. Mrs. Porter put her bag on the seat of the chair, took a sheet of the paper, saw watermark, and placed sheet so elbow remained on terra cotta pad. Dipped pen, then held in such a manner that halo showed around four-leaf clover like water bug skating on pool in shadowy glen. In not quite upper right-hand corner she put *Monday PM.*

The Deep Sleep

Dear Evelyn—

Howard gave up the losing battle Sunday a.m., just before dawn. Have just come from Clough & Bayard but very much doubt if you would recognize it, modern interior, euonymous (you-wan-imus) I think, in front. Found have fallen in arrears on many things. When yours passed away, viewing was out, now find it is in. "The bigger the man the simpler viewing," Mr. Bayard said. Plan quiet, simple, private viewing at home. Am here in S & C buying Howard black shoes as sent only other pair of blacks to James.

She had blotted what she had written, looked to see if it was there on bottom of blotter, saw that it was, but found it strain to figure it out. Looked to see if black modern inkwell was imported, saw it was not. Looked over antique-bronze railing at summer shoppers around Italian straw bag counter.

Right here below me—Notions side of Mezzanine—see three off-shoulders in group of seven or eight. Toujours perspiring, more of it showing, than conservative type. Eye-opener, of course, and notice men on escalator are *not* facing toward top. Lemon yellow straw bag, navy bleu gloves, pumps with butter-yellow plastic buckle, *no* stockings, runny suntan lotion, passing below. Looking for beaded bag in green or dull black. Too late, I think.

Katherine Porter, carrying man's white shirt in blue paper bag with gold emblem, stopped on the landing to look at books on stationery side. Showing brown shoes to all coming up, showing blue hat to all going down. Showing slip with dip at front to elevator man with back to light.

Children down from summer retreat on train last night. My own child, of all times & places, in blue frock of her mother's with medium brown walkers. Do notice she is no longer so easily upset. Might be living with successful artist makes for putting all, *all* cards on the table.

She let that dry, blowing on the wet periods, then dipped pen lightly and said—

Now as to why I didn't get your call. Long distance from Uncle Charles who said attack severe but minimal after effects, thanks to catching culprit in early stages and going to bed. Dr. Haemmel (spelling?) had his training under specialist at Harvard, and MD in pre-Hitler Germany. Case of Mr. Erskine, however, not producing any miracles.

Looking up she saw frock, organdie print with pearl buttons, just before it stepped into elevator.

Evelyn, must still find something suitable viewing, but not eyesore somewhere else. Weighing pros and cons of Nylon in black, but hear complaints of slippery shoulder straps.

Here comes my child!

In haste,
MILLY

The Deep Sleep

As I write Mrs. Sutphen in gray fur (imagine) to cover collar on black she has worn for years. If *any* body can buy it, old guard trend is to do without it. Old cars. *Old* hats.

She folded it neatly, put it in the tissue-lined envelope. At the stamp machine she reflected on three threes for ten, or four ones for five. Could not decide, put letter in pocketbook. On her way down the stairs she stopped to read the hours of collection on the mailbox, just as her daughter, slip still dipping, was on way up.

"Mother, where in the world have you been?"

"Lift the right strap just a *lit*-tle," she said. As Katherine didn't seem to hear she put her hand to the shoulder, gave the strap a lift.

"I was going to tell you something—" she said.

"Mother, if Paul is over there *waiting*—"

Mrs. Porter gave her daughter her gloves and her bag, then went back to the Mezzanine, back to the desk where she had left pen on blotter, not in place. Plastic tip pointed at note she had made, forgot.

Organdie. Yellow-green. Bamberger print.

She tore it off corner of blotter, and holding it in her hand she went back to the stairs where her daughter, slip still dipping, waited at edge of rug.

[179]

The Deep Sleep

When Webb took the gray suit from the hanger he
threw it on the bed, which was still unmade, while he
looked around for a clean white shirt, wool tie, and
socks. The Judge's socks were in the bureau drawer
that stuck. He put the socks in the pocket of the coat,
where he found some moth balls the size of bee-bees,
and a note on a piece of envelope in Mrs. Porter's
round hand.

> Jelly roll in top double
> boiler. Celery damp clo.
> tp. rear ice box.

Webb tossed the clothes over his arm, then got
down the stairs as far as the landing when the vest
slipped out of the coat and fell to the floor. It lit with
a thud, and something broke. Three of the pockets
proved to be empty, but in the fourth he found a
cheap dollar watch, and five or six pieces of broken
glass. The drop had broken the crystal, but set the
watch to running, and the loud alarm-clock tick
seemed to throb in his hand. The tip of the hour hand
had broken off. Webb gave the stem several turns,
absently, and on his way through the living room
dropped the watch and glass into the oval waste

basket with the Audubon print. On top of it, wadded up, he placed the comic section of the *Bulletin*. Then he left the house, threw the clothes into the car, and drove to where a procession of cars, a funeral, perhaps, blocked the road crossing the pike. He had to pull up and stop beside a bench for bus passengers in front of the sidewalk. Behind the bench was a small shady park, the grounds of the local library, and a woman and child were coming down the path toward the street. The woman carried several books under her arm, and held on to the child's hand. It was such a hot, humid day, Webb felt a sudden sympathy for the boy, and the hand that the woman would not let him have. He would tug to free it, forget about it, then tug again. The woman's face was shiny with sweat, and her blouse was stuck to her back. When she reached the bench she dropped down on it, without releasing the boy's hand, and with her free hand, awkwardly, she fumbled for a piece of Kleenex in her purse. With it she wiped the boy's damp face, then her own. She then spoke to him, or at him, but he did not speak to her as he seemed to have an obstruction at the front of his mouth. A metal cricket, as Webb could hear its half-smothered chirp.

Webb turned his head away, at that point, as it seemed he could taste in his own mouth the metallic flavor of a toy train wheel he used to suck. He went around for weeks with it cupped in his mouth, blowing a whistle through it. One summer night, lying flat on his back, he had all but swallowed it. It was not a memory that gave him much pleasure, and he honked the horn, stepped on the gas, but the procession heading west still blocked the street. He turned to look at the woman and child again. Hot and humid as it was, the boy had straddled one of his mother's legs. Her arm, drawing him toward her, circled his waist. It was clear that she suffered from the heat that the boy radiated, from the noise he was making, and the fact that he would not give her a moment's peace. Every now and then her distracted gaze would look down the street for some sign of the bus, for a horn that had honked, but would hurriedly return to the boy's face. As if in that brief moment of time it might escape, like a bird from a cage; or worse, that she might forget what it looked like. It was freckled, and sublimely commonplace. The head was knobby, the ears were large and thrust out from the sides like the handles on a pan, and the open mouth was like that of a fish. From it the chirp of the mechanical cricket was blown into her face. But she couldn't seem to get enough of it, her eyes clung to his lips, peered into his mouth, studied first one side, then the other, and passed like a damp, lightly soaped rag over all of it. They were, it seemed to Webb, not two people at all

but one joined person, and the child was a mirror in
which the mother saw herself. He did not have her
angular face, or her complexion, and to Webb's jaun-
diced eye there was no outward resemblance, and very
little sign of an inward one. But she searched him like
a map for some key word, some familiar sign, something that pointed to the past, or the future, some like-
ness of a lover or some conception of her better self.
They were not, for the moment, two people but one,
the child straddling the leg was still part of the mother,
as if the hydra-headed monster had learned to spawn
and admire itself. Nothing, it seemed to Webb, would
ever tear them apart. Through the clasped hands a
current seemed to pass, the same force that drew the
salmon up the river, leaping, and drove the lemmings
on their suicidal movement to the sea. *Thy will be
done*, Webb said aloud, *on earth as it is in heaven*, and
wondered if the nature of the day had made him soft
in the head. He just sat there, staring, till the man behind him leaned on his horn, then he went off in a
series of frog-like leaps.

He went off, but the chirping of the metal cricket
went along with him. The woman and the child, the
hook-up of nature that was both public and private,
seemed to sum up all the problems that he was power-
less to resolve. A Sphinx-like riddle, related, in some
way, to what he had been going through since day-

break, a battle with obscure forces he could feel, but never grasp. The core of the problem, if it had one, was like the dried melon seeds in the bird box, held in reserve for birds described as the *friendly type*. All other birds got a clip on the noggin from the lethal cane. Once the male bird broke away from the saddle on the hip, or the angular knee, or the sponge-like gaze that held him like a pair of forceps, he was free, and he was also more or less detached from *life*. From the female bird's private, functional life.

"I suppose it's all for the best," they said, since the only bond that mattered, the only cord that bled, had been cut many years before. All that remained was the proper burial of the dead.

He drove on down to Surburban Square, circled the Square till he found the Hot Potato, then circled it again until he found a place to park. He dropped his last penny in the parking meter, and with the suit, shirt and tie over his arm, he waited at the door while a small clucking covey made their way out. A slight gasp, from the one at the rear, made Webb wonder if his fly was open, until he realized that the goods he carried were out of bounds. Male feathers. A herring-bone suit, a white shirt, a wool tie. *Any*one—as Katherine would tell him later—*any*-one but the one she had married, would have had more sense than stick his long neck out like that. He had been seen, but not arrested, he might have turned right there and walked back to the car, but *that*—as even Webb could tell you—was not like Webb. He opened the door and let the blast of air-cooled air hit his face. He knew that he was overstepping the bounds, but what the bounds were he couldn't really tell you, just as he couldn't tell the gaps in the bird box from the slats. So he stepped inside, he swung around to the left and headed toward a sign that read REST ROOMS, just as the sleeve of the coat he carried dragged a place setting off on the floor. The silver rattled on the seat of the chair, something dropped into his cuff. He stooped over, he managed to pick it up, he muttered something or other to the woman at the table before he noticed that the woman facing him was his wife. At her side was Mrs. Porter, the menu concealing her face. Without moving her eyes Katherine said—

"Dry cleaning is delivered at the rear, Mr. Webb," and as if she had given the waiter his order, Webb turned and left. He went right back to the rear corner as he had been told. There were telephones, a nook stacked with phone books, and he just stood there turning the pages until one of the booths was empty, then he stepped in. He sat there, behind the closed doors, smelling the lure of the departed female, and listening to the voice of the one in the next booth.

"I know—I know," she began, "I know, but—" but

there she was cut off. Webb heard her scratch a match on the side of the booth, then blow out the smoke as if it choked her. "I know—" she said, and tapped with her nails on the glass in the door.

Someone had tucked a newspaper into the seat, and Webb pried it out, glanced at the sport page, then wrapped the Judge's clothes up in a piece of it. A smudged picture of the Judge turned up on the front. The smudge, perhaps, made him look strangely distracted, as if the Judge, as well as Webb, had just turned his gaze from the mythic, hydra-headed mother and child. The pair of them drawn together by the same force that drew the salmon, leaping, up the river, and men, as well as lemmings, to some fatal rendezvous with the sea.

With the package under his arm Webb came out of the booth, had a look at the phone books, then crossed the room and took a seat facing his wife at the table. The empty luncheon plates were there between them, the glasses full of water from the melted ice cubes, and the ashtray with the red-tipped cigarettes his wife had smoked. One of her hands idly fingered a soda spoon, one lay in her lap. Webb raised his eyes from the menu, wet his lips, and prepared to make a statement, but seeing the expression on the face of his wife he said nothing. Her gaze was beyond him. That of Mrs. Porter was the same. They seemed to be unaware that he had returned, and sat there facing them. Both women—he had never thought of them as a pair before—both women were gazing at the soda counter at his back. He turned his head and saw two girls, waitresses. Just a pair of young kids. One was slicing butter, one was placing the slices on paper chips.

"The shirtwaist doesn't really suit the dark one," Mrs. Porter said.

"You think they're twins, Mother?"

"I've been turning it over in my mind," her mother said.

With the handle of a spoon, Webb rapped sharply on his empty glass. Neither Katherine, nor her mother, looked at him.

"Is it all right if I have a bite to eat?" he said.

With the napkin from her lap, Mrs. Porter wiped her lips. She looked to see if what she was wearing had come off, saw that it had. The girl with the shirtwaist came to the table and Webb ordered a cheeseburger.

"A *what?*" said Katherine. "You're not going to eat *now?*"

Webb put the menu down, took a swallow of the water the girl had poured. His hand shook a little, and some of the water spilled into his lap. With the paper napkin he found on the table, playing for time, he dabbed at the water. He then raised the glass, had another swallow, and at the bottom of the glass, as in a faulty mirror, he seemed to see the woman with the hot sweating boy in her lap. Their faces blended. Their arms and legs intertwined. He closed his eyes, but he seemed to hear the chirp of the cricket in the boy's open mouth.

"Are you going to keep her waiting all night?" Katherine said.

Webb placed the menu flat on the table.

"What is he thinking of *now*?" Mrs. Porter said.

"He's always *thinking*," Katherine said. "He has a life of the mind you know, Mother."

Through the window, where he was gazing, Webb saw the red signal on the parking meter, and beyond the signal the cop standing there filling out the tag. He was reading the license at the front of Webb's car.

"Are you girls sisters?" Mrs. Porter said, and pushed back her chair to rise from the table.

"Yes ma'am," said the girl, and with the pencil she was holding fluffed out the curls in her dyed hair. "Don't tell me you don't *like* it now," she said.

"It probably goes with summer things," Mrs. Porter said, and with the girl leading, they all walked toward the front of the shop. Webb got up, then remembered in time to pick up the package he had wrapped in the paper, and about to walk away, he noticed the check.

He stood there, the check on the table, and as he went through his pockets looking for money the face of Judge Porter, the gaze still distracted, looked up at him.

KATHERINE

"A summons?" Mrs. Porter said.

From the windshield wiper, where it had been left, Paul removed the parking ticket. Without glancing at it, he slipped it into his shirt.

"You know how men are, Mother," she said, "they don't like to be rushed in the powder room."

"I didn't think artists cared about such things," Mrs. Porter said.

"I fully expected," Katherine said, "to see him step from the booth wearing Daddy's suit."

"I've known your father to forget and leave his vest," her mother said.

"Every minute of your life that is wasted, Mother, I suppose you know is lost forever. Every minute must needs be spent absorbing life, brooding on it."

"I suppose they can do that anywhere," Mrs. Porter said.

In the rear view mirror Katherine glanced at her husband's eyes, the sweat on his face, and saw that he was about to speak. Her right foot pressed down hard on the floor board as she heard his voice. She held it there, waiting, but all he said was, "Where to now, ladies?" She didn't like that. That was not like him at all.

"Since you've picked up a parking ticket," she said, "perhaps we'd better go by and pay it."

"Where is the station?" he said.

"Bryn Mawr or Haverford?" asked her mother.

"He means the police station, Mother."

"I'm afraid he is *not* dressed for it."

"Where to next, ladies?" he said.

"You know what?" Katherine said, "his feelings are hurt. That's what it is, Mother. *We* sit there waiting, but it is *his* feelings that are hurt."

"I meant to ask him," her mother said, "what in the world it was that caused the delay."

"You are perfectly free to, Mother, but I hope I'm not *that* curious."

Paul settled back, took a crumpled cigarette from the pack in his shirt pocket, put it between his lips, then searched through his pockets for a match. He found a match, lit the cigarette. With his fingers he picked at the shreds of tobacco on his lips. Never before had she seen him quite like this.

"Will you please stop acting?" she said.

"I know how you feel," he said, "for years I *have* been acting. I've been acting like a man. But now I'm not acting. Where to next?"

"Paul," she said, "are you crazy?"

"Children, children!" said her mother.

"He's just acting, Mother. He's trying to get us upset. Anything but admit that *he* made a mistake."

"I am at your service," he said, "where to next?"

"I think your father's suit had better be delivered," her mother said.

"Thank you, ma'am," he said, put the car in gear, backed from the curb. "Clough & Bayard, ma'am?" he said.

"Mother," said Katherine, "if he doesn't stop I am going to walk."

"If your father had done it, he would still be with us," her mother replied.

Paul drove them over to Clough & Bayard, swung the car into the drive, then walked around it like a chauffeur and opened the door.

"Clough & Bayard, ma'am," he said to her mother.

"Where did he put it?" her mother said. From the back of the car Katherine removed the package and passed it to her mother. "Why, there's your father!" she said, and turned the bundle around so she could see him. "*City Mourns Passing*," she read, "well now I wonder—"

"Mother, give it to him."

"I don't think I care for the wrapping," she replied, and opened the bundle, removed the suit, shirt and tie. Looking at the tie she said, "It's all you can expect if you don't do it yourself."

"The shoes, Mother—"

"If they don't seem to fit, we can return them."

"But where are they, Mother?"

Mrs. Porter lifted her handbag and looked at her lap. Then she looked within her bag, found the piece of blotting paper, and read it. "Mezzanine," she said. "Now I just wonder—"

With the suit, shirt and tie, Paul walked up the steps and rang the bell. A man, but not Mr. Bayard, answered it. Paul explained what the clothes were for, the man thanked him, and he came back to the car. As he climbed in he said, "Where to now, ladies?" and she hated him.

"They close at five on weekdays," said Mrs. Porter.

"Drive home," said Katherine.

"Home?" said Paul. "Thank you, ma'am."

As they moved into the street her mother said, "We need bread, eggs, Drano and melon." She read from a list she had found in her purse.

"Mother, we are going home *first*," Katherine said.

The Deep Sleep

"I wonder what C-L-P means," her mother said. She passed the list to Katherine, who examined it.

"It's your writing, Mother—" she said, just as they turned up the drive to the house. A green tarpaulin still covered the swing on the porch. The afternoon sun peered through the slats that went around the bottom of the porch, like a fence, and spied out the places where she and her brother had gone to hide. Where her father, too big to crawl under, had bargained with them. The afternoon paper lay on the steps, where the paper boy had tossed it, and as they came up the drive she recognized the picture on the front.

"Here you are, ladies," Paul said, and though she hated him so much she could hardly speak, her hand, against her will, went out and touched his knee. As her fingers dug into the flesh, the car jerked to a stop.

"Christ!" Webb yelled, and the sound of his voice, his real voice, made her face glow with heat as if she had blushed.

"Carter's Liver Pills—" her mother said, "you suppose that's it?"

Katherine felt the leg she still gripped stiffen out, press down on the pedal, but before anything happened the screen door opened and closed. There was Mr. Parsons, looking a little sheepish, but smiling at them.

The Deep Sleep

" 'Bout time you folks were gettin' home," he said, "I got a hungry boarder here."

PARSONS

When he heard the car brakes screech in the drive, Parsons woke up, saw the Grandmother before him, and as he rose from the chair several pigeons in the bird box flapped their wings. The racket they made did not disturb the Grandmother. Her chin rested on her chest, her hands were clutched around a twist of apron, and she might have been dead but for the long white hairs blowing on her chin. The down draft through her nose was directed at them. Parsons lifted the chair with him to keep it from scraping, took his hat from the table, set it on his head. In the kitchen he walked tiptoe on the paper-strewn floor. Through the screen door he could see Webb's Ford, the reflections vibrating on the windshield, and as he opened the screen he heard Mrs. Porter mention liver pills.

" 'Bout time you folks are gettin' home," he had said, before he noticed that Webb, staring straight ahead, had a strained expression on his face. He didn't get out of the car, but sat there with his hands grip-

[194]

ping the wheel. Nobody looked less like the Judge than Webb did, tall as he was, with his angular face, but the way he just sat there brought the Judge to Parsons' mind.

There were times when the Judge would drive into the yard, then sit there at the wheel, the motor running, until Parsons had come forward and opened the door. Sometimes there was a carton of groceries there, which Parsons would take out. Sometimes there was nothing, nothing at all but the *New York Times*, which the Judge would read later, and maybe his coat thrown over the back of the seat. When Parsons opened the door, the Judge would say, "Get in." Then the Judge would maybe back down the drive, which he did against Mrs. Porter's orders, and at the bottom of the drive they would turn to the right, instead of to the left. That road led away from town, and wound around through the woods toward Gulph Creek. As a rule, Parsons never so much as opened his mouth. He would sit back, his left arm up and along the back of the seat, his right arm on the door, and let the breeze, if there was one, blow in his face. He would say nothing. The Judge would say nothing, and they would go for a spin. No, not really a spin, as they would seldom go further than the ford in the creek. They would dawdle along through the woods, keeping clear of all the traffic, till they came to the point where the road dropped down and into the creek. Right down there at the bottom, with the wheels in the water, the Judge would stop. There they would sit, the motor idling, for sometimes as long as half an hour, or until some other car came along and honked at them. The water made a cool lapping sound on the wheels, and up to the left, just out of sight, they could hear it spilling over the walls of Pitter's dam. The Judge would smoke four or five cigarettes, maybe point out a bird or a flower if he saw one, and after while they would turn the car around and drive back. Parsons often wondered if the Judge ever did that by himself. He doubted it. He seemed to like someone along. He never troubled to explain to Parsons why he did it, or what they came *there* for, but it was often at a time when the Judge was under some sort of strain. As he was the spring the boy turned up missing, as he often was when he headed the draft board, and especially when he felt himself slipping, toward the last. He would hurry home, but then he would put off going into the house. If Parsons wasn't around, he would sometimes sit right there in the yard. The only thing he ever said about it, the only time he ever spoke openly about it, was the evening they had stayed down there until nearly dark. Mrs. Porter had been out in the yard when they got back.

"Now where have you two been *this* time?" she had asked, and usually the Judge would say for a spin, then go on to say what bird or new flower he had seen. But that time he had said—

"Been over to Porter's Island," got out of the car, and walked into the house. Parsons was left sitting there in the car. By the time Mrs. Porter had figured out what he had said, the Judge was gone. The screen had closed behind him on the porch. In nearly forty years it had been the only moment that Parsons would have called a situation; one, that is, where there was more to it than met the eye. It had been evening, the yard was dusky, and he just sat there in the car and Mrs. Porter just went on weeding out devil grass. After while he got a basket and picked up the pile she had weeded out.

"Little Liver Pills," Mrs. Porter said, as Parsons walked out toward the car, "bread, eggs, melon, Drano, and little liver pills."

"You like me to pick 'em up?" Parsons said.

"You men can go," Mrs. Porter said, and passed the list she was holding to Parsons, then climbed out of the car. Katherine got out beside her, and when Parsons got a look at her face he could see the lipstick her upper lip had left on the lower one. Peering into the car he saw that Webb was still staring forward, his hands gripping the wheel as though he thought it might get away from him.

"All set—Chief?" he said, as that was a way Parsons had of kidding the Judge. When the Judge was out of sorts, and looked a little grim, he would call him *Chief*.

"Don't mind him, Mr. Parsons," Katherine said, "his feelings were burned at the Hot Potato."

"Parsons," said Webb, "will you get in?"

Parsons got in. Webb let out the clutch, and Parsons could feel the grass edging the drive spewing out behind them. Like a dog, he thought, like a damn dog. He held on to the door and braced himself for the turn in the road. But right at the bottom of the drive Webb slammed on the brakes.

"Where do we get these goddam liver pills?" he said.

Parsons put up his hand, wagging it to the left, then he suddenly lowered it, coughed, and said, "Nope, I guess to the right. Liver pills to the right."

Webb swung the car around to the right, and they headed down grade. Parsons let him run wild since he knew that the curves would soon slow him up. He waited till they did, then he lowered the window, put out his head, and took a sniff of the air as if it was something special along that road. When he glanced at the rear view mirror he caught Webb looking at him. Leading *him* on a goose chase was taking quite a risk, but for an hour or so, which could seem pretty long, Parsons had had the feeling that he no longer had much to lose. Webb had already seen him at his worst. So he led him on, he led him down past the spring where the city people liked to come for water, and there were women sitting in the cars, fanning themselves. Just going by people who looked as hot as that relieved the strain. Parsons whistled. Webb began to ease his grip on the wheel.

"Smoke?" he said to Parsons.

"No, thank you," Parsons said.

Parsons watched him light it, and he could tell that he was going to talk after he lit it. He settled back, as he did with the Judge, and waited for it.

"What you got in mind, Parsons?" Webb said, and blew out a cloud of smoke.

"A little spin," Parsons said, "for some little liver pills."

He didn't mean that to sound as clever as it turned out. It just so happened that the spin and the pills were both that way. They went along to where they could hear, not far below them, the water spilling over Pitter's dam.

"Ever been to Porter's Island, Chief?" he said.

Webb turned his head sharply, looked at him.

"Porter's *island*?" he said, "what the hell you mean?"

Parsons didn't answer that, he just sat there, as they were coming down the long grade, and there at the bottom, running a foot of water, was the ford. Near the bottom Webb stopped the car for a look at it.

"This all right to cross?" he said.

"Let it in easy," Parsons said, "put it in low, then let it in easy."

Webb shifted to low, then let the front wheels ease into the stream. As the rear wheels dropped in, Parsons sat up straight, and said *Whoa!*

Webb did.

"Well, how you like it, Chief?" he said.

"How I like what?" said Webb.

"Porter's Island," replied Parsons, and opened the door on his side of the car. He sat there watching the water flow beneath. The Judge had once taken off his shoes, let himself down to where he sat on the floor, and let his feet dangle in the stream. The water was cool all summer long. Down the stream, maybe fifty yards, a man, his wife and two small children sat on a rock eating from a basket the woman held. The man had taken off his shoes, and rolled his pants legs up. It was shadowy and peaceful, the sound of the water was like friendly talk that passed between them, and Parsons saw a bird that the Judge often pointed out.

"That was *his* name for it?" said Webb.

"Yup," said Parsons, "Porter's Island."

"It's too good to be true," said Webb, "bygod, it's too good to be true."

Parsons wondered just what he meant by that. But not for long.

"Hear that?" he said. Webb did not reply. "That's the male brown thrasher," Parsons said. It was strange how he remembered, since he really didn't care for birds. "Long tail—" he went on, "stripes and wing bars."

Webb said nothing, so they sat there with the water flowing beneath them, and the smoke from the exhaust making a blue cloud over the stream. Now and then, on the opposite bank, a car passed. One of the boys, with a banana in his hand, waded in the stream. They sat there till a bread truck from Conshohocken, one that used the backwoods roads as a short cut, came down the grade that loomed up behind them and honked. The honking went on till Parsons thought that Webb must have fallen asleep. When he turned to look at him his eyes were wide, but there was so little strain in his face that he looked, right at that moment, like somebody else. Absently, as if the honking came from far, far behind him, way over some hill, he put the car in gear again and they slowly drove away.

THE GRANDMOTHER

Hearing the voices—neither Rindsfoos, Rautzen, nor any other speech that mattered—the Grandmother got the chair to rocking, rocked to her feet. Around the table, clear around it, her right hand just grazing the chair backs, she caught the beam where the sun seemed to set in the open front door. Toward it, as toward a bull's-eye, she set off. Her shoulder set the cord on the bridge lamp to swinging as she passed. She heard the rear screen door open and close, she heard them walking on the kitchen papers, then she heard the daughter say—

"OHhhhh—!" then again, "Ohhh—"

"*Some*-one has been at the bird," Mrs. Porter said.

"The chair, Mother! The chair! Look at the chair, it's rocking!"

The Grandmother heard Mrs. Porter come to the door.

"Your grandfather made it," Mrs. Porter said. "They don't rock like that anymore."

"It's positively uncanny," the daughter said.

Coming into the living room she said, "Oh—Oh, here she is, Mother."

"Pretending she's sound asleep more than likely," Mrs. Porter said.

"She's in her other chair," the daughter said, and the Grandmother heard her cross the room, then walk on the tile floor near the door. She heard her push open the screen, step out on the porch. Opening her good eye, the Grandmother saw her take the paper from the steps, open it out, and stand there reading it. Then she came back in, closing the screen quietly.

"Mother—" she said.

"I'm afraid we forgot about paper napkins," Mrs. Porter said.

"Daddy's in the *Bulletin* too, Mother. Is it all right if she sees it?"

"You think we're keeping anything from *her*?"

"It says, survived by his a-ged mother."

"Well, he certainly is," said Mrs. Porter.

The daughter stood in the back of the hallway, reading the article through.

"Don't think for a moment it was easy on your father," Mrs. Porter said.

The daughter folded the paper, then said, "Here's nylon blouses at Wanamaker's, Mother."

"It's a question of principle," said Mrs. Porter.

"You wear rayon, Mother. Rayon is synthetic."

"Four people," Mrs. Porter said, "simply have no business with a twenty pound bird."

The daughter left the door that opened on the kitchen and came to stand beside the Grandmother.

"Oh, Grandmother, you awake?"

No, she was asleep. As she was known to do in her sleep, she muttered a bit. As she was known to fuss in her sleep, she fussed a bit. The daughter folded the paper then placed it on the table where the light came through the Grandmother's eyelids. Then the daughter walked quietly out of the room, keeping on the rugs. At the kitchen door she said,

"She's asleep."

"You know the three monkeys?" Mrs. Porter said.

The daughter did not answer.

"See no evil, hear no evil, speak no evil so forth."

"What about them?" said the daughter.

"They've got nothing on your Grandmother." Mrs. Porter licked her fingers then said, "This is one of those new double-chested birds."

The Grandmother could hear them both picking at it.

"Ohhhh—" said Mrs. Porter, and there she was crossing the living room. At the far end of the room, in the fireplace corner, the Grandmother could hear her turning the dials. "I just hope we're not too late," Mrs. Porter said.

"Too late for what, Mother?"

"Lowell Thomas," said Mrs. Porter.

"Good evening, everybody," Lowell Thomas said.

Mrs. Porter left the room, and her daughter said, "But she's asleep right now, Mother?"

"You forget the three monkeys," said Mrs. Porter. "Your Grandmother can hear Lowell Thomas in her sleep."

Raising her cane from her lap, the Grandmother brought it down on the base of the lamp. It gave off a ring, it gave off a chime, and then for some time the loose shade rattled, and the Grandmother could see the tassels rock.

"What did I tell you?" Mrs. Porter said, then, "Go ask her what she would like to drink. We're making iced tea, but when you let her have it she chews on the ice."

WEBB

"Parsons—" said Webb, facing the parking meter, "I got one ticket already. You got any pennies?"

Parsons put a hand into his pocket, brought out several nails.

"Never use 'em," he said, "suppose that's why I got 'em?"

He tried the other pocket, found three pennies.

Two he put into the meter, one back into his pocket, then he turned, with Webb, to face the row of stores.

"Where you usually shop?" said Webb.

"Better get the perishables first," said Parsons, but when Webb turned to look at him, Parsons did not smile. "Five fifty-two," he said, "think the market closes at six."

Webb followed him into the air-cooled market, where the carts were telescoped at the front. He pried one loose and started off with it. Parsons did not follow him. When he looked back for him, Parsons said—

"Think that one's got a flat wheel, Chief," and loosened another cart from the pile himself. He tried three carts before he found one that he liked. Coming up beside Webb he said, "Can't stand the feel of that flat wheel a-thumpin'—" then went on by toward the shelf of Pepperidge Bread. Webb reached for a loaf of whole wheat, giving it a squeeze to test its freshness, then dropped it in the basket at his side. Parsons stood there looking at it.

"You don't like whole wheat?" Webb said.

"Don't she have a little of it?"

"There's about a third a loaf," Webb said, "that Martha Washington may have handground, but anything that old is too dam' valuable to eat."

Parsons did not laugh. He stood there gazing at the list.

"Chief—" he said, "it don't pay to buy it if she's got it on hand."

"Parsons, I'd like some bread around I can eat."

Parsons did not raise his eyes from the list. "You can bring it in fresh," he said, "but it'll be stale before you can eat it. She won't let you eat it till she's used up what she's got."

"Parsons," said Webb, "just tell her this loaf is on me. I'll buy it. I'll try and absorb the loss." Webb put a solemn look on his face that he meant to be funny, but Parsons did not look at him. He did not laugh.

"Chief—" he said, "you mind me puttin' it back?" Webb just stood there. "It ain't the twenty-four cents," he went on, taking the loaf from the basket, "it ain't the money at all, Chief, it's the principle." He returned the loaf to its proper place on the shelf. He took a loaf of the white and said, "Judge liked the whole wheat loaf himself, but guess Mrs. Porter didn't like so much roughage. So it got a little stale before he got around to finishin' it off. But he had to finish it off before he got a new loaf." He stopped there, wet his lips, then said, "Judge finally decided to do without it rather than go through all the fuss and bother. Whole wheat didn't mean as much to him as principle meant to Mrs. Porter. If he did without it, just made it easier for all concerned." Turning to the list, Parsons said, "Let's see now, guess it's eggs.

"Look—" said Webb, "why don't I get the liver pills?"

"Sure," said Parsons, "sure—" but not at all as if he meant it.

"Have roughage problems with the pills too?" Webb said.

Parsons didn't seem to hear that.

"You got to make sure they're *Carter's Little* liver pills," he said.

"Carter's make big ones?" said Webb.

"Not many people seem to have 'em," Parsons said.

"Well, I can start looking—" said Webb, and to keep from saying what he was thinking he turned on his heel and went down the aisle. He swung around the lines forming at the front, and without glancing back at Parsons pushed through the doors into the street. A drugstore was sandwiched in between the hardware and the A&P. A *Tabu* perfume ad filled the window, and a heavy sprinkling of dead flies spotted the streamers of crepe paper that lay on the floor. This shop was not air-conditioned, and a whining ceiling fan circulated the air and stirred the covers on a rack of magazines. A blonde girl in blue

jeans sat on the floor looking through a copy of
Flair. At the back of the shop Webb could see a long
row of dark bottles with paper labels, and a small neon
sign that read *Prescriptions Filled*. A counter divided
this section of the store from the front. Behind the
counter and a high glass partition, his eyes level with
a pair of druggist's scales, an elderly man stood gazing absently toward the street. His shirt was open at
the throat, and to absorb the sweat he had placed a
handkerchief around his collar. As Webb came up he
began to fan himself with a newspaper. Although
Webb blocked his vision, being five or six inches
taller, the man's gaze was not distracted by the fact
that it was cut off. It seemed to be fixed at some point
near the front of the shop. Webb took a few coins
from his pocket, let them clink on the glass-topped
case, and when that didn't work he let a quarter drop
on the floor. The man behind the partition heard that,
and came to the front.

"Yes sir," he said, "what can I do for you?"

"Would you happen to have any Carter's Little
Liver Pills?" said Webb. The man turned, started
away, then turned and said—

"I beg your pardon?"

"Liver pills," said Webb, "Carter's Little Liver
Pills."

He gazed at Webb as if he still questioned that.

Then he shook his head slowly and said, "I don't think I can give you Carter's."

"I've got my orders, and it's got to be Carter's," Webb said.

The man smiled, opened a drawer in the counter, and stood there gazing at it. He seemed to have forgotten what it was he had opened it for.

"You know how old people are," said Webb.

The man gave no indication whether he did or not. But from the corner of the drawer, where it was all but hidden, he picked up a small liver-colored package. He turned it in his hand as if to read what the label said.

"You mind my asking?" he said, "who they're for?"

Webb did. But he said, "What's the gimmick? The kids using them to spike Coca-Cola?"

The druggist did not smile. He seemed to be reading the instructions on the wrapper.

"If for some reason or other," said Webb, "you don't want to sell them to me—"

"Would it be—?" he said, raising his eyes, "would it happen to be for Mrs. Porter?"

"It would," said Webb, "and would you mind my asking why this seems to be so important?"

The druggist did not speak. He pushed up his glasses and rubbed at his eyes. His eyes still closed he said, "How is the old lady taking it?"

"With her meals, I suppose," said Webb, thinking that he meant the liver pills.

"I mean—" said the druggist, and passed his hand through his hair. "I mean the Judge—how is she taking that?"

"OHhh—" said Webb, "Oh, I'd say she's taking it pretty well." As the man seemed to be waiting, he added, "She's seen an awful lot of it in her time. She's seen so many of us come and go—"

"I know—" the druggist said, "I know, I know—" removed his hand from his eyes, and Webb was struck by how they seemed to have changed. They were large and shining, as if the rubbing he had given them had polished them. "I know—" he repeated, lowered his head for another look at the package, and a drop of water fell from his nose to the package itself. Then another, and the soft paper soaked it up. "If you'll excuse me—" he said, and placed the package on the counter, where Webb could reach it, then turned as if someone had called to him. He went around the partition, through the swinging half-door under the row of dark bottles, and disappeared in the darkness behind. That was all. The doors stopped swinging as Webb stared. He placed the coins that he held on the counter, picked up the package of pills, then stepped over a boy who was reading a comic book he had spread on the floor.

The Deep Sleep

A man with the Sports edition of the evening paper waited for Webb to hold the screen door open for him, and Webb saw that the Judge was no longer on the front. In that space was a picture of Eddie Joost, who had hit a home run. As he stepped out in front Webb could see that the A&P market was closing down, letting people out through one of the doors, but not letting them in. Parsons stood at the front of one of the lines. The checking girl, a grey-haired woman, had turned her back to the register and stood with her hands pressing the skirt of her apron to her face. Parsons stood staring at the coins in his hand, as if he had been short changed. From the vegetable counter, wiping his hands on his apron, a man stepped into the booth, patted the woman on the shoulder, and then took charge of the machine himself. He handed to Parsons the bag of food she had filled, and Parsons walked away. As he came through the door into the street Webb could see the old man's eyes were blurred, and that his lower lip, sucked into his mouth, was trembling. Though he seemed to stare directly at Webb, he saw nothing. He went right by him, right past the car which Webb had parked at the curb, and on down the street where the elms shaded the walk. Webb had his mouth open to call to him, and his right hand raised in the air, when the truth of the matter, if such a matter had a truth, dawned on him.

The man that Parsons was trying to avoid was Webb himself. Paul Webb more than anybody else. Carl Parsons didn't want to be caught showing this kind of emotion, or any emotion, before people who didn't seem to feel that way themselves.

Webb was still there, the pill package in his hand, when Parsons hustled around the far corner, the groceries hugged in his arms and the sweat-dark tail of his shirt hanging out.

KATHERINE

"In my bag," her mother called, "look in my bag," and Katherine took the bag from the handle of the door, released the clasp, and dipped in her hand. She felt around among the objects for one of her mother's missing gloves. There was no glove, but in the lining of the bag, the edges of the paper frayed and yellow, were several sheets of paper, a letter, in her mother's round hand. Katherine could see that the first page was missing, but at the top of the second, written in pencil, was the note, *Easter Sunday, 1908.* She closed the purse, and with the letter in her hand—hadn't she spent her life looking for an answer?—crossed the

[213]

kitchen and stepped out on the back porch. There she turned and said—

"Mother, I'm going to look in the drive. When you got out of the car it might have dropped out in the drive."

"I keep hearing a ticking—" her mother said, and Katherine left the porch and walked up the drive, then around behind the garage toward what had once been the compost pit. When the rats had come, they had stopped using it. If she had been upstairs she would have gone into the bathroom, a much better place to read a letter, as her father had warned them about the poison ivy near the pit. But Roger had gone there, with his helmet and his rucksack, when he planned to leave home and join the Foreign Legion, and Katherine had once gone there herself when she had been car sick. Her mother didn't believe in things like car sickness, and if she had come down sick in the house she would have had to go to bed and lie with a thermometer in her mouth. Now the pachysandra had overgrown the trail, but she went on ahead, through the tangled honeysuckle, into the clearing that had been made around the compost pit. There she stopped, facing the pit, but as her mother had a taste for pale inks and dark paper, it was two or three minutes, in the cave-like gloom, before she could read a word.

The Deep Sleep

Howard—it began—I must tell you what happened this morning at church. Dr. Scovell has been in the south, as you know, and he got Dr. Baker and Dr. Kelson to fill his place in the pulpit while he was gone. Dr. Kelson preached today, and he took as his text the following words, *I AM THE WAY*, and then he told us of a picture that he had seen at the World's Fair. The picture showed a young man he described as "the patient," and a Doctor he described as the "great Physician," and the Doctor had just made a deep incision in the young man's breast. Howard, you must remember that in this operation there was very little chance for the young man surviving, but his parents were acquainted with the "great physician," and they knew, come what may, that He was the only Way. The doctor was represented as holding the bloody knife that had just made the incision, and the blood had spurted to stain his hand to the wrist. Before going on with the incision, the Doctor had raised his eyes to the "great physician" as he knew he could not go on alone the rest of the way. Dr. Kelson had got this far, but no further, when Olive just put her head on my shoulder, and before I could say "Jack Robinson" she was in a dead faint. Imagine poor little me in a situation like that! Fortunately, we were right there on the aisle or I might not have had the presence of mind to signal to the young man across the aisle from me. With his assistance we managed to get poor Olive out. Mrs. Packer went ahead of us with her hat and opened the door. Dr. Mather, who was there, followed quickly, and did for poor Olive what he could, and just before she came to she gave three unearthly shrieks. They were heard above

The Deep Sleep

Dr. Kelson, who has a strong voice. There were those who said that the shrieks resulted from the fact that poor Olive knew that she was lying in the arms of a strange young man. Howard, if that should reach her ears, I am sure she will faint again. Dr. Mather said that I should tell you that I would make a good Doctor's wife because I had such excellent nerves and self-control. All the while, I was on the verge of fainting myself! We kept Olive in the reading room until the people had all gone home, then we made her lie down, for the afternoon, on Mrs. Packer's couch. Not till then did I hear that Mr. McCloskey, while we were absent with Olive, had sat up straight in his seat and looked around the church like a crazy boy. He was the next to be taken out. Then Mrs. Servel fainted, and Letta Whitten sat crouched in her seat, with a case of *hysterics*, clasping and clinching her hands until they were sore. Others spoke of a nervous chill, coming on after the sermon was over, but there was general agreement that Dr. Kelson had made his point. I heard Dr. Mather say that it was certainly "one for the books."

Genevieve will not go to Ohio, as they have just passed a law against the wearing of birds on hats. Nellie Cooper was arrested in Piqua, although her home is in West Virginia, and fined $5 when she had less than four in her purse. She had to telegraph for money and bring the hat back in a box.

Howard, right now we are planning a greenhouse picnic—

There it ended, and the voice of Lowell Thomas,

saying so-long to everybody, brought Katherine back
to where she was standing, her mother's faded, un-
mailed letter in her hand. Had she mailed off the missing pages? Why had she kept just these? Why were
they now in her purse? Why had her mother, of all
people, of all the sober and unsentimental people,
held on to these sentimental pages for more than
forty years?

Katherine looked around her, as if for an answer,
and saw, leaning on the wall behind her, the nail keg
that had once stood in the garage. The flannel rags
for washing the car had been stored in it. The keg
was there to sit on, she was sure, either by Mr. Parsons
or her brother Roger, and for the same reasons, perhaps, she sat on it. She had had the feeling, for a
moment, that her knees might bend both ways. But as
she dropped down on the keg something gave way,
perhaps the boards at the base had rotted, and she
sagged to the ground as the air stored in the keg puffed
out on all sides. Otherwise, she might not have noticed
the smell. An odor both honey-sweet and sickly, a
blend of fake perfume and real decay, but so strangely
familiar she knew just where she had smelled it before.
On the Paoli local. On the local nearing Bryn Mawr.
Her father had had a front seat on that train, the evening *Bulletin* had been spread in his lap, and beneath
the *Bulletin*, in a cellophane bag, he had a package

of cheap banana candy that he was eating, like peanuts, with a chomping sound. The sweet sickly smell
of the candy had spread through the car. And she
had been at the back, and in the seat beside her, coming home to spend the holidays with her, were two
school friends who had never set eyes on her father
before. She had been scared to death that he might
turn around and recognize her. Turn and smile at her
with his mouth full of the candy, his lips powdered
with the pinkish color, or put up his hand and wave
the sticky fingers that he had just licked.

There at her side, on the bottom of the keg, was a
transparent bag full of such candy, all melted together
like a single piece of lumpy flesh. In the tight glassine
bag the ants had not been able to get at it. A coke
bottle, tipped on its side, still had a swallow or two
of Coca-Cola in it, but the soft rubber stopper had
swollen like a finger and would not pull out. Someone had tried it. The metal grip on the stopper was
twisted and bent.

Her father, Judge Howard Rautzen Porter, had left
these things. Even during his illness, on the hot summer
days when he dozed in the yard, a paper spread over
his face, he had come to that spot to eat banana candy
and have a drink of the coke. Seated there on the keg,
in the dappled shade, the sweet scent of the privet
and the candy around him, what—Katherine won-

dered—what had been her father's thoughts? That he had failed? Yes, he had thought of that. That he had failed his son, he had failed his daughter, that he had also failed one Howard Porter; but it could not be said that he had failed his wife.

Of his wife, Millicent Porter, it could be said that she had failed her son, she had failed her daughter, and she had driven her husband from his own house, but it could not be said that she had failed him. No, it could not. Katherine Porter, who understood nothing, could still understand that. She could not, that is, see how it might have been otherwise. The unjust thing was that it was just. The horrible thing was that it was not horrible. They had each been true to some sort of conscience, they had each made some sort of peace with their souls, and the really senseless thing about it was that it made sense. It made a pattern that her husband, for one, would never puzzle out. He would never understand, that man, why the scent of decayed banana candy, and the sight of a half-empty coke bottle, would make her sit on a squashed nail keg and have a good bawl. She couldn't do it in the house, she couldn't do it in the car, she had to sneak off somewhere to do it, like her father, and make what terrible sense out of all of it she could. Nor could she do it very long, either, as she could hear, coming up the drive, the steps of someone walking very slowly, and when they stopped the voice of her mother speaking to him.

"Well—" her mother said.

"Guess I must've lost him," Mr. Parsons said, "guess I lost him in the rush, they were closin'—"

The screen door opened as her mother let him in, then closed again. When the lights came on at the front of the house, Katherine walked down the drive and entered the kitchen, returning the letter to where she had found it in her mother's bag.

"Is that you—?" her mother called from upstairs.

"I'm borrowing your comb, Mother," she said, and stood there in the kitchen, combing the leaves and cobwebs out of her hair.

PARSONS

The bag that he carried stuck to his shirt, and the shirt stuck to his body, but even in the heat Parsons liked the long walk down the grade. As a rule, if offered a ride he would turn it down. "Do me good," he would say to Andy Spatoli, who often went by him in the dry cleaning wagon. "Do me good to get a little exercise."

The Deep Sleep

Nobody ever questioned it. Nobody doubted, that is, why it was that Parsons walked. Nobody cared, or showed much concern if Carl Parsons, dawdling along the road, stopped to rest a bit and gaze at the houses back through the trees. It might be a big place, like the Wherry's, or it might be something modern, like the Troy's, or it might well be an old place that was now on the block, a big FOR SALE sign at the gate.

If the house for sale lay along the route that Parsons had followed for some fifty years, he would make a mental note of the firm that offered it. That day, or the following day, or whenever the time and the mood seemed proper, Parsons would give the firm a call on the phone. He would make inquiry of the house put up for sale. How many rooms? Baths? How many acres? What type of heating? And what would an estimate of the tax situation be? If asked for the name of the person calling, Parsons would oblige. He had several names, according to the nature of the property: Caldwell, for estate-type holdings; Crosby for suburban family accommodations; and Sloane for modern, or remodeled Colonial. As a rule, it ran Caldwell, three to one. The Sloane, C. F. Sloane Jr., was really just a favor to Mrs. Porter, as Parsons had very little interest in the modern-type home. But Mrs. Porter did him the favor of making certain inquiries for him, and he obliged by making certain inquiries for her. As a man, even as Mr. Caldwell, he hesitated to ask about the bedroom arrangements, but Mrs. Porter could do it without batting an eye. She could talk about bathrooms just as a matter of course. Most of the real estate people enjoyed talking with her. When Sydney Catlett, for example, had slashed his wrists while lying in one of his bathtubs, with Mrs. Porter's help Parsons had discovered what bathroom it was. The guest one. The one in the servant wing of the house.

Perhaps the peculiar house that he lived in had something to do with the fact that Parsons had a certain feeling for the small estate. Ten or twelve acres, with a house of about fifteen rooms. Field stone, with a lot of small windows, a tower or two at one end, and steep slate roofs with good copper gutters that had turned green. A two- or three-car garage was extremely important, as Parsons would point out over the phone, but of course he didn't go on to say why he thought it was. He didn't drive. He didn't really want a car for himself. But the people who bought a house like that and asked Parsons to keep it in apple-pie order, would have at least one car—and Parsons wanted one section of the garage for himself. He wanted a garage without the car in it, just a wicker chair perhaps, a small electric heater, and six or seven hundred dollars worth of fertilizer, mowers, and good garden tools. The interesting thing about all of these houses was that Parsons didn't plan to live in them himself—he just wanted to keep them in apple-pie order for somebody else. Somebody who could pay a little more than the Judge, but about the same type.

Parsons didn't want this grandeur for himself, but he believed in its existence, and if it existed somebody had to look after it. After it, as well as the people who lived in the house. He had had enough experience to see, and he had lived long enough to know, that these fortunate people were not in a position to look after themselves. They slashed their wrists, like Sydney Catlett, they took sleeping tablets like Mrs. Raeburne, or they simply went batty like Mr. and Mrs. Newcomb Erskine. There was not a house, of the ten great houses that lined the road where Parsons walked, of whom it might be said that the inhabitants could take care of themselves. Half of them were empty most of the year, except when the children came home for Christmas, when they picked up the troubles that made it even worse for them back at school. But from the road, where Parsons walked, only the FOR SALE signs indicated that there was any trouble in Paradise. That a man had bled to death in his marble tub, that a young mother, a college girl, had wrapped her child in an ice cream carton, packed it in dry ice, and then sent it to Santa Claus. That a childless woman had had five husbands, that a husbandless woman had

had three children, and that a great man, a pillar of the state, a father and a friend to hundreds of people, had passed on with a wild look in his eye, crying, *In the name of God, will you let me die?*

People who lived in such places seemed to need competent outside help. A member of the family, and an outsider at the same time. A man who bore, taken all in all, a certain resemblance to Carl Parsons, who now walked along the road with a bag of groceries in his arms. Porter's flunkey. That was the term some people used. When Mr. Kluger had passed him the melon, Parsons could see in one eye a tear for Judge Porter, and in the other eye a tear for Carl Parsons, an orphan now. Whose flunkey would he be next? It would no longer be proper for Mrs. Porter to keep him around. When he had pushed his cart into the checker line and Mrs. Reilly, the checker, had looked up and seen him, it was pity for Parsons that first clouded her eyes. He had seen it. It had been unmistakable. Everybody loved the Judge, but the way you first began to feel it was not through the Judge, but through the orphans that he left. What will *he* do now? That was the look. Over the years Parsons had given it a certain amount of thought, but he had had no idea that he was as poorly off, as helpless, as the looks people gave him indicated. It had revived an old pity he had once felt for himself. The only son

of a beautiful woman and a man who had bats in his belfry.

When Mrs. Reilly had looked in his eyes, just raised her head and looked right at him, it had been all he could do to keep his knees from wobbling. Up till then, he had simply not felt much. He had already felt it too long. But right at that moment he had felt abandoned, with nothing in the world to his name but the handful of packages there in the cart. It had also been too much for Mrs. Reilly, and by the time he got the stuff into the bag, and the right change from Mr. Kluger, he had been on the point of breaking down himself. When he saw Webb, Webb standing at the window gawking at him like some fool kid, there had been no choice but to walk right by him, or bawl in the street. Right on past him, on down the street to the underpass at the tracks, then on down the road toward the creek.

What would Webb think? Already he thought too much. It was a little nerve-wracking to pass the time with a boy like that. It was a relief to walk along the road lined with the fine homes of unhappy people, many of them worse off than flunkey Parsons, and needing his help. At the Catlett estate, where a low stone wall went all the way around their Japanese garden, Parsons leaned on the wall, in the shade of a willow, and looked at it. The people who had bought the place were tearing it down. A modern solar house, with all the gimmicks, would be built on the spot. But they were going to leave the garden alone, and in the wide green pool, shaped like a lily pad, Catlett's mad old setter named Mike stood in the water chest deep. He had asthma bad, and Parsons could hear him wheeze. He had also been running. Nobody had ever been able to make him stop. On his rust-colored face the hairs were turning gray, making him look quite a bit like a walrus, and his great jaws, snapping at the flies, caught his own loose jowls. A dozen people had dragged him off the place, but he had always come back. Now, it was said, they were leaving him alone. Some of the people in the neighborhood put out food for him. Mike didn't say yes, and he didn't say no, he just gobbled up whatever he was given, then rushed back to bark at the trucks that were coming up the drive. To chase all the foreign dogs off the place. He didn't have much more time to go, it was said, so why not let him do it? Why not let him finish what he had been obliged to start. Old Mike's hindquarters were rheumatic, and as he stood there in the cooling water Parsons could see his legs tremble as if the earth shook. Maybe Mike thought it did. He was that kind of dog. But the sight of it troubled Parsons, something of an old dog now himself, only he knew it was his legs, and not the earth, that he felt trembling. Way up on the rise, nearly a stroke before he heard it, a woodsman sank his axe into a log he was splitting, one of the big tulips that had grown up with the place. Parsons had the axe for felling such a tree himself.

At the crossing on up ahead, a car honked. Parsons could see the Dry Cleaning advertisement on the cab. That would be young Spatoli, so he walked on ahead and let himself be driven the last half mile.

"See you lost your chauffeur, eh?" Spatoli said, but he meant all right. He let Parsons out at the foot of the drive, and though they weren't there more than twenty seconds, Parsons saw Mrs. Erskine come to the window for a peek at them. Webb didn't so much as cross his mind until Mrs. Porter, opening the screen, asked him where everybody was?

"Guess I must've lost him in the rush," he said, and stepped inside.

MRS. PORTER

When he came into the kitchen she saw the sweat showing dark around his collar, and she took the Air-Wick bottle from the shelf, gave the wick a pinch.

"The melons were up a dime already, Mrs. Porter," he said.

She turned in his direction, her eyes on his feet, and he said, "We've already tried it, Mrs. Porter. Just one of those things. Small neck an' big feet. Judge had big neck an' small feet."

"I think it might prove cheaper in the long run," she said.

"When I was just a kid," Parsons said, taking the melon out of the bag, "I bought a big bundle of lisle dress socks for thirty-five cents. Dozen pair, dozen pair lisle socks for thirty-five cents. Now what would you say to a dozen pair socks for thirty-five cents?"

"We get what we pay for as a rule," she replied.

"Was a full dozen pair, no monkey business there, and there was even two of each kind, but wasn't a sock in the whole blame bundle that had a heel. Not a sock. Had a toe an' a top, but not one heel in the whole bunch. You've no idea how important a heel is to a sock."

Katherine came in from the porch and said, "Mr. Parsons, did you walk?"

"Does me good to walk a little now and then," he said. He turned from the table and looked for a place to sit down.

"If Paul ever thought of anyone but himself, I think I'd just drop dead," said Katherine.

"One out of seven now," Mrs. Porter said, "do."

They waited and she said, "Melon .39, eggs .84, bread .24, string beans—"

"Nice buy in string beans today," said Parsons. "Sixteen a pound, two for thirty-seven." He winked at Katherine.

"Eggs up, bread steady," Mrs. Porter said.

The phone rang. She waited for Katherine to answer it, and then she heard the voice of Mrs. Erskine.

"I've got my hands full now," she said, and picked up from the table the melon.

"All right?" Katherine said, "why, so far as I know. No, I think Paul had some special business, which would take him nearly to City Line, so Mr. Parsons thought he would just come on himself. He had some things we—"

"Let me speak to her," said Mrs. Porter, and passed the melon to Katherine. She seated herself, comfortably, then said, "I seem to think I hear a ticking. I suppose you're not troubled with small wildlife in your house—" There she stopped, and turned on the chair to face the living room and the front window. The Grandmother had the *Bulletin* open and was reading "Out Our Way." The evening was coming on, in all of its beauty, the dappled sunlight filled the cloak room hallway, and the feathered songsters could be heard bedding down for the night. Now the thrush, soon the whip-poor-will would take up the strain. At first whip-poor-will, whip-poor-will, whip-poor-will, but knowing ears would hear not poor-will but good-will to all men. On the table beside the Grandmother sat the lamp with the parchment shade showing the British Isles, with perforated stars marking all of their stops. On the wall above the lamp the hand-lettered Jurist's Credo, with illuminated initial letters, framed in a simple wood frame taken from a beam in the Rautzen barn. The wing-back chair was from Caleb Marshall Ordway, right leg repaired by native craftsman, and footstool with rush seat woven by Roger Porter at summer camp. Holy German Bible, forty-seven pounds, thirty-seven rare wood block illustrations, printed in Saxony 1769. Brought out by Emil Rautzen, under his frock, slung between his legs on leather harness, to Germantown in 1848. Tipped in at front water-stained copy of Emancipation Proclamation, and top half of Brooklyn paper announcing assassination of President. Bible resting on oval-shaped marble-topped table with claw feet grasping balls of onyx, estimated to be rare, hard-to-come-by piece by man from New York. Rug bought at auction second year they were married, upright piano from Uncle Charlie Ordway, and on it a photograph of Howard holding vireo with injured wing. Nothing pretentious, nothing ostentatious, nothing bought on time and not fully paid for, nothing that was not *connected* with something else. But on debit side, three non-matching throw-rugs too good to throw out. Three cigarette stains on cherry wood table, two cigarette butts in Dartmouth coaster, a scuff on the rug where someone had walked, a hollow in the chair where someone had sat, and an irregularity among the magazines.

"I'm afraid—" she said, into the phone, "that I hear Katherine calling me now," but Mrs. Erskine had already hung up. Through the living room window, where the Grandmother sat with the tip of her nose scanning the paper, Mrs. Porter saw the Erskine door swing open, stay that way. After a moment, a little man stepped from in back of it. He wore his green smoking jacket, with the Erskine monogram. The lower part of his face was tanned, but his head was a pasty color and he began to pat the top of it with the palm of his hand. From the hall at his back, walking on the mules that Mrs. Porter could hear clacking, Rosa Erskine suddenly appeared, carrying flowers. On the head of Mr. Erskine, like the lid of a pot, she clamped a soft felt hat. He did not trouble to check it, or set it straight, and with a nudge of her shoulder as she walked by him, she set him in motion, propelled him, through the door.

"Here they come!" Mrs. Porter said, and removed the cigarettes from the Dartmouth coaster, the hollow from the cushion, the scuff mark from the rug, and on her way out of the room, from the Grandmother's apron pocket, a piece of wadded Kleenex and a turkey bone.

WEBB

As he turned in the drive, Webb could see the lights were on all over the house. In the Porter house that usually indicated some emergency. That something was lost, or that the Grandmother had fallen down the stairs. She had never once fallen, anywhere, but they had discussed the possibility so often, and in such detail, that it seemed to have taken place. She would fall from the top, right at that point where she paused to hook her cane over her arm, and grope in the dark for the railing along the right hand wall. Every old lady, sooner or later, fell and broke her hip. But the Grandmother would not settle for something like that. They had discussed, time and again, putting a gate at the top, the kind used for small children, but the Doctor had advised them to leave well enough alone. The gate would simply be a new gadget, and trouble her.

It would be just like her, Webb was thinking, to pick this time to make a little trouble—to attract a little attention, that is. But as the car went up the drive he could hear some woman laughing, a booming man-sized laugh, but a woman's husky voice. Webb had heard it somewhere before. He sat in the car until he remembered. He had heard it *last* night. That seemed hardly possible, as last night seemed years ago. Last night he had got out of bed—he had been pushed out of bed, that is—to see what car had pulled up to a stop out in front. It may have been around two, it may have been three o'clock. So he had gone to the window, he was standing there, when Katherine suddenly cried—

"Don't stand there like *that*!" and maybe the woman in the street heard that, as she had raised her head. Webb could see her peering toward the Porter house. Before he could move, or duck, she had begun to laugh. A loud vulgar laugh, she not only made no attempt to conceal it, but she actually slapped the handbag she was holding on the top of the car. Webb had naturally concluded the woman was drunk. As he walked past the bed he had said, "Some drunken old bag in the street," then he had gone into the bathroom and smoked a cigarette.

From the porch off the kitchen he could see the platter of turkey sandwiches on the table, the tray of iced tea glasses, and the melon in the sink. No one was

there, however, and when the woman began to laugh
again he opened the screen, grabbed two of the sandwiches, then headed for the basement. At the foot of
the stairs he stood eating the sandwiches in the dark.
He gulped one in four, or five bites, took a little more
time with the next one, then stopped to think about
something to wash it down. He thought of it soon
enough. Inside the fruit cellar, he pulled on the overhead light. The bottle of Old Grand-Dad was still
there. He found a tall jelly glass, emptied the wax
and the jelly into the crock below the shelves, then
poured about three fingers of the whiskey into the
glass. He took a swallow of that, then filled it to the
mark again. Stepping back into the basement, he
turned on the water at one of the tubs, let it run cool,
then filled the glass to the top. As he held it to the
light, judging its strength, he saw, in the gloom across
the basement, Carl Parsons quietly seated on the basement stool. On the floor beside him was a half full iced
tea glass.

"I beg your pardon, Parsons—" said Webb.

"It's nothin'—" said Parsons, "I'm just sittin'."

Webb could see that was the case. He took a swallow from the glass, then said, "Well, it's cool down
here, for one thing."

"Cool in the summer, warm in the winter," Parsons
said. He raised his iced tea glass from the floor, and

took a swallow of it. Cool as it was, Webb could see
that the old man's face was sweaty, and that the thin
wispy hair was plastered to his head.

"You sure you feel o-kay?" said Webb.

"Oh sure," he said, "sure, I'm fine."

"I didn't mean for you to walk it," said Webb, "if
that's what you did."

"A little walk now and then does me good," Parsons said. He raised one hand to his face and said, "You
manage to find the pills?"

"Right here," said Webb, and slapped one hand on
the pocket of his shirt.

"I sorta think maybe she could use one," Parsons
said. "Notice she's a little off her feed."

"Bygod, I'm a little off my feed too," said Webb.
He took another swallow of the whiskey, then said,
"How about a swig of this, Parsons?"

"That the Old Grand-Dad?" said Parsons. Webb
nodded. "Been in there about thirty years," said Parsons, "ought to be pretty good."

Someone thumped a heavy foot on the living room
floor.

"What the hell is going on here, anyway?" said
Webb.

Parsons did not answer.

"Who are these people?" Webb asked.

Parsons shrugged, then said, "She's a noo-fo-rish."

Webb didn't challenge it. "You can't make a silk purse from an old sow," Parsons said.

Someone walked from the living room into the kitchen, passed over the spot where Webb was standing, opened the screen, and said, "Why, Mother, there's his car." After a moment, she called, "Paul— Oh, Paul!"

"Yes, dearrrr—" Webb replied.

She came to the basement door and said, "What in the world are you doing?"

"Do you really want to know?"

No, she did not. She left the door, then came and said, "Have you seen Mr. Parsons?"

"Nigh hide nor hair," said Webb.

She left the door and walked back across the kitchen to the living room.

"Well, I'll take it for a while," said Webb, "if you'll come up and spell me off later."

He meant that to be funny, but Parsons did not smile.

"You like me to bring you a sandwich?"

Parsons shook his head. "Nope," he said, "just think I'll sit here for a while."

Webb emptied his glass, left it on the drain board, and rinsed his hands under the faucet.

"You mind turnin' that light off again?" Parsons said.

The Deep Sleep

At the foot of the stairs, where the cord hung, Webb turned it off. He started up the stairs, and Parsons said, "I'd go on home if she hadn't asked me. So long as she asked me I better hang around."

"I know," said Webb, "sure, I know."

"If I'm *here*, I can say I was here," Parsons said.

"Sure," Webb said, and walked to the top of the basement stairs. A car was coming up the drive, and through one of the windows at the back of the kitchen he could see the lights bobbing on the closed doors of the garage. When the car stopped, and the lights blinked off, the dark window mirrored the kitchen, and Webb could see that a woman stood between the table and the sink. A large woman, as she blocked the aisle, she stood with her back to the window, and it crossed Webb's mind, since he felt that way himself, that she might be sick. Her right hand gripped the rim of the sink, and through her nose and mouth came a wheezing noise, as if she breathed with difficulty. But her head, half cocked toward the door, suddenly tipped back rather than forward, and over her head, like a cluster of grapes, she held four or five slices of the turkey, the white meat glistening like so many silvery fish. One at a time, the slices dropped into her mouth. All in, it closed on the catch, a blast of air wheezed through her nose, and from her mouth a muffled slobber like a dog with his head in a garbage

[237]

pail. Then she turned, without warning, and crossed the kitchen to the top of the stairs, where she wiped her hands, then her face, on the sleeve of one of Parsons' shirts. She did not see Webb, she did not hear him, but in spite of her own strong scent she smelled him, as her head screwed around as if to catch the wind. Webb stared into her face, shiny with grease, the mouth open on the remnants of the turkey, and the tongue that she had been passing around her gums. He waited for her to scream, but she made no sound. As if the doors to his own face stood open, Webb thought he could taste, as she stared through them, the green paint on the cricket and the train wheel on which he had nearly choked. He managed to make a noise, then said—

"Think I see lights out there in the driveway—" and when the woman didn't seem to hear, he pushed on by. He crossed the kitchen to the screen door, from where he could see the car parked in the driveway, and in the light from the dashboard he could see the man at the wheel. He was sitting there with his head in his hands. The head was narrow, well shaped, with the hair trimmed so close it looked boyish, and the hands were cupped as though he might be praying, or drinking from the palms. As the woman waited for him to do something, Webb opened the screen and stepped out on the porch.

"Yes—?" he said, and without surprise the man raised his head from his hands, and gazed through the laurel to where Webb stood on the steps. The lines around his mouth were strained, but his eyes and gaze were serene. "Why, Dr. Barr—" said Webb, and walked around the hedge to the side of his car. Dr. Barr smiled, and put out a hand for Webb to shake.

"Paul—" he said, "how are you?"

"How *am* I?" said Webb, and for a moment he wondered. He was awful, really, he had never been worse, but the Old Grand-Dad made it seem amusing. "Well—" he began, and braced himself to say that he was feeling no pain—which would be something of a shocker—when Dr. Barr said—

"I know—"

"How I am?" said Webb, and wondered if Barr had caught a whiff of his breath.

"Paul—" Dr. Barr said, "what are *you* going through?"

"Through?" said Webb, as it took him by surprise.

"Through—if possible," said Dr. Barr, and pushed the car door open, stepped into the drive. He inhaled deeply, and looked through an opening at the evening sky. Webb realized that Barr was waiting for him to speak.

"Going through—?" he repeated, to pick up the

question. "Well, I'm not too sure that I'm going *through* it."

"I was thinking of that," said Dr. Barr, "—sitting here."

A tall man, eye to eye with Webb, Dr. Barr stood straight over his heels, but, just a bit like a man who had inhaled deeply, stood holding his breath. Webb thought he might collapse like a balloon when he let it out.

"Privet—" Barr said, picking up the scent, "how is your wife's hay fever, Paul?"

"There hasn't been time, Dr. Barr," said Webb. "I haven't heard a sneeze."

"That is no jest," said Dr. Barr, with a touch of the pulpit in it.

"The ladies will be glad to see you," said Webb. "I'm afraid I'm not worth a dam' at this business."

Dr. Barr shrugged, raised his head to speak, then turned to see who it was that was choking. At the back of the kitchen, where Webb had left her, the woman was coughing and wheezing. But not long. As she inhaled, she began to laugh. A loud guffaw, like the one he had heard the night before, broke through the hand that she had clapped over her mouth. The hand still to her mouth, as if she was sick, they saw her round the sink corner and leave the kitchen.

"Well, I wish *I* could do that," said Dr. Barr soberly.

"I think Mother—" said Webb, "has asked a few people over."

"Erskine—" said Dr. Barr. "Mrs. Newcomb A.," as if he saw the name on a list of donors. "Newcomb A.—" he repeated, and had another look at the sky.

"You can come in this way, Dr. Barr," said Webb, and started around the hedge toward the porch, but when he turned Dr. Barr was not following him.

"Paul—" he said, "don't you think I better go around to the front?"

Webb knew that the moment he said so, but he replied, "Well, the family all use this one, and you're certainly one of the family."

"I know, Paul," Dr. Barr said, but he waited for Webb to come back to the drive. As they walked down the drive toward the front Barr said, "Mrs. Porter keeps the rules when she visits the Lord, and she expects the Lord to keep the rules when he visits her."

"You think the Lord is up to it?" said Webb.

Dr. Barr stopped in the shadow of the porch, but he did not reply. He put a hand on Webb's shoulder and said, "The Lord, Paul, is a mighty warrior—"

"Wouldn't you say that he owed it all to his mother?" said Webb.

Dr. Barr raised the hand he had placed on Webb's

shoulder, gazed at the palm, then dropped it to his side.

"How is she, Paul?" he said.

"She—?" said Webb, "which one?"

"The old one," said Dr. Barr.

"The only thing that fazes her," said Webb, "is a meal without her spreadin's."

Perhaps Barr didn't hear that, he had turned to hear the voice of Mrs. Porter, and behind it, somewhere, Mrs. Erskine's wheeze. He took Webb's arm, gave it a squeeze, then went up the steps to the open door, and as Webb walked away he could hear the ring of the chimes in the house.

He went around to the back, where he entered the kitchen just as Katherine, with a tray of empty glasses, came through the dining room door and walked past him. He stood there, smelling of sweat and whiskey, but she didn't notice him. She didn't look to see if he had combed his wild hair, or buttoned up his shirt. From the platter on the table she selected a sandwich, removed the top slice of bread and added more turkey, then dropped a fresh slice of lemon, after giving it a squeeze, into a glass of iced tea. But she knew that he was there, for she said—

"You needn't come in, dear, if you don't want to," then she left, holding before her the tray, the fragrant glass of tea, the overstuffed sandwich, and in the mirror on the door he saw her eyes swiftly appraising herself as she passed.

KATHERINE

There had been a time when nearly everybody wondered what it was that Dr. Barr seemed to lack, since he had, in most respects, nearly everything. A fine voice, a good mind, one of the best congregations in the country, and the devoted support of a lovely wife. When Katherine saw Dr. Barr with his *lovely* wife, or seated at the piano with his musical daughters, she knew, she really knew, what it was he lacked. He lacked just what Katherine Porter might have given him. Sybil Eames Barr was dark, she was pale, she was devoted, and she was musical, and she bore a great resemblance to Katherine Porter herself. The resemblance was certainly striking, but as Katherine knew Dr. Barr could tell you, Sybil Barr didn't bear much more than a resemblance to life.

Katherine never saw him, with his lovely wife, when he didn't look like a man who was dying—but when she saw him alone he always seemed to be getting well. In all the books she had read a man in that position was false to himself, or to the woman he had married, but this could not be said of Dr. Barr. He just seemed to drop right back, as she did, to the Young People's Service League, and the discussions they had as to just what music she should play. While they discussed, she would go on practicing. She had been working on "Lotus Land" at the time, which was the piece everybody asked for, and he had never once hinted at what terrible stuff it was. Four years later, in England, when she was playing Bach and knew better, she had written him to say she was working on the Preludes and Fugues. He had written to ask if she knew the Partita in B flat. So she had worked on that for nearly two years, but when she came back he was away on vacation, and when she saw him again Paul Webb, her husband, was at her side.

"How did that Partita ever work out?" Dr. Barr had asked. So she had sat right down at his piano and played it, right before his lovely wife, who was something of a harpist, and Paul, the ninny, thought that she was playing it for him. She had never played it so beautifully, he had said. Right in one piece if the truth were known, she was playing two kinds of music, but perhaps only in music could you get away with something like that. Only in music could you be true to what Paul called life. He liked to point out that the beauty of childhood was limited to those who had outgrown it, and she would like to point out that this was

also true of a love affair. All the young men she had
known as lovers had never grown up. They were
trapped in her past, just as she was very likely trapped
in theirs. It was like the first chapter or two of a book
with all the important chapters missing, leaving the
lovers trapped in a hopeless, foolish predicament. It
had a good deal to do, she was sure, with the silliness
in books, poems, and music about the notion that love
was out of this world. That it was never meant to
come to anything. But if it didn't, if it couldn't, it
was like having a bad appendix, and with his lovely
wife that was exactly how Dr. Barr looked. Something, obviously, was poisoning him. But when he
came to see her he came alone, since he knew how
much good it did him, and it was one of the reasons,
sick as he was, that he was holding up. He had faith,
they said, and one thing he had faith in was herself.

"Dr. Barr," she said, going toward him, "whether
you have had your dinner or not—"

"As a matter of fact, Katherine," he said, "I am
almost starved."

She thought he looked it, frankly, although he had
always more or less looked it, but now his stilt-thin
legs seemed attached to his sides, like the legs of birds.

"I hope I'm right about the lemon—" she said, and
under his arm, as he sampled the tea, she saw that Rosa
Erskine, her eyes bugging, was not missing a trick. To

keep Mr. Erskine from patting his head, she had squashed his hat down low on it, but his right hand tapped the arm of the chair like a metronome. "You don't *act* like you're starving, Dr. Barr," Katherine said, and when he took a bite of the sandwich she suddenly remembered the chomping sound that he always made. Eating and talking, he often spewed out food like sparks. It had been the first thing that Paul liked about him. He said that any man who ate like that had something on his mind, and was no pious boob.

"Dr. Barr," her mother said, handing him a paper napkin, "I'm afraid we may seem a little light-hearted—"

"It is easier to weep than to laugh," said Dr. Barr.

"I think you should do as you feel if there's no harm in it," said Rosa Erskine. "You come and you go. It makes you go quicker to hear people weep."

"Would you call that mind over matter?" her mother said.

"Honey—" said Rosa Erskine, "I just don't give a hoot what you call it. If you want to call it what you said, it's all right with me."

"Who's been eating chocolate?" her mother asked. She stooped to pick a flattened piece of it up, her backside toward Dr. Barr, who said—

"Without a name, Mrs. Erskine, we may hardly know *what* it is we feel. We all feel something, but without a name, without a suitable custom, we may not feel it clearly enough to know what it is. It is the purpose of language, art, and religion to help us out."

"How do *you* feel?" said Rosa Erskine.

"I feel a great loss," said Dr. Barr. "I feel the need of an arm to lean on to help me sustain that loss."

"That's what *you've* got an' I *don't* have!" Rosa Erskine boomed.

"Why, I thought Christian Science took care of that too?" her mother said, and picked at the chocolate stuck to the rug.

"I suppose it does," Rosa Erskine said, "if you read in it far enough. All I really want is to stop runnin' to doctors all the time."

"Well, I think it can be a real help there," said Dr. Barr.

"Except for this ulcerated tooth—" said Mrs. Erskine, running her tongue back to sound the hollow, "I haven't had to fall back on *any*body for more than five years! It got me to see there wasn't *any*body to fall back on. Till it did I was a nervous wreck about half the time."

"It seems to me we need something—" said Dr. Barr, "to have around *all* of the time, not only when we need it to fall back on. Otherwise, when we fall back on it, it might not be there. It might not support the burden we drop on it."

"I'd like Mr. Parsons to hear that," said her mother, and stood up straight to look around for him. "Katherine," she said, "where did he go?"

"You have to watch all of 'em like a hawk!" Rosa Erskine cried.

Dr. Barr cleared his throat, then in his pulpit voice said, "I'm going to eat this food, I'm going to drink this tea, then I'm going to have a long heart to heart talk with the oldest Republican lady in the USA."

They all turned to gaze at the Grandmother. "Humph," she said.

"May I?" said Dr. Barr, bowing to the old lady.

"You may," she said, but with such authority, funny as Katherine thought it was, nobody laughed. Not until Dr. Barr drew up his chair, and tucked up his trouser legs to show his bony ankles, did she realize that he was seated facing *her*. To look at him, she would have to turn her head. But his gaze, if he had that in mind, would pass undisturbed over the Grandmother's head, and she knew, without turning, that he had that in mind. She did not need to look to see if this was so, for the Grandmother, as if her name had been called, crooked her head around to see who it was in back of her.

"Well—" said Dr. Barr, "I don't need to ask how *you* have been."

The Deep Sleep

THE GRANDMOTHER

The Grandmother's standards, elevated as they were, had not had to lower themselves, in her opinion, when she passed the time of day with Dr. Barr. He talked slow. He listened to sound advice. He did not talk or listen to everybody at once. When she had heard the voice of Mrs. Erskine in the cloak room she had slipped her teeth right out of her mouth, but then she had to slip them in again when she heard Dr. Barr. Of all the men who came to visit her, writers and statesmen, governors and public figures, only Dr. Barr, in her opinion, was just as big when he straightened up as he was before he stooped and took her hand. Some of the others shrunk up to a foot.

"If I don't talk to someone," she said to him, "I think I'll lose my wits."

"What kind of language is this, Mrs. Porter?" Howard's wife said.

"It's plain talk to them that understands it," the Grandmother replied.

"I think I understand it," said Dr. Barr, "and I also think it was very well put."

"With all the people there is in this house," she said, "you would think one of them would listen to an old lady." She stopped, then said, "If I don't talk, I forget."

"I haven't noticed any sign of your memory slipping," Howard's wife said.

"If it ain't, it's because I sit an' talk to myself!" she said.

"If it *is*-unt," said Mrs. Porter.

"We all do," said Dr. Barr, "but I don't think I know many people, if I know one, who really have so much to talk about."

"I won't have if they let me forget it," she said.

"I tell you what," said Dr. Barr, and took from his inside pocket a wallet, opened the wallet, and took out a card. He looked at the card and said, "Mrs. Porter, are you free on Tuesdays and Thursdays?"

"I am allus free to them that wants me," she said.

"Say we make it around four-thirty," he said. "Tuesday and Thursday, rain or shine, around four-thirty."

"The rain is usually over out here by then," Mrs. Porter said.

"Now—" said Dr. Barr, putting the card away, "I want to hear all about Uncle Billie."

"Oh, pooh—" the Grandmother said.

"I don't think I ever heard of a more gallant warrior," said Dr. Barr.

"Oh, pooh now—" she said.

[250]

Turning from her Dr. Barr said, "Have all of you people heard of Uncle Billie's Last Battle?"

"It's no such thing!" she said.

"I'd tell it," said Dr. Barr, "but I'm not going to tell it and spoil it."

"Grandmother," said the daughter, "I don't really think Mrs. Erskine has heard it."

A good thing, the Grandmother thought, but she was too polite to say so.

"I've heard it," said Dr. Barr, "but I like it better every time I hear it. It's the finest war story I ever heard."

With the back of her hand, the Grandmother slowly wiped her lips.

"Oh, pooh—" she said, but not so you'd notice it.

"Is this the Civil War?" Mrs. Erskine said.

"What other war was there?" said Dr. Barr, saving the Grandmother the trouble.

"Let me get Paul," the daughter said. "I don't think Paul's heard it." She went into the kitchen and they heard her call, "Oh Paul?" From upstairs somewhere he said—

"What now?"

"Come down," the daughter said, "Grandmother's going to tell about Uncle Billie."

"She hasn't much voice," Howard's wife was saying, "so if you'll move your chairs just a little closer—"

[251]

The Deep Sleep

To save what voice she had, the Grandmother held her peace. She could see the movement as they gathered around her, and when Mrs. Erskine, a large egg-shaped blur, dropped down in a chair, the Grandmother could smell what Mrs. Porter called her *lure*.

"I've just never been able," Mrs. Erskine was saying, "to work myself back to the Civil War. Don't it seem far away to you?"

"Grant does, but not Gettysburg," Mrs. Porter said.

"It does and it doesn't," said Dr. Barr, "but when I sit right here, when I am facing the woman who once gazed upon Abraham Lincoln—"

"Why it just makes me feel goose-fleshy," said Mrs. Erskine, "don't it you?"

"He was out on the rear platform," the Grandmother said.

"I think we better go on without Paul this time," the daughter said.

"Well—" said Dr. Barr, "we'll hear it again when he comes down." He turned to the Grandmother and said, "Should I just sketch in a little of the background?"

"You may," she said.

"Well," said Dr. Barr, "the picture is something like this." He paused, then spread out his hands. "We have the nation in the midst of this terrible turmoil, this life and death struggle. We have men in the midst of the battle, and then we have Uncle Billie—"

"He was not much good for anything," the Grandmother said.

"Well, now I don't know," said Dr. Barr. "We *do* know that he enlisted. We do know that he went off to win this war. He left his loved ones, his little farm, and walked across the mountains with his trusty musket, and we know that he—"

"Fired two shots!" the Grandmother said.

"I hear you say he fired two shots?" said Dr. Barr.

"He fired two shots—" the Grandmother replied, then closed her eyes, pressed her lips together, and let them wait till she hoped they'd bust.

"Yes?" said Dr. Barr.

"Fired two shots," she repeated, then peered over the top of her isinglasses, blinked, and said, "One at the enemy, and one in his britches!"

Mrs. Erskine was so startled she forgot to laugh. Then she didn't laugh, she exploded, and the spray reached as far as the Grandmother, who was pushing the knee she had raised back to the floor. Dr. Barr, his handkerchief to his face, was wiping away tears of laughter, and Mrs. Porter was straightening the rug where he had wrinkled it. The first time people heard about Uncle Billie they were amused, and some of them even laughed. But when they heard it again and again, with Dr. Barr supervising the battle, something in the story, or the telling of the story, seemed to grow on them. As for Dr. Barr, it was almost more than he could stand. Mrs. Porter, a napkin in her hand, dabbed up tea Mrs. Erskine had spilled, and moved the glass she had left on the floor to a safer place. That's where they were, when the daughter cried—

"Paul!"

The Grandmother couldn't see, from where she sat, what the trouble was.

"Speaking of stories—" she heard him say, in a voice that didn't sound much like him, "any of you had a look at Hamlet?"

"O-livey-aaa," Mrs. Erskine said, "don't you love O-livey-aaa?"

"Well, it's quite a little play," he went on, "it's really quite a little horror story. Take this, for example—just listen to this—"

"Paul!" the daughter said, "are you—" Then she stopped.

"Listen to this—" he said, and the Grandmother could see him on the stairs at the front of the room. He was on the landing. He held up his hand as a preacher would.

"Ohhhhhh, what a rogue and peasant slave am I!" he said, which was not just how the Grandmother would have put it, but she could certainly agree with

the gist of it. But that was all she heard, that was all
there was, and she saw the daughter cross the room
toward him and then the sound as if a hymn book
had snapped closed. It was so quiet in the room she
thought maybe they were waiting to pray.

"Katherine," Mrs. Porter said, "I do hear a ticking.
Right in this room."

PARSONS

When Parsons heard Katherine calling his name he
had a small piece of ice in his mouth, otherwise, out of
habit, he might have cried out *Here!* He spit the ice
into the glass he was holding, where a piece of lemon
rind was floating, and waited till she walked from the
kitchen into the living room. He had never heard such
a commotion in the house. Furniture had been moved,
he had heard them all gather in one corner, and he had
heard the old lady croaking at them before they
laughed. There had never been anything like it in the
Porter house.

When the Grandmother came up from the country
she had brought along with her three or four scratchy
records, none of them really music, and all of them

just the talk of The Two Black Crows. She didn't croak so much at that time, and when she heard the Black Crows talking about O-hee-O, when what they meant was Ohio, and a-Fricka, when what they meant was Africa, it was just about more than she could stand. Mrs. Porter didn't laugh because in her estimation the records were nothing but concealed propaganda, and a serious discredit to the peoples of the colored race. Down in the basement, where he often was, Parsons often had to step into the fruit cellar, where he would laugh so long and so hard he thought his ribs would crack. But there had been no laughing like that in the house since Mrs. Porter came home with the new Console Combination, and the Grandmother was not allowed to play her old records on it. It would ruin the sensitive needle, Mrs. Porter had said. Then a year or two ago, maybe longer, Parsons had found all four of those records on the pile of junk Mrs. Porter had put out for the Good Will people, and though he didn't have a phonograph Parsons had taken the records home. Just to read the names printed on the labels made him laugh. He had hoped Mrs. Porter would throw out the machine that she no longer had any use for, but she liked it around in case the newer model happened to break down. She really didn't have much confidence in the newer things.

The Deep Sleep

Leaving the glass on the floor—he had sat there so long he could see pretty well without the lights on—Parsons rinsed his hands and face at the tub, and combed his hair. At the top of the stairs, from the hook beneath the raincoats, he took an oversize seersucker jacket that somebody had left in the back of the Judge's car. Nobody had ever asked for it. It was small for the Judge, and large for Parsons, but not so large he couldn't wear it, and Mrs. Porter often said it made him look like a southern gentleman. Now the funny thing about *that* was, that was how Parsons felt. When he was in the jacket, that is. He liked to droop his handkerchief over the collar, as he had seen men do it in the southern movies, and Mrs. Porter also said that his speech was more refined when he wore the coat. He used a broader *a*, and usually said doesn't when he meant *don't*. He hadn't worn it at all for a year or so as he didn't need a coat to watch the Judge dying, and it *wasn't* the type of coat to walk up and down some highway in. He took it off the hook, shook the rubber smell out, then turned up the collar of his shirt so it would help keep the collar of the coat a little clean. Also, he didn't want to give the Erskines the false impression that he was dolled up, that having iced tea with the Porters was anything unusual with him. It was, but not the way they would think, and he happened to know that Newcomb Erskine, in twenty years, had never once set foot in the Porter house. Not until tonight, when he was so old and feeble-minded it no longer meant to him what it might have, and the Judge himself, who would have been bored stiff with him, was not in the house.

In the kitchen he stopped to eat a bite of turkey, but when the house dropped quiet, dead quiet, he slipped back into the cloak room at the top of the stairs. He heard Mrs. Porter say that she heard a ticking, but otherwise nothing much happened, and when the house began to stir he walked through the kitchen to the dining room door. He could see Dr. Barr, leaning forward on his knees, listening to the Grandmother tell him, for the thousandth time, just where it was in Würtemberg the Rautzens were from. Just to one side, as though she were listening, Katherine was sitting with a platter in her lap, and when he stepped through the door he naturally thought she would speak to him. "Mother, here's Mr. Parsons," was what she usually said, but she didn't say a word. She seemed to have her eye on what was going on at the far end of the room.

Parsons put in his head to where he could see, down at the stair end, Mrs. Porter and the Erskines huddled around Webb, with old man Erskine, propped on his cane, just off to one side. He had one of the canes people take to the races, that open out at the top so

you can sit on them, as nobody knew just when and
where it was he might have to sit down. Stuck in his
mouth, like a cork, was a cigar, and Parsons never saw
him that close up but what it made him think of the
faces he had seen on coconuts. Whatever he had inside
of it was slowly drying up.

Webb stood with his back to Parsons, but he looked
so strange in Mrs. Porter's front room, with his hair up
wild and his sleeves rolled, that it was no wonder that
Katherine was sitting there eyeing him. He really
looked a sight, but Mrs. Erskine, as if she couldn't
hear what he was saying, was standing so close that
his tie hung down and folded on her front. She was
telling him about her maid, Eloise, the only maid she
ever had that lasted out the winter, but left in the
spring when the mad robin wouldn't leave her alone.
It kept pecking on the window till it gave her the
willies, as Eloise said. It would shame most people to
live in a house where the birds went crazy, let alone
talk about it, but Mrs. Erskine told that story to everyone. Webb had already heard it, but he looked like
he could hardly wait. He was using one of his dirty
fingers to dunk the ice cubes in the glass he was holding, and it crossed Parsons' mind that maybe it had
more than tea in it. It might have been the orange
light on the piano, which made nearly everybody look
a little funny, but if Parsons could believe his eyes,

Webb was a little drunk. He watched him put his right hand, wet finger and all, on the shrunken shoulder of Newcomb Erskine, and then give him a shake, like he was a pup.

"Don't they make a pair though!" Mrs. Erskine said, and stepped back so she could look at them better.

"You hear that, Newcomb?" Webb said, and shook him so hard he nearly fell over. "You hear that? They think we make a pair!"

"Katherine—" Mrs. Porter said, "where do you suppose he has been?"

"I don't think I really care to know," Katherine said.

"Been—?" said Webb. "You really want to know where I've been?"

"You been to see O-livey-aaa!" said Mrs. Erskine.

"Nope," said Webb, wagging his finger at her, "guess again." He lowered the finger he had been waving, dunked an ice cube.

"Where were you, baby?" Rosa Erskine said.

"At twenty minutes past two, Madame—"

"I don't want to hear!" said Katherine.

"—until twenty-seven minutes to three, I was in a cozy phone booth at the Hot Potato, very nice view of the ladies' john."

"He was too late," said Mrs. Porter, "for the daily luncheon platter, and it was too near mealtime for what he ordered—" but there she stopped, as Mrs.

Erskine was choking on something. "He was too late—" Mrs. Porter continued, and Parsons saw Katherine, looking like she was car sick, turn from her mother and look wildly around the room. She turned to Dr. Barr, who was gazing at the fireplace, then she turned to Parsons, as if he had spoken, and came toward him with a tray of sandwiches.

"Mother!" she cried, in a voice that wasn't like her. "Look, Mother, here's Mr. Parsons. Just look at his new glamor jacket!"

MRS. PORTER

As Mr. Parsons crossed the room toward her she saw that he had buttoned it wrong, as usual, and she kept her eyes on the *right* button till he buttoned it.

"Mr. Parsons," she said, "tell us about the material."

"Think it's seersucker," said Parsons, looking at the sleeves, "guess you can wash as well as dry clean it."

"Newcomb won't wear anything," said Mrs. Erskine, "that might make life a little bit simpler. He wouldn't think of it, would you, lamb?"

"Racer," said Mr. Erskine. "Border's racer."

"Baby!" said Mrs. Erskine, "what did I tell you? Didn't I say not to bring it up?"

The Deep Sleep

"He wants an *ee*-raser?" said Mrs. Porter.

Mr. Erskine shook his head.

"Think maybe what he wants is a light," said Webb, and struck a match, held it out toward him. Mr. Erskine did not want a light. He took a step back, removed his hat from his head, but Mrs. Erskine took it from him and slapped it back on.

"Baby," she said, "what did I tell you?"

"Border's racer," he said.

"Doll—" said Mrs. Erskine, bending toward him, "you forget what I told you? Didn't I tell you it was no time to bring it up?"

"What the hell's he want?" said Webb.

"You want me to tell the people what it is you want, baby? You want all these people to know how little sense you got?"

Mr. Erskine wagged his head up and down.

"I told him I wouldn't bring him over if he was going to ask for it," said Mrs. Erskine. "I told him this was no time to bring it up."

"If he would state his wishes," Mrs. Porter said, "we would be happy to oblige him."

"Border's racer!" Mr. Erskine said.

"He's collectin' old razors now, Mrs. Porter. Can you believe it? When somebody dies he wants his old razor!"

"That isn't my department," Mrs. Porter said. "I'm afraid that's outside my jurisdiction."

"Parsons," said Webb, "you know where there's any razors?"

"Ain't my department either," said Parsons.

"Mother—" said Katherine, "would there be one in the fitted bag?"

"A gift of the Law School," said Mrs. Porter.

"I think the bag is in the attic, Mother."

"Why don't I go take a peek at it?" said Paul.

"If we're going to Finlay, Mother," said Katherine, "we're going to need all the bags we've got. They are *all* in the attic. If we can get Paul—"

"Mrs. Porter—" said Dr. Barr.

Mrs. Porter turned and looked at him.

"We have a request over here," said Dr. Barr, "for the messenger to the attic. A black net shopping bag with pine cones in it, is that right?"

"It's where they told me they put it!" the Grandmother said.

"Well, I'll peer around for it," said Paul.

"Dr. Barr—" Mrs. Porter said, "I hope you're not giving certain people ideas. I hope you're not suggesting that they might be going somewhere."

"We've just been discussing it in the abstract," said Dr. Barr.

"Is Howard goin' to Finlay?" the Grandmother asked.

"There are no final arrangements," said Mrs. Porter.

"Mr. Parsons," the Grandmother said, "is Howard goin' to Finlay?"

"Mrs. Porter—" said Dr. Barr, rising, "I think she may be a little overexcited. If I can be of any help on the stairs—"

"Katherine," said Mrs. Porter, "you want to go ahead and look at her room?"

"Oh Chief!" Parsons called up the stairs. "If you see a black umbrella with a bone handle—"

WEBB

In the ceiling of the master bedroom, papered to resemble a section of panelling, a trapdoor opened into the attic of the house. A full-sized door, it was pulled from the ceiling by a chain that resembled a light cord, and as it dropped toward the floor a set of stairs slid down the tracks on its back. The stairs operated on a pair of weighted cables, so that it took a man-sized pull, and then a man-sized weight, to hold the contraption to the floor. Roger Porter, when almost a man, had got the door from the ceiling all right, but when he sat on the stairs they disappeared into the ceiling with him on board. His sister, Katherine, had been left alone in the room. Like a ghost speaking from the attic, Roger had warned her to keep her mouth shut, and then he had piled on the door what were known as the Grandmother's effects. To top it off, he got on himself, and as the door slowly dropped from the ceiling he had looked to Katherine like a carpet-traveler from another world. Everything had spilled into the room, as down a chute, then the door had gone back before they could stop it, and the Grandmother's effects had been carried to the basement, where they still were.

Ever since he had heard the story, Webb had wanted to try the stairs himself. When Katherine had suggested that he look in the attic, he had his chance. He stood there in the room, the chain in his hand, wondering how hard he would have to pull on it, when he noticed the smear of oil at the top. He gave a tug on the chain, a very light tug, and the door budged. It had certainly been opened since Roger Porter had gone up with it. Webb cleared the floor in the center of the room, then stepped behind the door, in case the stairs were loose, and drew it down toward the floor. Door and stairs dropped to the floor without a squeak. The wheels and hinges were oiled, the weights had been reset. Webb stood there, gazing into the loft where a large oil painting hung from the rafters, a seascape, a rather bad one, and his own. A dozen or so hot, humid summers had not improved it. A long cord, lumpy with flies, suspended from the small bulb near the ceiling, where it could be reached by whoever mounted the stairs. As Webb started up something about it made him think of going up a gangway, the last of the animals, perhaps, to enter the ark. Near the top he gave a pull to the cord, and as he stepped into the attic the stairs arose from the room below him, the door eased closed. He was in the crow's nest, the Captain's walk, he was cut off from the yawping he heard below him, and the steps that he could hear coming up the hall stairs. He had gone to that part of the barn where the ladder was no longer nailed to the rafters, and the last man up pulled the rope in after him. The ship was at sea. The gangplank was no longer in touch with the shore.

High above him in the rafters the bulb glowed, but gave off little light. Around the point where he stood there were piles of shoe boxes, suit boxes, and cartons that had collapsed. Seen from the stairs below, the attic looked like a crowded place. But what there was, and there wasn't too much, was gathered like the dirt around an ant hole, and back away from the hole the attic was an empty place. An Irish Mail, a Flexible Flyer, a small collapsible billiard table, were stored against the rafters back from the center of the floor. At one time, from the way it looked, something had been planned. Someone had come up here and swept clean the floor, perhaps drawn a map. There was room in the attic for a game room, a club room, or something like that. At each gabled end was a window, the one to the east was overgrown with ivy, but the window on the west let in some light. Webb could still see the glow in the western sky. Beside that window, which sat close to the floor, was a three-legged stool, a fine cowhide bag, a small box of Robert Burns cigars, and a chamber pot with a wreath of blue flowers on the lid. On the floor beside the stool was a box of kitchen matches, and a Gem razor blade. As he dropped down on the stool Webb could see the nail parings scattered on the floor.

The cowhide bag was locked, but the key hung on a string. Webb inserted the key, unlocked it, then left the key in that position while he searched through his pockets for a cigarette. In the pocket of his shirt he found the liver pills. He put them on the floor beside the matches, and as he struck a match he could see, in the box with the matches, a small pack of mints to sweeten the breath. *For the removal of tobacco and liquor odors,* the label read. Webb pried one of the sticky mints loose, dropped it into his mouth. It had a sweet unpleasant odor, but one that might make a favorable impression on somebody else. He sat listening to the voices in the house. Through the window he could see the living room lights on the lawn. It reminded him of what he had come for, and he pried open the bag, saw that it was fitted very handsomely. On each side were silver plated, monogrammed toilet articles. Military brushes that had not been used, bay rum that had never been smelled, a mirror perhaps unlooked at, and a brush that had never lathered a face. In a case labelled RAZOR, a razor that had never been stropped. Webb took it from the case, passed the blade through the air, then placed it on the floor beside the pills. The case he returned to its place in the fitted bag. When it didn't go easy, he put in his hand to see what the trouble was.

Another case. This one of leather, morocco leather, square in shape with a gold clasp, and the initials H.R.P. stamped in gold on the front of it. In the case, in a bed of cream satin, a gold watch. There was a light at his back, but Webb struck a match to look at it. In the lid of the case, tipped in, was a card, and written on it—

GOLDEN SWISS TICKER
Lost by me, found by Mother
May 17, 1939

Webb had seen it before. He had seen it lying in the Judge's broad hand. Just fifteen years ago, in

Chicago, the year before he had married the Judge's daughter, he had heard the watch chime as the Judge flicked the lever at the side.

"Nice, eh?" the Judge had said, and when Webb had agreed, the Judge had added, "Three hundred seventy-five simoleons, son."

That had been the summer night Webb had called for Katherine—she was staying with her father at one of the clubs—and he had found the Judge sitting alone in the lobby when he walked in. When he saw Webb, the Judge had patted the cushion at his side. That was very characteristic, as Webb learned later, and part of his role as a good listener, a man you could turn to who made no demands himself.

So Webb had taken a seat, and the Judge had first told him some nearly naughty story about a goose and a gander, and Webb had laughed pretty hard to please the Judge. Then the Judge had asked him if he planned to visit Italy. Webb said he didn't think he would as he didn't have the money, and he planned to spend what time he had painting. The Judge said that he could appreciate that, then he went on to say that he and Mrs. Porter had spent several weeks at Lake Como, and Webb got the impression that Lake Como had figured in the Judge's life. But just an impression, as right at that point the Judge had taken out his watch, as if he had an appointment.

"I hope I haven't kept you, sir—" Webb had said, but the Judge had wagged his head as if a fly had buzzed him. He muttered something or other, but kept his eyes on the watch. So Webb had glanced at the watch himself, and saw that it was small, thin as a dollar, with a lever at the side that the Judge liked to work.

"Nice, eh?" the Judge had said, and when Webb agreed the Judge nudged the lever with this thumb nail. He held the watch to Webb's ear and he could hear it chime out the correct time.

"Well, I'll be damned," Webb had said, as he had been honestly impressed.

"Bought it at Lake Como," the Judge had said, then let it slip back into his vest. "Dollar watch," he went on, "keeps about the same time, but guess I wanted to commemorate the occasion."

"You were on your honeymoon?" Webb had asked.

"Not strictly speaking," the Judge had replied, "had our actual honeymoon back in this country, but guess it was there, there around the lake, that things came to a head."

That had been all, he put a hand on Webb's knee, pushed up from the couch, and Webb felt his fingers brush his shoulder lightly as he walked away. That had been all. That is to say, that had been everything. The Judge and Mrs. Porter, as it turned out, had made the

Grand Tour in 1913, and the following spring, in Bryn Mawr, Katherine Porter was born. Things had come to a head, that is, in the fifth year of their married life.

From the box on the floor Webb took a cigar, snipped off the end with a razor, and sat there smoking, the *Golden Swiss Ticker* in his lap. There was a tapping in the floor, but he hardly noticed it. Then he remembered where he was, and said, "Yes?"

"What are you up to now?" said Katherine.

He dropped the watch, case and all, into his pocket. Looking around for a place to drop the cigar, he saw the nightpot and removed the lid. Floating in the water at the bottom were both butts and cigars. He dropped his own into the pot, returned the lid.

"Oh, Paul!" Katherine said. He stood on the trapdoor till it started down, and as it opened into the room below he said—

"Having a quiet little smoke, dear. Like to come up?"

KATHERINE

"Paul—" she had said, and she could see Dr. Barr gazing at her with admiration, "Paul, would you look in the attic for the fitted bag?"

[271]

Without creating a scene, without raising her voice, she had got rid of him. If he hadn't been too drunk to appreciate it, he would have known, like everybody else, what a real stroke of genius it was. It gave him, as well as the rest of them, a way out. If it had not been for the rest of them she would have left him to stew, as he was so fond of putting it, in his own juice. But poor Mr. Parsons looked like he would die of shame by himself, and Dr. Barr would certainly never have forgiven her.

And then the Grandmother, shouting at her mother, had had one of her attacks, which would have been her last if it hadn't been for Dr. Barr. Right at that moment she had had the feeling Paul had outwitted her again, as if he had known *that* was coming, and had left her holding the bag. But there had been no time to think about it, and all this time, every moment of it, somebody had to act *as if* everything was all right. Her mother did. Her mother had been simply remarkable. Any other woman would have had an attack herself. But her mother took it right in her stride, she kept the damper on a woman like Mrs. Erskine, and in less than ten minutes they had the Grandmother quieted down. It was nearly hard to believe that anything unusual had taken place. Dr. Barr had stopped to speak to Mr. Erskine, to assure him that a razor, *some* razor would be forthcoming immediately. And where was her mother? She was trying on Mrs. Erskine's hat! They were both down at the end of the room facing the full length mirror on the back of the door.

"Katherine," she had said, turning from the mirror, "would you ask Paul to bring down my hatbox? Mrs. Erskine is in the mood to try on some hats."

So she had said yes, yes, of course, and had gone up to get the box herself. But when she stepped into the bedroom and saw the trapdoor up tight in the ceiling, for just a moment she thought she might be sick. There was not a sound from the attic, not a thing. She wet her lips, but she couldn't bring herself to speak. Then she looked around the room for something she could rap on the door with, and on the wall behind her, beside her mother's bed, was a billiard cue. It had come along, years ago, with Roger's billiard set. Without getting out of bed—if she had the cue— her mother could tap on the bedroom window and frighten off the squirrels that came to the winter feeding box. With the point of this cue she tapped on the ceiling, and when he answered she said, "What are you up to now?" When he didn't answer that, and she stood there waiting, she thumped on the door harder than ever, and the next thing she knew the door suddenly opened, and he was looking at her.

"Paul," she said, "how could you?" and when he

said something silly to that, she said, "Mother would like me to get her hatboxes," and walked up the steps. He stood right there at the top, waiting for her.

"And what are *you* going through?" he said, and struck a pose.

She pushed by him, through the tiers of boxes, and stepped into the empty room.

"Why!" she said, in spite of herself.

"Quite a little hideout, eh?" he said.

"Where is everything?" she said.

"Guess it slid down the hatch that day with Roger," he said. She didn't like the way he looked. He didn't look drunk *enough*. She left him there and looked around the room for her mother's hats. There had been a fine leather box from Vienna, containing hats from Budapest, London, and Paris, new hats that her mother had never worn. They were too high-class for a Professor's wife, she had said. She saw this box behind the Flexible Flyer, but when Paul saw where she was looking he walked over and removed the sled himself. He would never have done that if he hadn't been interested.

"Having a little floor show, dear?" he said.

"Isn't that what they have *after the drinks*?" she said.

When he rose up suddenly to look at her, he bumped his head. When he didn't howl, she said,

"You must be practically numb with it."

He didn't reply to that, and she took a piece of tissue from one of the cartons, and wiped the dust off the top of the hatboxes. There were others from Best's, Wanamaker's, and a young matron's shop in New York. He just stood there watching her. As mad as it made her to have him carping, or swearing at every other mouthful, it was somehow worse not to have him say anything.

"And *where* did you get the cigar?" she said.

"It's quite a little story," he said. She waited, and he said, "After leaving my wife and her lovely mother, I drove the hired hand down to the crossing, pushed him out in the path of an oncoming train, then I drove into town and bought myself a box of fine see-gars. Then I drove down the street to a bar, where I had myself a bottle and ten or twelve straight ones, then I came out and drove wildly back to my lovely home. There I hid for a while in the basement, chatting with the hired hand while he sat on the crapper, then I heard the bells ring as the Reverend father entered the house. I saw the rosy flush of morn on the cheeks of my pale little wife. Then I went to read in a book called *Hamlet*, noting well who was slain behind the arras, the rosy pallor of the fair Ophelia, and the anggg-wisht sor-rowww of the Queen. Then I—"

"Then you all but killed your Grandmother!" she cried.

He stood there.

"If you would just shut up I wouldn't talk like that!" she said.

He turned away, he walked back to the window, and took a cigar from the box on the floor.

"I am going to ask you not to smoke in *this* attic," she said.

"Out behind the garage be o-kay?" he replied.

Was he smiling at her? The light was so bad she couldn't see his face. He was seated on the three-legged stool that belonged in front of the fireplace, the one her mother was sure the rug cleaning people had made off with.

"Just what do you mean by that?" she said.

"Just wondered," he said, "if out behind the garage would be o-kay. Know it's against the law in the house, and since you don't seem to have an outside crapper—"

"Would you feel more at home if we had one?" she said.

"Well, a man *has* to go somewhere. Sort of makes it hard for a man to know *where*."

"All any of you ever think of is yourself," she said.

"It's a full time job," he went on, "but when I'm workin' overtime, as I am now, I often get around to somebody else." She waited, and he said, "It isn't everyday a man comes face to face with a perfect human bein'. It's even rarer when it turns out to be a member of the fe-male sex."

"We have Mrs. Erskine to thank?" she said.

"Nope—" he said, "Mrs. Howard Porter, the only livin' woman without a human failin'."

"I'll thank you to keep your opinions to yourself," she said.

"T'ain't mine," he said, "got it from the horse's mouth."

"That woman has her nerve—" she began.

"Said *horse*," he said. "Not cow. Got this straight from the horse's mouth."

She waited, but of course he wouldn't go on.

"Well, I'm waiting—"

"Mistah Carl Parsons," he said, "a dam' good man."

"You're both just a pair of gossips!" she said. "I can see you sitting in a bar somewhere, the pair of you, just chewing it all over—"

"It's quite a statement when you think it over," he said.

"You can sit and think it over all you like, you've been sitting and thinking since you got here, you leave the work and the trouble to the woman you sit and think about."

"She's a very remarkable woman," he said.

"I am leaving," she said, "but I am not leaving till you put out that cigar."

"Seen the latest in ashtrays, *Doll?*" he said.

"You call me that just once more," she said, and watched him take the lid from the nightpot, dust his cigar, then return the lid again.

"If Grandmother saw you do that, old as she is, she would choke you. I just wish I had my Grandmother's strength."

"I was just sittin' here—" he said, "mindin' my own business, when I just happened to look for a place to drop my see-gar. So I just happened to lift the lid—" He lifted it.

"Yes—"

"If you're curious," he said, "you can come an' look for yourself."

"That's just what you've been hoping," she said, "that's just what you've been sitting there planning. You think I'm so curious that I just can't resist. Well, I can. I can and I'm not going to give you a particle of satisfaction—"

"Well stated," he said. "That's the first law of the house."

"What do you mean?"

"The first and last Commandment of the House," he said, imitating Dr. Barr's pulpit manner, "the first

Commandment of the House reads— Thou shalt not give a particle of gratification. Thou shalt drive from the Temple the man who smokes, and he shall live in a tent behind the two-car garage, and thou shalt drive from the bed the man who lusts, and he shall lie in tourist camps with interstate whores, and thou shalt drive from the bathroom the man who farts, and he shall sit in a dark cubbyhole in the basement, and thou shalt drive from the parlor the man who feels, and he shall make himself an island in the midst of the waters, for the man who feels undermines the Law of the House!"

"Paul!" she said.

"Such are the Commandments, but alas, men are mortal, the tables of the Law are cracked and broken, and in the nightpot in the attic float the sins of the sinner, great and small. In the darkness of the basement sits he chambered with his carnal thoughts. On the Beauty Rest mattress lies he in uneasy pneumatic bliss."

She said nothing.

"My love—" he went on, "as I was sewing in my closet, Lord Webb, his doublet all unbraced, no hat upon his head, his stockings foul'd, pale as his shirt and his knees knocking together—"

She turned away from him, picked up the three hat-boxes, but when she tried to leave she found the trapdoor stuck. She kicked at it, but it took more than her weight.

"Lady—" he said, "I hear you lost a father?"

"You will pleave leave *him* out of this," she said.

"Left out of it he certainly was, Lady—out of bed, out of board, out of life, out of mind—"

"Will you open this, or will I have to call someone?"

"We both lost a father, lady, but methinks it can't be said that we lost a tear."

"You!" she cried. "You! You, of all people, talking about tears!"

"Just talk, Lady, mere words. I try to observe the rules of the house. The rules of the house indicate that there shall be no tears."

"For the last time—" she said.

"Lady," he said, holding up his hand, "I have here a portion of Little Liver Pills. They are soiled, alas, they are tarnished, indeed the salty tears of the druggist have so dampened the wrapping that they may have the taste of brine."

"Parsons!" she cried.

"But Lady, what's the Judge to him, or he to the Judge, that he should weep for him? What would he do had he the motive and the cue for passion that I have? Drown the stage with tears, cleave the air with horrid speech, make mad the guilty and appal—"

"Par-sons!" she cried. "Ohhhh, Par-sons!"

"How now, Ophelia?"

"PARSONS!" she cried, and she could hear him below her, she could hear him on the stairs, hear the chain snapping, then the trapdoor opened and there was Dr. Barr!

"Katherine!" he cried, "Katherine!" but as she stepped forward, as she started down, one of the hat-box strings snapped off in her hand, and the hats, four or five of them, tumbled all over him.

"Exeunt Ophelia!" Paul roared, and on the third or fourth step from the bottom she stepped on a hat. She stepped right through it, that is, she tripped, and in order to catch her Dr. Barr had to throw up his arms and release the stairs. As she fell toward him, hats and all, she heard the trapdoor rise toward the ceiling, just as it had done with her brother Roger still on board. Up it went, stairs and all, shutting off the light and his terrible cackling, but he was not drunk at all. When *he* was drunk, really drunk, he never laughed.

PARSONS

Parsons saw her, hatboxes and all, topple from the stairs toward Dr. Barr, and then the stairs go up like a drawbridge and leave them alone. So he turned to leave, he took a step on the stairs, but down there on the landing was Rosa Erskine, her eyes like saucers and a barmaid's leer on her greasy face. So Parsons crossed the hall to the bathroom, closed the door. Even there he could hear Webb's wild crazy laugh.

"Baby—!" Rosa Erskine called. "Oh, baby, you all right?"

"It was the boxes," Katherine replied. "The string broke on one of the boxes. Dr. Barr is helping me pick up the hats."

"Well, that's awful sweet of him, baby," she boomed. "He *is* the nicest man—" then her voice trailed off, and Parsons could hear them going down the stairs.

"Well—" said Mrs. Porter.

"Mother—" said Katherine. "If Dr. Barr hadn't been right there to break the fall . . ."

"I know what you mean, baby—" said Rosa Erskine.

"There was a box from Bonwit's," Mrs. Porter said.

"I am not going up those stairs again!" said Katherine.

"They're not intended for a woman," said Dr. Barr. "I'm afraid that some man of evil genius—"

"Border's racer?" said Mr. Erskine.

Parsons could tell by the silence that they had all

forgotten about it. So had he. Everyone of them.

"Doll—" said Mrs. Erskine, "didn't I just tell you not to bring it up? Didn't I just tell you for tonight once was enough?"

"Border's ole racer," he said.

"Paul is still looking for it," Katherine said, "he is still up there looking for it."

"If he doesn't find *that* one, I know where there is one," said Dr. Barr.

"You see what an awful old hen you are?" Rosa Erskine said.

"I don't remember that one," Mrs. Porter said.

"That's the one I *stepped* on, Mother—"

"Though I must say I have seen worse," Mrs. Porter said.

"Look at all those stickers!" said Rosa Erskine. "Don't it just kill you to see all those stickers? Cans! Is Cans one that's still there?"

"Ap-fel-dorn," said Mrs. Porter. "I don't remember it. Bâle, don't tell me we were there?"

"Mother—" said Katherine, "we are all waiting to look inside."

They moved away from the stairs, and Parsons left the bathroom, crossed the hall. From the door he could see that the attic trapdoor was up tight. Parsons had never been to the attic, but he had often stood on the ladder, holding it to the floor, while he passed up cartons to the Judge. Parsons had offered to do it, but the Judge had said if he did it himself, there was some chance of his remembering just where things were. Standing beneath the trapdoor, he said—

"Oh, Chief—?"

No answer.

"Anything I can do, Chief?"

Did he hear him laughing? It was hard to say. Parsons knew the bedroom, *this* room, better than the one where he slept himself, as when he wasn't sleeping in his own room he got out of it. But in this room, for weeks on end, he had to sit. He faced the Judge, who had been propped up on the inside bed. Parsons couldn't read, as the rattle of the papers disturbed the Judge. Anything that disturbed him made it harder for him to breathe. He couldn't seem to get enough air into his lungs. So Parsons would take his hands, like you do a baby's, and pull him so he could sit up, and the Judge would sit there with his big head in his hands. As his body got smaller, his head seemed to grow. It was probably just the wildness of his hair, which you couldn't keep down because he kept stirring, and the fact that he was always holding that big head in his hands. It made Parsons think of Bible pictures he had seen. John the Baptist, with his head right there on the platter, the eyes closed. Whatever the Judge saw didn't make him feel better as he would often moan, not from pain, but like a dog howls when he is tied up on a rope, or left in the basement or a woodshed somewhere.

Parsons was there in the room so much that he got to be part of the room itself, and the Judge more or less forgot that he was there. Toward the last he didn't seem to care. When Parsons shaved him he had the feeling he was working on something that no longer mattered. Parsons had got to wondering, at the time, what goes on in the people who take a dead man, slick and comb his hair, and then doll him all up. He didn't wonder about it so much anymore. He had come awfully close to doing just that himself. The man inside the Judge was so far away from the beard that he was shaving, that he often wondered what it was that made it grow. It wasn't really the Judge's. It had a life of its own.

"You waitin' for the call, Parsons?" Webb said, and this voice, coming from the attic, gave Parsons such a fright that for a moment he couldn't speak. Then he got hold of himself, and said—

"You got those little pills on you, Chief?"

Webb didn't reply, but Parsons could hear him cross the floor. Not to the trapdoor, but along the wall to where there was a ventilating grill in the ceiling. He opened it and said, "Heads up, Parsons," and dropped the pills through the opening. They fell into Mrs.

Porter's Indian pot, and Parsons fished them out. Looking up at the grill, Parsons said—

"When she gets excited she don't take her food well. Don't think one'll hurt her. She don't look too good."

"She's been on the frail side," said Webb, "for about ninety years."

Parsons tried to think of an answer to that, but nothing came to mind. He heard the steps in the ceiling go back across the attic to the gable end. Walking loud enough to indicate that he was leaving the room, Parsons left it, then he stepped into the bathroom for a glass of water, and opened the pills. He'd never done it before, but he took one himself. Then he filled the glass again, took another pill from the package, and put it on the chair that sat beside the Grandmother's bed. Her breathing seemed pretty regular. He closed her door, then got down the stairs to within a step or two of the landing when he heard the sound of people on the front porch. The door chimes rang, and he heard Katherine go to the door.

"Why, Mrs. Crowell!" Katherine said, "won't you come in?"

"This is Muriel, dear," said Mrs. Crowell, "she was at Smith when you were in England."

"You got the better of that deal all right," Muriel said.

"Mother," said Katherine, "here is Mrs. Crowell and Muriel."

"We've been eating your bird," Mrs. Porter said, "and I'm ashamed to say that we are somewhat frivolous."

"Heavenly Peter!" Mrs. Erskine said, from the far end of the room, "will you look at that?"

"Piccadilly," Mrs. Porter said, "Liberty's, I think."

"My God," said Muriel, "and they actually wore it. They really did."

"I don't think you ever wore it, did you, Mother?"

"They were very popular," Mrs. Porter said.

"Looks like an English cop!" Mr. Erskine suddenly said.

There was a pause.

"A London Tommy, perhaps," Mrs. Porter said.

"*Did* you ever wear it, Mother?"

"Your father—" said Mrs. Porter, "didn't think it was particularly—"

"A turtle!" said Mrs. Erskine, "—under a rock!"

"—becoming, and when we got back they were wearing something else."

At the foot of the stairs Parsons turned left, took a piece of the turkey as he crossed the kitchen, then opened the screen and stepped out on the porch. The light from the attic made a pattern on the leaves over his head. He put the piece of turkey into his mouth and chewed it all the way to his own place, where he let himself in, and then undressed in the dark. He could hear the women's voices and see that the light in the attic was still on.

WEBB

When the voice of Parsons came through the floor, Webb was seated on the stool, near the gable window, with a postcard mailed from the Gondolier Room of the Alcazar. It was dated June 9, 1927, and said—

DEAR HOWARD:
Yesterday saw Pokeweed Pottery exhibit in lounge, but back in time to add my vote to waterways. Two president's sons in our group, Richard P. and Charles P. Taft. Food here worthy of special comment: rhubarb juice for breakfast, side of applebutter. Light brown potatoes, in strings, new to us all.

The card was from a small packet labelled *Letters from My Wife. Letters from My Daughter*, and *My Son*, were still in the bottom of the fitted bag. When Parsons called again, Webb thought he could hear through the window where the vines were tangled,

The Deep Sleep

the voice of Mrs. Porter carrying on from where the card left off.

My day as an election official very interesting. Very small vote in our booth, but quite an encouraging turnout across the hall, where the League of Women voters diorama attracted young and old. Found myself bombarded with flattering comments on simplicity of my costume, which was in keeping with dwarf iris and sprigs of forget-me-nots.

In twenty-five years *that* voice had not faltered. The tone had not changed. It had been above certain human failings from the start. On the front of the card was a four-color picture of the new Alcazar Roof Garden, with "couples of the younger set dancing to the strains of the Gondoliers." A sound below reminded him that Parsons had spoken to him, so he said something. Parsons was still there, asking him for the liver pills. He didn't want to see anybody so he dropped the pills through the ventilator, then he came back and sat down on the stool. He could read, without opening the packet, the first letter from *My Daughter*.

Dear Daddy:
The towns of Pennsylvania are mostly mining or factory towns. Today we were at Independence Hall and I put my finger in the crack of the Liberty Bell. Tonight

we got to hear the Philadelphia Orchestra under the direction of Nikolai Sokoloff.

Aunt Nettie has her hair bobbed and it looks wonderful.

Love,
KATHY

He read a card from Camp Ottawamatomie, a girl's summer camp on the Cape somewhere, and part of a letter she had written *from the roof of My Grandmother's chicken house*. He read one or two more, then he stopped reading, as he had stopped feeling anything. Anything. He took off his shirt so he would feel some of the breeze that stirred in the yard. A door lamp burned at the Erskine house, and every now and then the voice of Rosa Erskine went across the street, then seemed to bounce back again. The cigar and the heat of the attic didn't mix too well. He had seen a lot of food, but he hadn't eaten much of it. On an empty stomach the cigars were not so good.

He thought he might lie down for just a bit, while the women were out of the bedrooms, but when he made a crack in the floor their voices came up from below. He let the trapdoor close again, and looked around. In the pile of junk at the back of the door, where it had been left after the last outing, the folded legs of an army camp cot were sticking out. He pulled it out, loosened the straps, and working with a certain urgency got it spread on the legs that were still coated with mud. He didn't trouble to put in the bars at the head or the foot. His head and his feet hung over, but that proved to be something of a blessing, as the draft along the floor was almost cool. He was not sick, just a little queasy, and if he could lie quiet for five or ten minutes, just lie quiet, he would be all right. He lay out on his back, his arms dangling, his eyes on the light bulb high in the gable, like a glow worm embedded in a piece of dirty glass. Without the head and foot bars the camp cot sagged, the canvas hugged him like a hammock, and the pincer legs gripped him gently, as if lending support.

He was asleep when Mrs. Crowell and her daughter left the house at ten past ten, nor did he hear, around eleven, Mrs. Erskine almost fall from the porch. He was still asleep when Dr. Barr took his leave at a quarter to twelve. He was also in the dark, as the bulb in the ceiling had burned itself out.

KATHERINE

Her mother closed the screen, hooked it, and said, "If she thought I would give it to her, she would take it."

"Well, if you're not going to wear it, Mother."

"She is a shrewd customer," her mother said. "If *she* looks at a hat, the hat is coming back." Crossing the room her mother stopped to pick up a piece of Kleenex, but she stayed down there. "Chocolate," she said, "who's been eating chocolate?"

"Did this Muriel get her divorce, Mother?"

"I'm afraid I don't keep track of such things."

"Well, I've never seen a woman work on a married man any harder. If we had a place for her upstairs I think she'd have fainted just to let him carry her somewhere. *Doct-tah Bahhh*—honestly, do they talk like that at Smith?"

Her mother picked up two glasses and said, "I suppose you noticed Mrs. Crowell didn't finish."

"She probably wasn't thirsty, Mother. I didn't finish mine either."

"I don't think she approved of the color of the glasses," her mother said. "If a Crowell approves, they never fail to mention it."

"Right now I don't care whether she approves or not," Katherine said.

Holding the glasses in her hand, her mother stood there listening.

"That ticking—" she said, then, "Who do you suppose has been eating chocolate?"

"Mother, it's after midnight. I'm going to bed."

"If you would listen to her talk," her mother said, "you would suppose she never touched chocolate. But mention Toll House cookies and watch her eyes roll." Her mother put the two glasses on the tray, and then carried the tray into the kitchen. Katherine put the chairs back in place, turned off the lights under the shades, then turned to hear the water running into the sink.

"Mother!" she said.

No answer.

"Mother, we are going to do that tomorrow morning. We are not going to stay up and do it now."

Didn't she hear? Katherine could hear the silver rattling in the pan. She went out into the kitchen where her mother stood leaning on the sink, her hands in the water, working up a suds with a piece of Fels Naptha soap. Behind her the day's plates were stacked, and in a tray at her side was the silver.

"Those new suds are not for me," her mother said.

"Mother, I am not going to argue. I am going to bed."

When the suds appeared her mother said, "Your Grandmother washed and rinsed her dishes. It won't hurt you to listen to what your Grandmother says."

"I am going to be perfectly selfish," said Katherine, "and say that I am the one who is tired. I am the one who wants to go to bed. I've just got to get some sleep for tomorrow. I'm completely worn out."

"I suppose that's where he went," her mother said.

"I don't know or care where he went, Mother, but I know where I am going. But it will do no good if you're going to stay up and wash. You can't sleep in a house where somebody is rattling dishes around."

"Your father and I," her mother replied, "can not sleep in a house where the dishes are dirty. There has not been a dirty dish in this house in thirty-seven years."

Katherine did not reply. She placed her hands on the sink board, and her knuckles turned white from the way she tried to grasp it, but neither the sink, nor her mother, said anything. At the top of the stairs, in the room where the Grandmother now lay sleeping, Katherine had spent most of her childhood lying awake. Lying awake in the morning listening to her father squeeze the orange juice and make the coffee, and lying awake at night listening to them wash the day's dishes. After the guests had gone, and the children had been put to bed. Then the dishpans that had been hung up the night before would be taken from the hooks and refilled with water, and the dishes that had been rinsed and stacked would be washed again. The silver that had been rinsed, scalded again. Every dish soaked in the soapy water, scrubbed down with the small raddled mop, then dropped into a dishpan of warm water, from where her father picked it up. Every dish, every piece of silver, every piece of glassware, every pot and every pan, passed through this treatment, passed through her hands, then through his. Every faded pink plate with the Willow pattern was carried into the front room and put in its place, and every piece of silver was returned to the silver drawer. Every pot was hung under the sink, or put in the lower shelf of the oven, or placed over the pilot light so it would dry out. And every single piece of it had its own sound, every piece of glassware had its own tinkle, in and out of the water, and every pot had its own rocking motion on the shelf or the wall. Without ever being there, Katherine lived through it all. And all of it without a word, without a *human* sound, as talk or speech was thought to wake them, and the ten thousand noises were supposed to put them to sleep. She never missed a one. She hung on to the last sleepy squeeze of the rag. She could hear the slushy whisper as it made a final pass over everything. Over the top of the stove, over the bread board, over the sink board, over the table, and then the wet flap as her mother hung it up to dry. Spread it out, like a fishnet, between the handles of the faucets, where it gave off an odor like a clogged drain. Then her father would

come up the stairs first, carrying his shoes so as not to
wake them, and some time later her mother would
pad around the house. Trying all the doors, checking
all the windows, opening or closing the radiators, and
then, but not till then, turning off the lights. And then,
but not till then, Katherine would hear the sound of
her brother's breathing and the dragging of the
weights in the clock that once stood at the foot of
the stairs. With her father's snoring, with her mother's
silence, she would go to sleep.

"Thirty-seven years and twelve days to be exact,"
her mother said.

If she went to bed she would lie there awake, just
as she had thirty years ago, feeling sorry for her parents, and feeling ashamed of herself. She would lie
there awake, curled up in the hole she had lived in
most of her childhood, listening to the sounds that
came to her from the mouth of the cave. She would
sift every sound, every fumbling movement, through
her mind. She would sort it all out, like the stuff in a
drawer, looking for the key. She would live all of it
over, she would bring it up to date for the last twenty
years, and then she would be right back again where
she started from. There was no key, there was no
explanation, there was no solution to the game in the
kitchen, to the rules of the house, or to the laws of her
mother's world. But they were there. The laws and

the rules had not changed. While in the house the only solution was to follow them.

"Where are the dish towels, Mother?" she said.

"Right where they always were," her mother replied.

Why had she asked? To make conversation. To break the spell. Something might be said, just *might* be said, that might explain something. She walked around the table to where the morning dish towel was spread on the radiator, and the lunch towel was fanned out on the rack. It was dry, as today there had been no lunch. Her mother took her hands from the pan of suds, placed her knuckles on her hips and said, "Why, over in Hershey—" she pointed, "the entire plumbing system was endangered by the use of detergents in one day's wash." She paused there, then said, "Pedlars left it on the porches, I suppose."

Hershey, Katherine knew, had not suffered from detergents, from some new soap or some new gadget, but from the collapse of moral fibre from within. An un-American shrinking from an honest Fels Naptha wash. A bombing attack that they were unable to resist. Her mother returned her hands to the suds, giving them a stir that made them fizzle, then carefully, as if for a baptism, she dipped the first glass. When Katherine picked it up her mother said—

"Does that have the stamp on the bottom?"

"Yes, Mother—"

"Your Grandmother's jelly glass," she said.

That glass went into the cupboard across the kitchen, where there were five other such glasses, and Katherine and her brother had drunk their milk and orange juice from them. They were cheap brittle glasses, water too hot or too cold might break them, but after seventy years six of them were still there.

"I won't have her thinking we don't take care of her things," her mother said.

In the glass door of the cupboard Katherine could see the light over the sink, and her mother's gray head, her rounded shoulders, bent over the pan. She was worn out. There were dark circles under her eyes. But there was no indication whatsoever that what she was doing was a tiresome chore, or that she merely did it to get it done. There was every indication—if Katherine could believe her eyes—that her mother's hands, elbow deep in the suds, were where they belonged. That every washing motion had a meaning, and accomplished something. After a long day of nothing done, nothing *really* done, just a day that slipped beneath her, she could come to grips with something solid every night. What had been dirtied during the day could be cleaned up. Another day, if and when it came, could be started afresh. One cup at a time, one glass at a time, one spoon, one fork, and one knife at a time, were just so many necessary worthwhile accomplishments. Had it been possible, Katherine wondered, that for more than thirty years her mother had *enjoyed* what Katherine had believed to be the bane of her life? The ten o'clock till midnight daily wash? A time when everything in the house that had been sullied—including the lives of the inhabitants—could be put through three cleansing waters and made pure again. Had she pitied her mother for one of the real joys of her life? Running the water, stirring up the suds, dipping and rinsing the assorted objects, each one of which had some special meaning for her. The Grandmother's jelly glasses, the Willow Ware from the shop in Surrey, the bone-handled knives from the store in Munich, operated by a man named Rautzen, and the family silver that would always lack the bouillon spoons.

"Your father and I," her mother said, washing the can the ripe olives had come in, "always found the time to run our own house."

Her mother, God knows, understood nothing, neither her husband, her son, nor her daughter, but perhaps it was not beyond reason to understand her. Perhaps *that* was just what her husband had done. Perhaps that explained what could not be explained about him.

"What do you do with your extra fat these days?" her mother said.

"We just throw it out, Mother. Nobody seems to want it."

"Well, I will *not* throw it out," she said. She turned to gaze at the Crisco can on the stove, the lid tipped back so the fat could be poured into it. "The people who are pouring it out will be crying for it next," she said.

"That's human nature, Mother."

"It is not *my* nature," her mother replied, and Katherine, a tumbler in her hand, felt it slide down the towel then strike the radiator. The pieces dropped and scattered on the floor.

"One of the amber?" her mother asked.

"I'm awfully sorry, Mother—"

Her mother turned from the sink, stooped to reach beneath it, and came up with a brush and a dust pan. "I am almost positive," she said, "that Mrs. Crowell didn't care much for them."

"Let me, Mother.

"No, I *know* that radiator." She let her mother slip by, and watched her sweep up the glass. "It gets around the leg. It chews up the linoleum." Her mother swept it up, carefully, then seeing other spots of dirt around her, she went over the general area with her brush. "You see that corner?" she said, and Katherine bent over to look at it. "He comes in and just stands there. He's worse than your father on a piece of rug."

"Mr. Parsons—?" she said.

"If I ask him to sit down, why, then he'll just sit till I ask him to leave."

"I don't know what we would have done without him," Katherine said.

"Your mother would have done whatever she was able," she replied. With the dust pan and the brush, she pushed through the screen to the rear porch. She emptied the broken glass into the waste can, firmly put on the lid, then stood there looking across the yard at the summer night. Katherine could hear her deeply breathing the cool night air. Absently, as if fingering her hair, she removed the sheet of towel paper from the clothesline, and slipped the plastic pin into the pocket of her dress. The summer night was very lovely, and her mother, while her hands were busy, seemed to be listening to the music of the spheres.

"I don't know what I'd do," her mother said, "if other people didn't go to bed."

Katherine waited a moment, then said, "Is it all right if I go now, Mother?"

"Your father would go to bed, but he never slept until I was there."

"Good night, Mother," Katherine said, and when her mother didn't answer she started for the stairs.

"Which one is Orion?" her mother said.

"I'm afraid I've forgotten it all, Mother."

"I'm going to miss your father," her mother said, and Katherine turned, her hand on the stair rail, as if another person, not her mother, had spoken. A voice, perhaps, from one of the letters she never mailed. Katherine wanted to speak, but now that this voice had spoken to her, broken the long silence, she could hardly believe what she heard. She went on up the stairs, entered her room, then closed the door before she remembered, before she noticed, that Paul wasn't there. Still, she would have called to him except for the fact that she had no voice, her throat ached, and he had been the one who had cried that this was a house without tears.

MRS. PORTER

The cool of the evening came to Mrs. Porter from the Poconos, from Valley Forge, from the slopes where Washington's men were quartered, to where she lay in the dark on the cot on the screened-in porch. At her feet was Conshohocken, at her head Bryn Mawr, on her left was Paoli and on her right

was Mannyunk. On the bed at her feet was what she
had taken off, and on the chair at her side was what
she would put on.

Black straw hat with grosgrain ribbon, spider veil
Dark two piece shantung suit
Black faille purse
Black mesh gloves
Black kid pumps, medium heels
In bowl on sideboard pearl necklace, matching earrings.

Her body at rest, her mind at ease, her day in the
hands of Clough & Bayard, she closed her eyes, she
stopped resisting, but she did not sleep. Above the
sawing of the crickets she could hear it, Tick-tick-
tick. *Mrs. Porter, your hearing is very remarkable*, Dr.
Lloyd had said. Anyone might hear the ticking in the
house, the ticking in the cupboard, the ticking in a
pocket, but who could hear the ticking in the woods?
Would you believe it, Dr. Lloyd? she had said. I am
prepared to believe anything you tell me, Dr. Lloyd
said.

A safe place. He had put it, he said, in a safe place.
In the quiet she could hear it very plainly, tick-tick-
tick. There was no tick in the electric clock, there was
sometimes a tick in the shade of the lamp, and there
was once a tick in the horseshoe crab that Katherine
brought from the Cape. *Tick-tick-tick* he had said, so

they had thrown him out. She had observed Mr. Parsons take him out of the barrel and go off with him.

All around her, like the sound of dripping, tick-tick-tick. She arose from the cot, took from the drawer of the sideboard the candles that were there in case of power failure, and the matches that were there in case the gas went off. The house was dark, but she did not scratch a match. Through the window of the living room she could see the light beside the bed of Rosa Erskine, where she lay reading the back issues of fashion magazines—and from where she could see, if she raised her eyes, a match flare in the Porter house.

With the candle in her hand, but out, Mrs. Porter crossed the living room rug to where Mr. Erskine had left his iced tea glass on the floor. He had hidden it under the skirt of the floral print on the chair. As she passed his chair Mrs. Porter kicked the glass, then she stepped into the water, into the tea and on the slice of lemon, before she heard the glass roll across the tile floor and thump on the door. It struck the woodwork, it struck the lamp, then it rocked back and forth, like a saucer, until she got down on her knees in the water and felt around for it. The glasses were no good for color, but after all of that it hadn't chipped or broken, and she made a mental note to call Mrs. Crowell and point that out. With the candle in the glass she went up the stairs to the second floor.

The Deep Sleep

WEBB

When the rolling tumbler struck the door Webb opened his eyes, tried to move, and thought for a moment that he had been buried alive. In the cave of the attic there was not a crack of light. One arm had gone to sleep, and in the grip of the cot he felt paralyzed. He closed his eyes. He waited for the trouble to go away. Webb had often seen his cats try that, and sometimes it worked. While in this condition, his eyes closed, he heard the faintest creaking in the room below him, and the soft cat-like padding of bare feet. On the attic rafters, when he opened his eyes, was a flickering light. It waved about on the ceiling directly over the ventilator grill, which Webb had left open when he dropped Parsons the liver pills. He did not move, he watched the light flicker and blow on the ceiling, like smoke, until he detected the unmistakable smell of fire. That got him up. On his hands and knees he crossed the floor. With his face pressed flat to the grill he saw Mrs. Porter, in her nightgown, peering around the room like Lady Macbeth. In her right hand, like a lantern, she held an iced tea glass which contained a smoking candle. Her eyes were wide, there was nothing in her face but the shifting light of the candle, and Webb was sure she was walking in her sleep. That she had returned, in this fashion, to the scene of the crime.

With her back to him, she crossed the room and opened the top drawer of the dresser, rummaging her hand into the back corners, where she found more socks. She then drew it out, as he had, and pushed her hand into the drawer beneath it, rising on her toes to increase the length of her reach. The same with the next drawer, then the next, whereupon she turned as if Webb had spoken and crossed the room to a large bowl on the sewing machine. She put her hand into the bowl, felt around, and drew out a round flat object, which she held near the candle to watch the three bee-bees moving around. She played the game for a minute, perhaps, then she put it away. In the left top drawer of the sewing machine, she found a bronze baby shoe. Webb thought that might be what she wanted, as she kept it, grasped tight in her hand, and crossed the room into the hall, but there she put it down, like a paper weight, on the memo pad. Gazing back into the room she saw the beds, and stepped in far enough to poke around at the mattress, fluff the pillow, and look beneath the pottery lamp on the nightlight stand. There she found four or five sugar-covered hoarhound drops. She took them along with her, into the hallway, and as she started down the stairs her shadow swelled and filled the landing at the top.

That was all, nothing there but the shadow, but the sight made the hair on Webb's neck rise, and if there had been blood left in his veins it would have run cold. As it had once before, as it did the winter morning that he had broken into the house, and with Dr. Barr right at his heels he had run up the stairs. Up to the landing, up to the point where the specter appeared from the Judge's doorway—appeared then disappeared without a word or a gesture—and Webb had been swept with both pity and terror for this man and his wife. Pity for the man, but terror for the power that made itself known in the woman as she passed before them, flesh and specter, down the hall.

Had it been the sight of death, or the sight of life, that had terrified the Judge? The powers that had shaped whatever it was that he had lived? And the terror he had felt, the terror he had known, that he might live the same life over, and the powers that had made and broken him once, would make and break him him again. This might look like pity to Webb, but it would look like something else to the man who could see himself stretched, who could see himself broken, on the same wheel of life.

The shadow was still there, filling the hallway, when the door to the guest room opened, and Webb caught a glimpse of his wife's distracted face. She followed her mother down the stairs, and a moment later, in the rooms below, he could hear the sound of drawers being opened and closed, as if Mrs. Porter had forgotten what time of night it was. It made it easier for Webb to leave the attic, to get the trapdoor down and then get it up, and when he stepped into the hall it was empty. Katherine was not there. He made his way slowly down to the landing, and from there he could see, at the far end of the room, Mrs. Porter with the sputtering candle in her hand. She was removing certain books from the fireplace shelves. Webb could see that she was somewhere in the Harvard Classics, and in the opening she had made, in the brick wall at the back, the latched door to a secret chamber of some kind. She drew up a chair to stand on before she opened it. The door stuck, she had to strain, and then it suddenly opened with the sound of a cork, and a cloud of dirt and soot, sucked in by the draft, filled that end of the room. For a moment Webb thought that the candle had been snuffed out. In the darkness he could hear Mrs. Porter coughing, then the cloud seemed to pass, and he could see her fanning at the streamers of soot with one of the books. As the air began to clear, she carefully returned the books to the shelves. They were all in place, it seemed to Webb, when she discovered the order of their arrangement, and then she rearranged them, properly, on the shelves. She was not impatient. He could her her muttering the alphabet. One book falling open, she paused to read the passage, her lips carefully forming the words, and her head nodding in agreement to what she read. To *know* that book, to mark that place, she crossed the room to her memo pad, tore off the top sheet, and filed it with an inch showing at the top. But on that inch she had written something, and reading it over she said aloud—

"Clorox, Air-Wick, digitalis—"

"Mother—" said Katherine, softly, "Mother—are you all right?"

Mrs. Porter did not raise her head. She was not alarmed. Stepping from the kitchen door Katherine said, "You want to scare a person silly, Mother?"

"I think that must be an old one," Mrs. Porter said.

Katherine walked into the living room beside her, and when her mother did not turn, or seem to hear her, she stepped forward and lifted a slipping strap on her mother's nightgown. In the dim light of the room, the sputtering candle behind them, the gesture struck Webb as very familiar, and he realized that it was just what Mrs. Porter would have done. First things first. First, last and all the time. The Harvard Classic still in her hand, but closed firmly on what she had marked, Mrs. Porter observed that her daughter's long tight braids were down.

"You don't comb them out?" she said.

The Deep Sleep

"I was just too tired to bother," Katherine replied.

Mrs. Porter reflected that that might be so, studied her daughter's face for a moment, and then, as if Webb had spoken, turned to look at him. Not at him, but in his direction, at the oval shaped basket in the piano corner, where Webb had dropped, several hours before, the cheap dollar watch. Without speaking, Mrs. Porter crossed the room, dipped her hand into the basket, scrounged it around beneath the paper, and came up with the watch.

"I knew I heard a ticking," she said soberly.

"Honestly—" said Katherine, "is everybody crazy? Who in the world's watch is it?"

"Your father's," she said, simply. Then, "Nine twenty something—can that be right?"

"Mother," said Katherine, "it's after two thirty."

"Your father loses them," Mrs. Porter said, "your mother finds them."

"I have had all I can stand, Mother," said Katherine, "and I am not going to leave this room until you do. Nobody can sleep while you are up padding around the house."

"I just knew I heard the ticking," Mrs. Porter said.

"Mother," said Katherine, "give me that watch," and she walked up to her mother, took the watch from her. "Now I've got it, and there will be no ticking if you go up and sleep in your own room. I'm going to sleep down here whether there's any more ticking or not."

She took her mother by the arm, and as they came toward the stairs Webb stepped from the landing into the kitchen, and standing there in the dark he saw them make the turn, slowly go up. At the top of the stairs Mrs. Porter said, "A safe place. That's where he said he put it."

"Put what, Mother?"

"The Golden Swiss Ticker," Mrs. Porter said, and then she stepped into the bedroom, padding softly across the floor directly over his head. A moment later, the springs creaking, she got into bed.

Webb remained in the kitchen until he was sure she would not come down again. Then he groped through the house to the screened-in porch, felt his way around the chair hung with her clothes, and lay out on the cot from where she had just got up. He smoked the last crushed cigarette in the pack, and when the light appeared in the eastern sky he watched the Porter bats, as Parsons called them, winging back through the broken windows of the garage. He remembered, before he fell asleep, to do one more thing. The Golden Swiss Ticker, in its morocco case, he put into the sideboard, behind the chest of silver, not a very safe place but one where Mrs. Porter might come upon it. If she didn't, he would stumble on it himself.

The Deep Sleep

"Mother," he would say, "what in the world is this?" and he would stand there, with the case open, until she came toward him and looked at the watch.

That was quite a picture, one that pleased him, and whether he heard the ticking or not, something kept him awake until he heard the Grandmother coming down the stairs.